# DEATH IN HIGH
# HEELS

## CHRISTIANNA BRAND

Carroll & Graf Publishers, Inc.
New York

The action and characterizations in this story are purely
imaginary and no reference to any living person or existing
organization is intended.

First Carroll & Graf edition 1989

Carroll & Graf Publishers, Inc.
260 Fifth Avenue
New York, NY 10001

ISBN: 0-88184-546-9

Manufactured in the United States of America

To
ROLAND
—of course

## THE STAFF AT
### CHRISTOPHE ET CIE

| | |
|---|---|
| Mr. Frank Bevan | *proprietor and manager* |
| Mr. Cecil | *dress designer* |
| Miss Gregory | *Mr. Bevan's Right Hand* |
| Miss Doon | *Mr. Bevan's Left· Hand* |
| Macaroni | *Doon's secretary* |
| Mrs. Irene Best | |
| Mrs. Rachel Gay | *'vendeuses'* |
| Mrs. Victoria David | |
| Miss Judy Carol | *mannequins* |
| Miss Aileen Wheeler | |
| Mrs. 'Arris | *charlady* |

# One

IRENE was always the first to arrive. At ten to nine precisely she clicked-to the door of her neat little, dull little bed-sitt. and caught the tram for the corner. There was sure to be a crowd waiting for the bus, but if she got there a few minutes before nine it wasn't so bad and she could at least wedge herself in and be permitted to stand, one of five privileged sardines, clinging to a strap and fumbling with one over-occupied hand for the ever-elusive threepence. Usually a good many people got out at Warren Street, and she could nip into a seat before the bus filled up again. It was a struggle alighting at Oxford Circus, squeezing past the succeeding batch of sardines, but at last she was out and if all had gone to schedule (Irene was very fond of schedules), with five clear minutes in which to walk along Regent Street and down the area steps into the basement of Christophe et Cie.

Mrs. 'Arris, the charwoman, would be there already, flicking a casual duster over the office furniture. Upstairs in the great gleaming showroom, with its golden carpet and shimmering curtains, its crystal lights and flattering mirrors, the silver glittered and the parquet shone and the glass was clear and bright; but in the basement, where the gilded staircase gave way abruptly to an unwholesome chocolate brown, a flick and a promise would do; and a flick and a promise was all Mrs. 'Arris vouchsafed. She was usually dusting the cloakroom when Irene arrived, having planned her work so as to 'ave a bit of a chat with the girls while they changed into their overalls of elegant turquoise blue; Irene dreaded these chats but never failed to ask politely after Mrs. 'Arris's stomach, which was known to be an unruly member, and to listen with an air of suffi-cient interest to the history of its vagaries since the preceding day. "You really do have a bad time, Mrs. Harris, don't you?" she would say, patting into place her soft, dark hair, polishing up her neat little shoes; and, "Musern't grumble," Mrs. 'Arris would reply, who seldom did anything else.

Victoria, meanwhile, would be taking leave of her husband on a scale that suggested a parting of at least a week. Victoria's husband was a painter and, though his Christian name was James, was invariably referred to as Bobby Dazzler; they were accustomed to explain to anyone who would listen that Victoria had awakened one morning on their honeymoon and been quite dazed by his beauty; a tribute rather to devotion than to judgment, for the Dazzler, though a personable, was by no means a handsome young man. He looked less handsome than ever on this particular morning, clad in a pair of outsize green pyjamas, looking vaguely round the studio in search of her handbag. "You had it last night, because I remember you taking it out to pay the beer."

"Here it is," cried Victoria, snatching it up from behind a pile of canvases, and bestowing upon him a second impassioned embrace. She tightened a suspender, perched her hat at a perilous angle upon her shining head, and started off down the stairs. Half a minute later she was back: "*Do* remember to ring up your mother, darling, because if you don't she'll be certain to say it's my fault." The Dazzler promised that he would ring up his mother at once, decided to take one look at yesterday's picture before so doing, and five minutes later was hard at work on it.

Irene and Victoria and Rachel were the sales staff at Christophe et Cie. Rachel was big and dark and handsome in contrast to Victoria's golden frailty; she said as they met on the corner of Regent Street: "We're as late as hell, darling. Irene'll be in a flap."

Doon did not care whether she were late or not. Doon was in charge of the stockroom; she assisted with designs and chose materials and doled out needles and pins. Irene, watching through the great glass windows her unhurried progress toward the shop, supposed that it was her artistic temperament that caused her to indulge in the romantic garments, the strange silks and barbaric jewelry that became her so well. One had to admit that she "could wear" them; but Irene had been born and bred in a cathedral city and she had a deep distrust for artistic temperament. Victoria, now, she could draw quite as well as Doon and she had ever such a good eye for colour; but she was as natural and ordinary as could be. Rather irresponsible, of course, but then she was married to an artist and everybody knew what artists were. Irene's own husband had been a bird fancier; a steady enough occupation you would have thought, but one of his less attractive fancies had pecked him on the hand and, blood-poisoning setting in, he had incontinently died, leaving Irene at twenty-five a widow and penniless. That was five years ago, and now she was in charge of the showroom at Christophe et Cie and with ever such a good chance of being sent to the new branch which Bevan was opening at Deauville . . . she fell into a reverie in which highly coloured umbrellas grew out of flat, bright-yellow sand, and the air was drenched with Chanel Five.

Judy, the mannequin, disturbed her, pounding up the stairs: "Irene! has Aileen arrived yet? Have you seen her?"

Irene came back with a start to grimy London. "No, dear; unless she was here before me. She may have gone up to the workroom."

"Not she! And that grey model has got to be finished to take to Lady Whatsit at the Ritz this afternoon, so that means that *I* shall have to go up and have the damn thing fitted on *me*, just because . . . oh, there she is! Aileen . . . Oi, Aileen . . . can't she hear me, the silly cow?"

"Not through the glass, dear, of course she can't," said Irene mildly.

Judy made wild signals; Aileen turned a face of exquisite beauty, lifted a streamlined eyebrow, and looked blank. Judy jerked a finger upwards, indicating an urgent summons to the showroom; Aileen looked first heaven-

wards, and then, interrogatively, at her umbrella. Judy
made a gesture in response which sent her tripping round
the corner with a look of refined disgust on her lovely
features; Victoria and Rachel came tearing upstairs,
zipping their blue overalls as they ran, and somewhere a
clock struck ten. Irene solemnly unlocked the silver
door: at Christophe et Cie the day had officially begun.

"Do you like this red frock in the window?" said Irene,
when apologies and explanations for their lateness had
sufficiently abated. "I thought it looked rather tasteful
with just the grey hat and the parasol. What do you
think of the grey?"

"I don't think it matters at all, darling."

"No, but Rachel, do *say*."

"What does it matter, Rene, my pet? It looks all right'
Yes, there, I think it's marvellous: does that please you?".

"No, it doesn't a bit," said Irene, fussily. "If it doesn't
look right Gregory'll——"

"Oh, damn and blast Gregory," said Rachel, crossly.
"This whole damn place is in everlasting fear of Gregory.
It's nothing to do with her, Rene, what you put in the
window. Whatever you do, she'll tell her darling Bevan
that it should have been something else, so why worry?"

"Stinking cat," said Victoria, calmly, plastering lipstick on her lovely mouth. "I wish to goodness Bevan
would send her to the new branch at Deauville, and then
we'd be free of her."

"You don't think Gregory will go, Toria?"

"I think it's practically certain, darling. Cecil rang
me up during the week-end. It's all set."

Doon wandered up from her basement office and Victoria, who had an eye for beauty, thought she had never
seen her look more attractive. She was a tall, well-
modelled creature, and every line of her body was outlined
and emphasized by the clothes she wore. Her thick
auburn hair was caught, with an illusion of simplicity,
into a twist at the nape of her neck; beneath wide, wing-
shaped brows her eyes glowed, dangerously green. She
propped herself against a pillar, and, lighting a cigarette,

asked without curiosity what they were gassing about.

"We were wondering about the job at Deauville," said Rachel, evasively. "Have you heard anything?"

"Oh, it's me that's going. I'm having lunch with the boy friend to-day to talk things over."

"We thought there was some idea of Bitchy Gregory getting it after all."

"I don't think so," said Doon, comfortably. "Bevan promised me I should go. That's the best of being girl friends with the boss," she added, laughing. "I'm afraid Gregory's chance was all washed up the day she first brought him to one of my parties."

"Is that when Bevan began to get keen on you?" asked Irene, inquisitively.

"Yes; she was an ass, wasn't she? I'd been in the shop all that time, and Bevan never bothered about me at all, though I was always a bit sweet on him; he was all taken up with Gregory, and then the fool wraps him up in a parcel and hands him over to me!"

"What on earth did he ever see in her, Doon?"

"My dear, he thought she was unattainable; after all, if ever there was a craggy virgin it was Gregory. The moment I set eyes on her I knew what her trouble was, and I actually had her round to a few parties and tried to get her off, as you know . . . but nothing doing. It never occurred to Bevan that she would succumb if he tried it on, and he couldn't resist the temptation: he told me he was shaken to the core when she fell without a struggle! Then, of course, she got really keen on him, and when I appeared on his horizon it was a bit awkward to get rid of her. I don't believe she realizes yet that he wants to."

"Doon, you *are* awful, telling everyone," said Irene, enjoying it thoroughly.

"Well, my dear, it's perfectly obvious; everybody knows it already. Why be silly about it?"

"Don't you mind knowing that he used to be keen on her?"

"Not in the least—he'd been keen on dozens of women before her, and I've been keen on dozens of men; as long as he doesn't love anyone else now, that's all I mind about."

Irene looked sideways at Rachel. "Won't you miss him if you go to Deauville?"

"Oh, he'll be coming over a lot; it's only a couple of hours if you fly . . . my God, I believe I've left a cigarette burning on the edge of my desk!" She unpropped herself from her pillar and ran downstairs.

"Evidently it's definitely between those two," said Irene, frowning after her. "I seem to be quite out of the running for the job."

"Should you be very disappointed, Rene?" asked Rachel, kindly.

"Oh, Ray, you know I would. After all, you two have something to keep you in England: Toria's practically a bride still, and Rachel couldn't leave her little Jessica without her mumsey; but what have I got? Nothing; and my rotten hanger-on of a brother's turned up again."

"*Irene!* No!"

"Yes, he has. I had a letter from him last night. The truth is that I shall never be rid of him till I can get away from here and he doesn't know where to find me. I wish I'd made a clean break with him years ago."

"Like me," said Rachel, thoughtfully.

"Yes, Ray; this is why I've always been so keen for you to get your divorce and be done with it. It never pays to go on with these half-and-half arrangements; you don't love your husband and he doesn't love you and he was unkind to you—well then, finish the whole thing and be free to start your life all over again."

"Yes, you were quite right, darling; it was far the best thing to do; but I'd never have had the courage to go through with it, if it hadn't been for you making me, and I shall always be grateful to you for helping me so much; only three months now and I'll get my *decree nisi* and it'll be all over."

"I hope you're behaving yourself, my girl?"

"I've got no one to misbehave with," said Rachel, smiling. "My life at the moment is a model of monotonous virtue. The only thing I worry about is that time I went out with Bevan . . . you see the way he talks, he tells Doon everything. Still, it's ages ago, before even Gregory's time, and I don't see how the King's Proctor could nose it out. Please heaven!" she added, piously.

"How's the kid?"

"Oh, she's all right, Toria. It's a bit rotten for her in London, but I'll get her away on Wednesday to her Granny's and she goes back to school after that, poor brat."

"Doon seems very certain of going to the new branch," said Irene, reverting to the only topic which, at the moment, really interested her.

"She's going to be disappointed; but still, she can't lose either way. If Gregory goes, Doon gets a rise in salary and can at least stay in London with her precious Bevan—not like poor old Rene; it really does matter to you, doesn't it, darling?"

"I'd give anything to go," said Irene again. "This place gets on my nerves these days with Gregory always carping and criticizing . . . if it was only to Manchester, I'd be crazy to go. But think of Deauville! Blue skies and sunshine and gaiety, and everybody rich and idle and beautifully dressed . . . and I've only to give a week's notice at my digs, and pack a suitcase to be as free as the air." Her injuries clamoured for utterance and she added, in a whining voice: "And talking about digs, my dear, I must tell you—*again* this morning a filthy black rim round the bath! It's those women in number six, I told you about . . . ."

2

"If Rene tells us just once more about those women in number six, I shall scream," said Victoria ten minutes later, as she sat down with Rachel in their little cubbyhole. "Bless her heart, she is the sweetest thing, but it does rather get on one's nerves."

"And I do wish she wouldn't call me Jessica's mumsey.

Jessica would be sick if she knew—she's a very tough child for six. Look, Toria, darling, what am I going to do about this *blasted* hat? I've hardly worn it, and it's filthy already. What cleans panama? Rene—Oi, Rene," she called across the empty showroom. "Do you know what cleans panama?"

"Rachel, dear, don't shout across the *salon* like that; supposing there was a customer!"

"There isn't a customer, so what does it matter? Honestly, Toria, Irene's getting as nervy as hell these days."

"She's worried about Deauville, and of course Gregory's getting her down, always saying sweetly catty things to Bevan—still, she does that about us all. Rene, darling, stop worrying about the window and come and advise about Rachel's hat. Look what a muck she's made of it."

"Oxalic acid's the best thing for that," said Irene, judicially, taking up the hat and holding it to the light. "You just rub it in and then brush it off again. It's supposed to be marvellous."

"Oh, that's fine. You always know these things. What did you say it was called?"

"Oxalic acid. You get it from a chemist, I should think. There's nobody in at the moment, and Bevan and Gregory won't be here till late—go across and see if the man in Mitchell's will let you have some," suggested Irene generously, anxious to make amends for her recent irritability.

"I'll go now—thank you, sweetie. Come on, Toria, you come with me."

They rushed bareheaded across Regent Street, dodging the traffic with accustomed ease, and the chemist bobbed up from behind the counter of his little shop to greet them.

"Good morning, young ladies, and what can I do for *you* to-day?"

"I want some oxalic acid," said Rachel.

"Oxalic acid crystals? What did you want them for?"

"She wants to murder Miss Gregory," said Victoria, laughing. "You know Miss Gregory—she's the one that made all the flap about your giving us tick for the showroom soap; don't you remember?"

"Oh, yes, I remember Miss Gregory," said the chemist, a trifle grimly. "I think everyone knows her in the small shops around here. But I can't be a party to her murder, you know."

"Don't listen to Mrs. David," said Rachel, "she reads too many detective stories. I want to clean a straw hat, that's all it is."

"Ah, yes, I believe I've heard of oxalic acid being used for that. How much would you want?"

"How much would kill a person?" asked Victoria, sticking to her point.

"Well, let's see—about a drachm, I should say. Not quite a teaspoonful."

"Then we'd better have nine teaspoonfuls for Gregory," said Toria, laughing. "How does one buy it? By the ounce, or what?"

"I think an ounce would be enough for the hat, certainly. That would be about—er—about four big teaspoons."

"Righto, we'll have an ounce. Can we weigh ourselves for nothing on your scales?"

"You always do, so why bother to ask?" said Rachel. "She only does it to annoy, Mr. Mitchell, because she's so much lighter than me. Don't we have to sign the poisons book or anything?" she went on, as he handed the little packet across the counter. "I'm quite willing to, in fact I'd love to."

"No, no, nothing like that. I know you ladies, you see; it isn't as if you were strangers to me—I believe I've even seen Mrs. Gay's panama hat!" They were out of the door by the time he added: "Anyway, you don't have to sign for oxalic acid."

They plonked their pennies down upon the counter and dodged their way back across Regent Street. "Easy enough to kill anybody, wouldn't it be?" said Victoria, strolling in through the showroom door, "as long as you weren't too particular about being found out; I suppose they could always trace you through the chemist, though. Look at this mouldy little packet—it's only a flimsy bit of paper and it's got a hole in it already. Oh, Rene, I'm so sorry, I'm dropping poison all over the carpet; look, a little paper-chase with Rachel's oxalic acid—isn't it sweet?"

"Don't be silly, Toria, there's only a few grains there," said Rachel as Irene bustled forward. "Put the rest of the stuff on my table and I'll help Irene pick up the bits. Here you are," she added a moment later, tipping half a dozen grains of crystal on to the rest of the heap; "that's most of it. Sorry, Rene, my pet, but it wasn't very bad."

Irene threw two or three crystals on to the little pile, and dusted her hands over it. "Supposing Mr. Bevan had come in or a customer, and found us picking dirt off the carpet!" she said, irritably. "I do think you two are inconsiderate. It's so childish." She went off to her desk in the corner of their little room and turned her back on them.

Rachel and Toria tipped the crystals on to a sheet of paper and began rubbing feverishly at the hat. Twenty minutes' work showed little improvement. Judy strolled over from the mannequins' room and stood watching them, automatically going through her tummy exercises and inquiring anxiously as to the reduction of her almost non-existent behind. She was a curly-haired blond who would one day be Rubenesque and was for ever pre-occupied with the postponement of this tragedy. Aileen, who ate heartily without ever suffering the slightest deviation in her measurements, was her envy and despair; she said so now as the elegant figure drifted past, on a languid progress down from the workroom.

"It's no use being cross with me, dear," said Aileen, unruffled. "If I went to fat like you do I'd just starve, I wouldn't eat a thing; not a sausage," she added, applying this phrase literally for the first, and probably only, time in her life. Her wandering attention was diverted to the panama. "What on earth are you doing to Rachel's hat?"

"Cleaning it," said Rachel, "but it's still pretty mucky."

Aileen picked up the hat and perched it on her red-gold hair. "It looks like a million dollars on you," said Rachel, with a characteristic mixture of chagrin and laughter. A twang of Hoxton came out in Aileen's carefully modulated Mayfair voice as she said with studied indifference that she would give ten bob for it.

"Got any money?" asked Toria, before Rachel could reply. Aileen confessed, unconcerned, that she hadn't a sausage, and strolled away with Judy, grumbling without rancour about the new grey model.

Cecil came through the silver doors with a customer and stood clapping girlish, impatient hands. "Miss Irene, Miss Irene . . . . I want you, please. And Miss Aileen, fetch Miss Doon . . . . ask her to bring up the new peacock silk we got in last week. You're going to adore it, Lady Bale, you really are. It's the loveliest thing, it'll suit your delicate colouring down to the ground, I'm really quite excited about it . . . . ," He danced round her, draping and pinning, pushing back his smooth, fair hair from his forehead. Lady Bale raised leaden eyes in a mud-coloured face and said that she was sure she would like anything Mr. Cecil chose for her. "Only nothing elaborate, Mr. Cecil, just cut quite plain, with a vee neck; you know I don't like these naked shoulders!"

Cecil, nearly swooning at the idea of his peacock silk creation with a vee neck, nevertheless controlled himself into a semblance of acquiescence, and Doon at last gathered the lengths of satin and chiffon into her arms and prepared to descend to her basement; on her way she paused at the door of the salesgirls' room to ask what they were doing.

"Cleaning Rachel's hat. There hasn't been a soul in all the morning, except this old cow with Cissie, and we've had nothing else to do."

"The workroom would have done it for you."

" Oh, the showroom's rather out of favour upstairs since that idiot Aileen smuggled out the new chiffon model to wear at a party and tore it right across the hem and had to take it up to them to be mended. Gregory found them doing it and asked awkward questions. Then Irene seemed to think that this stuff would do the trick, but it hasn't—not the hat trick, anyway."

"You're very humorous to-day," said Rachel, laughing. "She made a lovely one this morning in the chemist's . . . what was it you said, Toria?"

Victoria proudly related her joke about Gregory and the nine lives.

"Would it be any good for a plain white straw, do you think?" asked Doon, having paid suitable tribute.

"Goodness knows, my dear. You can have some and try, if you like."

"I may as well if you don't want it all. I can't take it now, with all this stuff in my arms, but I'll send Macaroni up for some."

Macaroni was Doon's secretary, so christened for reasons obscure enough in the beginning but now lost in the mists of time. She was a plump, dark maiden, who giggled and wept with equal facility and she professed a sentimental attachment for Doon, who treated her with kindly contempt. She arrived now, lumbering up the stairs on her half-comprehended mission, and pocketing the small screw of paper which Rachel gave her, picked up the sheet containing the remaining amount of crystals and asked with bovine playfulness what they were.

"They're poison, that's what they are," said Rachel, sharply. "Put it down, child, for goodness' sake." She swung round as she spoke and Macaroni, startled by the irritation in her voice, fumbled to return the paper and finally dropped it, crystals and all, on to the floor.

At that moment Bevan, accompanied by Gregory, appeared in the doorway.

3

"What's going on here?" said Bevan, angrily. "What's all this mess? and what did I hear you saying about poison?"

"It's my fault, Mr. Bevan," apologized Rachel. "It's oxalic acid and I've been cleaning a hat with it, and I'm afraid it's got spilt."

"Oxalic acid? Good heavens, what are you doing with that stuff all over the place? Where did you get it?"

"We—I bought it at the chemist's, Mr. Bevan."

"Rachel and I did," amended Victoria.

"But, my dear Mrs. Gay, this is most terribly dangerous stuff," said Bevan, ignoring Victoria and addressing himself to Rachel. "Half of what you've got there would kill a man. Surely you can't just buy it at a chemist's?"

"Yes, you can, Mr. Bevan. He has to know who you are, but you don't have to sign for it or anything."

"Nonsense, they have no business to sell you such stuff. Which chemist gave it to you?"

"It was Mr. Mitchell, across the road, Mr. Bevan. But honestly, I'm sure it's quite all right for him to let us have it; he doesn't know our names, I suppose, but he knows us very well: we're always going in there for soap and things——" Rachel cast a glance at Gregory, who stood behind Bevan, just outside the doorway.

Bevan stooped and picked up a few grains of the powder in the palm of his hand. Gregory, looking over his shoulder, said, with a virtuous sniff: "I'll clear it all up for you, Mr. Bevan."

"No, no, don't touch it. Mr. Cecil—Mr. Cecil, come here, please. Did you know the girls had this dangerous stuff in the showroom?"

Cecil came bounding across the room. "No, I didn't, Mr. Bevan. I don't know anything at all about it; I've been with a client all the morning, and really, Mr. Bevan, it does take all one's mind creating for a customer, especially when one doesn't feel well, and I don't feel at all well this morning; I can't be looking after the girls *and* contacting the customers, Mr. Bevan, really——"

"Well, see to it that this stuff is cleared up and destroyed—destroyed, please."

"You don't expect me to brush it up my*self*, I suppose, Mr. Bevan?" cried Cecil, on a rising note. The tears came into his eyes and he wrung his hands hysterically.

Bevan turned away impatiently and marched downstairs. Gregory took Cecil by the arm. "There, Mr. Cecil," she said, fixing him with her unsmiling grey eyes, "don't bother about it any more. I'll send Mrs. Harris to sweep it all up and then she can hand it over to you and you can get rid of it. I really do think, Rachel, that you might be a little less childish, when Mr. Bevan has so much to think about just now, what with the new branch and so on; this isn't a nursery, dear, is it? You should try not to be so irresponsible . . . . " She hurried downstairs in deep disgust to give orders to the charwoman. Victoria muttered rudely; Irene, from her corner, stared angrily after the retreating form; Rachel made a vulgar grimace; the two mannequins appeared from their room and said that, honestly, Gregory was a perfect bitch; even Cecil, who owed her nothing but gratitude over the whole affair, looked after her with indignant, querulous dislike, and Mrs. 'Arris, labouring up the stairs with her dustpan and broom, announced that there was two ways of asking a body to do anything, a pleasant way and an unpleasant way, and that that Miss Gregory fairly made her boil.

But it was Doon who died.

## 4

Victoria and Rachel sat in a clean, impersonal little room in the great hospital, and waited for Doon to die. "It's strange to think what a lot of emotions must have gone on in this room," Victoria said, gazing round at the blank green walls and rows of stiff-backed chairs. "It looks as if nobody but us had ever even been into it; but I suppose as much agony has gone on in here, agony in people's minds, I mean, as in any other place in London. It always seems to me as if all the thoughts must be tangled up just under the ceiling in a place like this, not able to get out. Have you ever felt like that?"

"Don't be whimsical, my pet; and you look awful, you've got an absolute moustache of dirt!"

"It's because I will keep on rubbing my nose on the back of my hand," said Victoria, ruefully. "I've always got a filthy face at the end of the day. What time is it?"

"Nearly eleven. This is hell, Toria. Why did we ever take it on?"

"We couldn't very well help it, could we? After all, poor Doon, it would be a bit off if there was nobody at all to worry about her; her friends aren't the kind of people who are much good in a crisis, and anyway, we've no idea where any of them live. It's funny how little you can know about a person, even when you work with them all day long."

"All we really know is that she lived in a lousy room in Guilford Street and put up with an awful old landlady, because nobody minded what she did there."

"And we also know what she did there. She certainly made no secret about it. And we know that she came from Australia."

"New Zealand, darling."

"Well, New Zealand; she hasn't got any relations over here, has she?"

"Not a soul. We couldn't have left her to die all by herself."

"Do you really think she's going to die?" said Rachel

"The Sister seemed to think so, Ray, didn't she? I feel awful about the oxalic acid."

"I don't see how she could have taken any, Toria, honestly I don't. It wasn't as if we left it lying about; and we told her it was poison, so that she could hardly have eaten any by mistake . . . . I wonder what happened to the lot we gave her to do her white straw with. She couldn't have taken any of that, I suppose? You don't think for a moment she could have done it on purpose, do you?"

"Why on earth should she, Rachel? She was perfectly happy; even if Bevan *was* sending Gregory to Deauville instead of her, it meant that she would get a rise and be kingpin at the shop, and she'd have been able to stay near him, which was all she really cared about just lately. There was nothing to commit suicide *for*."

"I suppose she was just as keen on the old swine as ever?"

"Oh, I think so, darling, don't you? or if she wasn't it only meant that she'd fallen for somebody else; she never fell out of love for any other reason, and she was always doing it."

"Perhaps it was because Bevan's going off her a bit?"

"I don't think so," said Victoria, thoughtfully. "I don't believe she saw it, any more than Gregory realized that she'd been completely cut out by Doon. Doon was awfully blind in that way—is, I mean—how awful ! I keep talking about her as if she were dead already. What I was going to say was that she's quite insensitive to other people's feelings and reactions and things. After all, she goes blithely through the shop and never realizes that she isn't beloved by everybody, and, when you come to think of it, she isn't beloved by anybody."

"Oh, *I* like her; and you like her, don't you?"

"Well, I do, Ray. I can't say I approve of her goings on, but I can't help being rather fond of her and she can be the best company in the world. Macaroni loves her, of course, though even she's a bit scared of her—but no one else. Judy's never forgiven her for pinching her fiancé, and Aileen detests her because she's afraid of what she'll tell her young man, and of course Gregory loathes her, since they stopped being so thick together; Mrs. 'Arris has never liked her and she's foul to the old girl sometimes; Cecil hates her because she's cruel and sarcastic and makes fun of his boy friend; and even Bevan the beloved is starting to make sheep's eyes at you again. None of them really care for her, but I'm sure she'd be terribly surprised if you told her so. She goes barging through life and because she's got rather a crude sort of mind herself, and no funny feelings to get hurt and no pettinesses like the rest of us, she never thinks that she may be hurting people, or that they may bear small grudges against her. If Judy had pinched one of *her* young men, she'd have been furious, but in a week she'd have got a new one and forgotten all about it—so she couldn't understand that Judy hasn't."

"Ah, but Judy couldn't just 'get a new one'."

"Oh, no, I'm not saying it as against Judy, Rachel. Poor darling, I think she went through hell, and I think she still does in a quiet way; she isn't changeable like Doon; I'm simply saying that you couldn't make Doon understand a thing like that."

A Sister came into the room, spruce and immaculate, with gentle eyes in a mask-like face. "I'm sorry, I'm afraid I have to tell you that your friend is dead."

They sprang to her feet: Victoria took two or three steps towards her, holding out unconsciously pleading hands. . . . "Dead!—she can't be dead?"

"I'm afraid so; I did explain to you, didn't I, that there wasn't any hope?"

"Yes, I know. I'm sorry, Sister, only—couldn't we have gone to see her or something?"

"She was quite unconscious. It was better not to, wasn't it?"

"Yes, we know that, really," said Rachel, miserably, "Thank you, Sister, for coming and telling us and for letting us wait here and all that. Do we—what do we do now? Shall we just go home?"

"Yes, I think you'd better go and get some sleep. We'll arrange all the rest. You aren't relations, are you?"

"No," said Rachel. "Just friends."

They went down the broad steps and walked in silence along the deserted pavement. "I can't help howling," said Victoria at last, half apologetically. "Poor Doon . . . somehow one can't believe that she of all people can be dead. That Sister must have thought I was an ass—she'd explained to us that Doon was going to die."

"I couldn't think of anything, when she was telling us, except the little wart on her nose," said Rachel, reminiscently. "I didn't realize it at the time, but I can see it now, a horrid little brown wart on her quite nice face. It's funny how things take you—I was really fonder of

Doon than you were, and yet when I hear she's dead all I can think of is a little brown wart on somebody's face. You'd better take a taxi, darling."

"Yes, I can't face a bus with my eyeblack all running and a moustache of dirt, as you so kindly put it. Good night, darling; go to bed like the nurse said and try to forget about it for a bit. I'm afraid it's going to be hell to-morrow."

Rachel dragged herself up her stairs and opened the front door of her tiny flat. Here were the relics of her first happy years of married life: two good, comfortable chairs covered now with an inexpensive linen; a Persian carpet, a couple of water-colours, silk brocade curtains that once had framed windows looking out on to country fields. The chairs had been made up into some sort of bed for herself; from her divan in the corner a small voice greeted her: "Mummy! I thought you was never coming."

"Oh, Jess, darling, couldn't you have gone to sleep?"

"Well, I did but then I woke up, and I've been waiting and waiting for you."

"I had to go out, my rabbit; I'm so sorry. That's the worst of Mummy working in London, isn't it? It's very boring for you stuck here all day long with Alice."

She sat down on the edge of the bed and took the child into her arms. Jessica wriggled free and, moving up to the top of the divan, perched herself on the pillow and regarded her mother with shining, precocious eyes. "I don't like being mauled," she said, deliberately.

Rachel flinched. "Jessica *dar*ling! What do you mean? Where did you learn to say that?"

"I've heard you say it to Daddy."

"Have you, Jessica? But that must have been a long, long time ago. We haven't seen Daddy for a long time now. You ought to forget those things."

"I saw him to-day," said Jessica, her voice full of an uncomprehending hostility against she knew not what.

"You saw Daddy to-day? Where?"

"He came and saw me here. Alice went to answer the bell and there was Daddy. He told Alice she could go

24

out for half an hour and he stayed and played with me. He gave me a lovely book—look, Mummy!"

Rachel snatched the book, and with a vicious twist, sent it flying towards the wastepaper-basket. "You can't have it, baby. I'm sorry but you can't keep it. I'll get you another one to-morrow." She looked at the child, afraid of the effect of her anger on the delicate mind, and said more gently: "Daddy ought not to have come here to see you, darling. You know we decided long ago, three months ago, that he was unkind and unfriendly to Mummy so he couldn't be your Daddy any more; Mummy went and told the Judge and he agreed with her and said that you and Mummy must stick together and do without a Daddy. . . ."

"What's the King's Pocket?" interrupted Jessica, paying not the slightest attention to the carefully chosen words.

"The King's Pocket? What on earth do you mean?"

"Daddy said where were you? and I said you hadn't come home from the shop but you rang up and told Alice to put me to bed, and Daddy said, 'Does Mummy go out with Mr. Bevan from the shop?' and then he said that that would be nice for the King's Pocket."

"The King's Proctor?" said Rachel, faintly.

"The King's Pocket," insisted Jessica.

It was nearly midnight.

## *Two*

### 1

At Scotland Yard Mr. Charlesworth's Chief pressed several buzzers and bent again over his morning reports. As each buzzer was answered, he handed out a file of papers, hardly looking up from his work; but to Charlesworth he murmured, "A dress shop!" and regarded him with a twinkling eye.

"A dress shop!" cried Charlesworth in accents of deep dismay.

"Well, knowing your genius for handling young women. . . ."

"I'm not genius enough to make one of them take any interest in me," said Charlesworth, bitterly.

The Chief looked anxious. "My dear boy, you're not still grieving over that affair? You mustn't let these things get you down. Miss Humphreys was a charming girl, of course—I remember meeting her one week-end at your father's place; but . . ."

"Miss Humphreys!" cried Charlesworth, quite overcome by surprise. "Good Lord, sir, it isn't Miss Humphreys I'm worrying about. Jane was the sweetest thing, of course, and I'm the greatest possible friends with her to this day; but—Good Lord, no! This is much more serious than that, though I know I thought that was serious at the time. I mean this—well, I beg your pardon, sir. The dress shop?"

"Ah, yes. Well, here's the report, Charlesworth, and I'm putting the whole thing into your hands. One of the hospitals has notified the coroner that a girl was brought in yesterday afternoon, and died during the night. They suspect corrosive poisoning. Sergeant Bedd seems to have been on the job and he reports, as you'll see, that the whole thing looks a bit fishy; and furthermore that the young lady worked in a dress shop. Probably an accident, I should think; wouldn't you, on the face of it? but still, there's nothing much doing at the moment, so you'd better run along and clear it up as best you can. Take your mind off your troubles, eh?" He forebore to smile until Charlesworth had left the room, for he had a very soft spot indeed for that young man.

2

Charlesworth cleared off odds and ends of work, did some telephoning and arranged a meeting with Sergeant Bedd. The post-mortem had been hurried forward and while he waited for the report he strolled down to the mortuary and asked to see the body. The attendant, who knew him well, jerked a thumb at one of the slabs, and bent again over his grisly task. Charlesworth pulled back the sheet.

The auburn hair and strong, sweeping brows looked as though they had been painted over the magnolia skin. Doon had died in torment and her mouth was still ugly with pain. Her blunt white hands were clenched at her sides, though the lovely body had been mercifully straightened out. He made a note that her hands and feet were manicured, her skin delicately cared for, and her whole person eloquent of the most meticulous attention. Sick and depressed, he flung back the covering to hide the ugly seam pulling together the thick white skin, and began to jot down remarks in his little black book.

"Who did the p.m.?" he asked the attendant.

"Dr. Littlejohn, sir."

"Oh, thank the Lord; he's a fellow I know. Can I have a word with him?"

Littlejohn appeared, wiping fastidious hands. "Hallo, Charlesworth, what do you want?"

"Somewhere to be sick, said Charlesworth, promptly.

"Good heavens, you've been here often enough; it isn't like you to be squeamish."

"Well, I've been looking at the girl, and she was a nice-looking wench."

"Oh, are you on that job? Yes, poor kid, she had enough oxalic acid in her to slay an ox."

"Oxalic acid, was it?"

"Tons of it."

"You haven't got the report out yet, I suppose?"

"Have a heart, man, I've got half a dozen more of 'em to do. I'll send it up to you as soon as I can. It's quite straightforward, anyway; lots of oxalic acid, probably in crystal form."

"How do you know it was crystals?"

"Well, I don't actually; only she seems to have had

access to some, according to the history, and she certainly died of oxalic."

"Was it taken with food?"

"I think so, yes. About seven or eight hours before death."

Charlesworth did rapid calculations. "That would bring it down to about lunch-time."

"Round about."

"Anything else?"

"That's what it all boils down to; actual quantities and so forth will be in the reports."

Charlesworth took his leave, but returned on an impulse. "Littlejohn, for my private information—was she a whatsa-name?

"For your private information, Charles, she was not."

"My faith in human nature is always getting these jolts," said Charlesworth and cheerfully went his way.

Sergeant Bedd met him outside and they stood together on the steps of the mortuary, poring over the notes, a tall, fair, smiling young man and a grizzled, thick-set, middle-aged one. Charlesworth's eyes are an honest and friendly grey; but Bedd's are as blue as the summer skies, set deeply in his square, brown face. He wears plain clothes, the coat straining across his broad shoulders, the trousers not quite wide enough in the leg. Charlesworth is in grey, a well-cut suit, chosen last year with care, worn for a week with uneasy pride and thenceforward without any consideration whatsoever. Bedd has one new suit a year with unfailing regularity; he pays five guineas for it, off the peg, and its pockets bulge with pens and pencils, foot-rules and tape-measures, an over-stuffed wallet, a fat cigarette case of inferior silver which he would not lose for a fortune, and finally the notebook which he now produces for Charlesworth, full of details and information. The girl's parents are in New Zealand and have been notified. He has called at Christophe et Cie and informed the principals that an officer from Scotland Yard will shortly be calling to ask a few questions about Miss Doon's death. He has advised that the routine of the shop shall continue, and has asked that all members of the staff shall remain on the premises. He has called upon Miss Doon's land-lady and made similar arrangements....

"Jolly well done, Bedd," says Charlesworth, relieved of much dirty work. "You must have wings to get about the way you do."

"I used one of the cars, sir," says Bedd, whose mind works along literal lines.

They transferred to Charlesworth's own car and Bedd suggested starting off at the shop. "She spent most of the day there, sir, and if she died of poison she must have taken it while she was there, I suppose."

"Oh, she died of poison all right," said Charlesworth comfortably, as they started off. "I've just seen Little-john and he gave me the result of the p.m. Oxalic acid. Easy enough to come by, isn't it?"

"Get it at any chemist's, sir; no restrictions. It's used for cleaning brass and various things like that. Shall I check up and see if she bought any?"

"Yes, sometime; but I'd like you to stick to me for the moment while I ask questions of all this dress shop lot; and see that I don't drop any bricks. Talking of bricks, Bedd, I've a nasty feeling that this may be one of yours. The whole thing looks mighty straightforward to me: I bet it was nothing but an accident—muddled up the oxalic acid tin with the slimming salts, or something—though, by gum," he added reminiscently, "she had nothing much to worry about in that direction. What's this something fishy you're so set on?"

"Something fishy? *I* never said nothing about some-thing fishy, sir," said Bedd, earnestly. "It wasn't anything in perticular, but just this: the first report from the hos-pital said that they suspected corrosive poisoning in crystal form, and as far as they could tell it must have been taken not long before she was brought in. Now, I thought to meself that there isn't much in crystal form that you take in the daytime, is there, sir? Salts and them things you take first thing in the morning; of course, that's very broadly speaking—there might be lots of stuff a woman would take, but I couldn't think of any. I wondered if it could be suicide by any chance, so I thought I'd better make a note of it; it wasn't anything you could call fishy, sir.''

"Have you inquired at her home?"

"I was only there a minute, just to tell them not to disturb things. It's not very far in the car; would you like to drop in before we start at the shop?"

They stopped at a dubious-looking door in a Bloomsbury street. An old woman, consumed with curiosity, showed them into a large and rather musty room, still in the state of almost incredible disorder in which Doon had left it. "I done nothink to it, sir," said the harridan, observing Charlesworth's look of surprise. "Miss Doon she used to leave it till she come 'ome in the evening as often as not. I did it out two days a week for 'er, and I would 'ave come in and straightened it up a bit to-day, though it's not my day, properly speaking; but this gentleman 'ere, 'e told me not to touch it." She started automatically to pick up a few scattered garments and fling them on to the bed. "She was a one and no mistake," she went on, regarding the confusion with an indulgent eye. "Poor girl, this is a terrible thing, sir, 'er dying so sudden. Oo'd 'ave thought it? Accident I suppose it was, if you'll pardon me askin'?"

"I suppose so," said Charlesworth, abstractedly, his mind occupied with the discrepancy between the expensive scents and lotions on the dressing-table, the profusion of extravagant clothes and possessions, and the cheap and dingy appearance of the lodgings. "You have no reason to think it was anything else, have you? She wasn't depressed or anything?"

"Oh, I don't think so, sir. Oh, no, nothink like that, sir, I don't think. Why, only yestidy, as she was going out in the morning, she says to me, ''Ow do you like me new 'at, Mrs. Briggs?' she says; 'pretty good, isn't it?' she says. 'It is, indeed, Miss,' I says; 'that'll fetch the boys,' I says, 'aving me joke, like. 'That's good,' she says. 'I've got a lunch date to-day that's going to change me 'ole life,' she says."

"But she had lunch at the shop," said Bedd.

"Well, I don't know nothink about that, sir. Them's the words she said to me, 'I've got a lunch date to-day as'll change me 'ole life,' she says. . . ."

"Had she lived here for long?" asked Charlesworth

"Best part of a year, sir. It isn't nothink grand, but she liked it; she wasn't one to fuss, Miss Doon wasn't, and if she could 'ave 'er parties and make a bit of a row now and agen and nobody to arst any questions, she didn't mind if a lick of paint was missing 'ere and there. She paid well, she did, and I've nothink to complain of."

"Funny thing about the lunch," said Charlesworth, as he and the sergeant climbed into the car again. "I do believe it's beginning to look a bit fishy after all."

"Well, I couldn't 'elp wondering."

"I hope your wondering comes off, anyway. We should look a couple of fools, ferreting out a bit of carelessness among a pack of women—my God!" exclaimed Charlesworth as they pulled up at the silver door. "What's this—this isn't the shop?"

"Pretty 'igh class, sir, isn't it?" said Bedd, with proprietary satisfaction.

High blue heels pattered across the floor. "Can I show you something?" asked Victoria with her sweetest smile.

"I am an officer from Scotland Yard," said Charlesworth, severely; "and I should like to see the manager. Did she think I'd come to order my trousseau?" he muttered to the sergeant, as they followed her across the thick carpet.

"I rather doubt it, sir," said Bedd, innocently. "She's seen me 'ere this morning, and she must know who we are. I'm rather afraid, Mr. Charlesworth, sir, if you don't mind me saying so, that the young lady was pulling your leg!"

Bevan was in his office, a slim, grey-haired man of middle height, in an obtrusively well-cut suit. He had an odd trick of turning his head with a sharp movement away from the speaker, and looking at him out of the corners of his eyes. He did so now while Charlesworth

31

introduced himself and explained the reason of his visit.

"We have definitely established the cause of Miss Doon's death, and I hope you can make it convenient to allow me to ask some questions of the people who worked here with her."

"Yes, yes, the sergeant was round here this morning and arranged all that. This is a ghastly thing to have happened." He swung himself round in his black and chromium chair and glanced sideways at Charlesworth again. "I hope to goodness there's not going to be a whole lot of publicity. It'll be terribly bad for the business."

"I'm afraid that simply depends on the Press," explained Charlesworth. "If they get hold of a story and plug it, we can't stop them. Lack of information from the police is the last thing they'll worry about. However, if it turns out to have been just an accident . . ."

"Of course it was an accident; what else could it have been?"

"Well, Mr. Bevan, Miss Doon died of corrosive poison, taken in crystal form. She took an awful lot of it, and it's difficult to see how she can have made a mistake about it. Of course she may have thought she was taking something else and that's the easiest answer; but we're bound to make sure that she mightn't have taken it deliberately."

Bevan went grey, and Charlesworth followed up the lead. "Or, of course, that it wasn't given to her deliberately . . . ."

"That's simply nonsense!"

"Yes, it may be, but as I said, we're bound to find out. I suppose you couldn't think of any motive there might have been to get Miss Doon out of the way?"

"My dear Inspector, this is simply fantastic. Girls don't murder each other in respectable dress shops."

"Well, it has been done," said Charlesworth, nonchalantly. "And, of course, it needn't necessarily have been someone in the dress shop. Do you know any of her associates outside her work?"

"No, I don't."

"You didn't know her outside the shop, I suppose?"

"No, I didn't—that is, I saw her occasionally."

"How did you come to employ her in the first place?"

"She answered an advertisement for a sales assistant, but she was much too valuable to be left in that kind of post; she did some secretarial work for me and a certain amount of buying and two years ago I gave her the management of the stock—models and materials and so on. Heaven knows what I shall do without her; I was going to . . ."

"Were you going to say something?" asked Charlesworth, sweetly.

"Well, I was going to promote her to being my personal assistant."

"It's certainly odd, under those circumstances, that she should have taken her life."

"Good heavens, man," cried Bevan, as much exasperated as Charlesworth could have wished. "Why do you keep harping on that? Of course she didn't kill herself." There was a pause and he went on more quietly: "The girls were messing about in the showroom with a lot of stuff which they said was poison. She probably took some of that, by mistake."

"Oh, ah, this is a bit more like. What sort of poison was it?"

"It was oxalic acid, and they were using it to clean a hat. I had it cleared up and thrown away."

"Who did the throwing away?"

"My showroom manager, Mr. Cecil."

"Oh, did he? Well, I shall want to have a word with Mr. Cecil before I go very much further. You might go down and get hold of him, will you, Bedd? Now, Mr. Bevan—when you say 'they" who exactly had the stuff?"

Bevan hesitated. "I hardly know," he said. "The three salesgirls were sitting together, as far as I remember: Rachel Gay, Victoria David, and Irene Best—no, no, Mrs. Best was at her desk, in the corner."

"Was Miss Doon there?"

"No, she wasn't. I went on downstairs to her office and spoke to her."

"Is it true that she had lunch here, in the shop?"

Bevan looked uncomfortable; he had been going to take Miss Doon out to lunch, he said, to discuss matters of business, but—er—he had had to alter his plans.

"Did you yourself have lunch in the shop? I ask you, because it will be necessary for me to get some sort of an account of what went on during the luncheon hour, so that I can discover whether it was possible for the girl to have taken poison with her food."

Bevan, for reasons of his own, had made most careful inquiries as to what had happened while he was out; he had foreseen the questions of the police and, for all his apparent surprise and distress, was not unprepared for suggestions of either suicide or murder. He embarked now upon a résumé of the hour from one to two.

It seemed that it had been Irene's 'day' to take the twelve-to-one lunch hour, and afterwards to remain on duty in the *salon* while the rest of the staff was downstairs. This entailed the duty of helping Mrs. Harris to juggle with the plates and dishes and serve out the portions of food, afterwards placing them in hot cupboards, from which the girls helped themselves on their, often belated, release from the showroom. On this occasion, as she counted the plates, Cecil came finicking up and announced that he would carve.

"There's nothing to carve, Mr. Cecil, thank you very much," said Irene. "It's curry."

"Well then, I'll serve out the curry and you can do the vegetables; and I shall stay and have mine down here with you girls—so you needn't lay a tray for the office, Mrs. Harris. Mr. Bevan's going out."

"He's taking Doon out, I believe," said Irene. "That'll be only seven plates, then, won't it? yourself and Victoria and Rachel (I've had mine), and the two mannequins and Macaroni and Gregory. Put that fat bit on Gregory's, Mr. Cecil, will you? She's such a fuss-pot, she'll scream the place down if she doesn't get the best helping."

Toria came running down the stairs. "Rene, you're wanted in the *salon*. Lady Norman's here. What's for lunch? Curried rabbit? How nice. Can I have this lovely fat bit, Mr. Cecil?"

"That's booked as a sweetener for Miss Gregory," said Cecil, giggling; "but I'll keep a special bit for you."

"Will you? Thanks awfully. And did you both remember that Doon'll be out? Come on, Irene, the old girl will be gnashing her teeth. I'll send Ray down to help you, Mr. Cecil."

Rachel arrived, panting. "What's for lunch? Curried rabbit? Good. Can I have this bit of back, Mr. Cecil?"

"No, you can't—that's reserved for Miss Gregory," explained Cecil, patiently. "Here's a nice bit for you."

"Oh, thank you, Mr. Cecil, my pet. Mr. Bevan!" she called as Bevan emerged from Doon's office and walked past the table. "You *are* going to be out to lunch, aren't you? because we haven't counted you."

"Yes, I shall be out," said Bevan, "and don't serve out any for Miss Gregory; she's having lunch with me." He leant across the table and murmured something to Cecil before proceeding on his way upstairs.

"There now, isn't that tarsome," cried Cecil, all flustered. "We've already done a plate for Miss Gregory, and now we shall have one too many."

"No, we won't, Mr. Cecil. If Gregory's having lunch with Mr. Bevan, then Doon isn't, so she can have Gregory's. Hallo, Macaroni, what do *you* want, my chicken?"

"I came to tell you that Miss Doon won't be in to lunch. I believe she's going out with Mr. Bevan," said Macaroni, sniggering delightedly.

"Well, as it happens, my child, she is not going out with Mr. Bevan, because Miss Gregory is. I suppose that means," added Rachel, *sotto voce* to Cecil, "that Gregory's definitely going to Deauville?"

"Yes, she is. Mr. Bevan told me so when he whispered across the table. He rang me up over the week-end about it, and he said that he thought after all he would send Miss Gregory."

"I wonder if she knows?"

"Well, they were together all this morning, before they came to the shop; I expect he told her."

"Why has he decided on her, Mr. Cecil, do you know?"

Cecil tossed back his fair hair, and gave her a confidential look. "Perhaps Miss Gregory was becoming rather tarsome . . . ."

Aileen and Judy strolled downstairs. "Isn't lunch ready yet?"

"No, I'm sorry," said Rachel. "Mr. Cecil and I are in a huddle together. Put the rest of the vegetables out for me, one of you, will you, like a darling? That's yours, Aileen, with extra potatoes—how you can do it, I don't know! None on this one for me and only a little for Victoria and lots of greens here for Doon. Not all *that* lot, you idiot," she added, as Aileen half-emptied the vegetable-dish on to Doon's plate. "You do it, Judy, for goodness' sake. Macaroni, don't stand like a lump, child! Help Mrs. 'Arris put the plates in the hot-cupboard; better keep Miss Doon's apart till we see what she's doing. . . ." She returned to her confidences with Cecil.

Gregory came downstairs. She looked rather white and excited and Rachel felt sure that she knew of Bevan's decision. She could not stifle her complacency at having a luncheon date and went off with a good deal of parade to tell "poor Doon" that Bevan had changed his arrangements.

"She needn't look so damn delighted," said Rachel to Cecil, scowling after Gregory's cocksure back. "As soon as she's well away, bang will go what little chance she ever had with her precious Bevan. Doon'll have him good and proper then."

"Or somebody else," said Cecil, insinuatingly.

"Good heavens, don't palm him off on *me*," said Rachel, laughing. "They can tear him to bits for all I care, and have half each."

Victoria came downstairs again and collected her lunch from the hot-cupboard nearest the table. "Don't forget, Mr. Cecil, that you have to be at the Ritz by two. Irene'll be all ready, she's got her hat and things upstairs." She sat down at the dining-table and the others joined her, each carrying a plate of food; they had started their meal when Gregory returned with a troubled and angry Doon. "Is my lunch in the hot-cupboard . . . . which, the further one?" She went to the cupboard and got out the plate. . . . "Here, Doon dear, take this. I'm so sorry about it, but Mr. Bevan just wants to talk over a little business with me—I expect he'll ask you out to-morrow to make up for it. . . ." She advanced to the table, half-propelling Doon, who wriggled uncomfortably in her grasp. "Judy, make room for Doon. Now, you sit down here, my dear, and have your lunch. . . ."

"Oh, for God's sake shut up, Gregory," cried Judy, in a fury. "Doon's got a mind of her own; she knows whether she wants her lunch or not. Silly bitch," she added long before Gregory was out of earshot; "I'd like to wring her ruddy neck."

"Stinking cat," agreed Toria automatically, her mouth full of curry.

All this, with the exception of the actual conversations and of a certain amount of detail which Charlesworth unearthed later in the morning, Bevan was able to relate. "I think that'll help to clear matters up a lot," said Charlesworth, privately thinking nothing of the sort. "Oh, here's Bedd. Is Mr. Cecil ready, Sergeant? Good. Now, perhaps you'll just let us have your full name and private address, Mr. Bevan; and then would you ask Mr. Cecil to come up right away?"

"Yes, certainly; and—er—before I go, Inspector, I'd like to thank you very much for the—er—the very decent way in which you've conducted this interview. It could have been pretty disagreeable and, of course, I'm worried and upset about the whole affair. You must forgive me if I was a bit irritable."

"Good lord, yes," cried Charlesworth, pleased. "I quite appreciate your feelings. . . . rather a pleasant chap," he added to the sergeant as the door closed.

"Very pleasant, sir. Funny thing, though—he *wasn't*

particularly irritable; not to make a song about, was he? nor was you particularly inoffensive, not while I was in here."

"Bedd, you're a psychologist! The gentleman's worried, eh? And now I come to think of it—did you see what I saw when I trotted out the idea of murder?"

"A shade of relief, Mr. Charlesworth?"

"Funny thing, wasn't it, Bedd?"

They were nodding their heads sagaciously at one another when Bevan returned; but they broke off and Charlesworth sat staring, with his mouth wide open, at the vision of his remarkable companion. Bevan broke the spell with a brief introduction and then left them and Cecil sat himself down at the extreme edge of a chair and twisted his delicate hands. He was a slim, fair man, with huge, brown, long-lashed eyes, a well-modelled nose and over-feminine mouth; at first sight one took him for a youth, but soft living had given him, too early, pouches beneath the eyes and a suspicion of a paunch. His trousers were draped over girlish hips and his suit and shirt were a miracle of lavender grey; over his forehead a lock of yellow hair was trained to fall, and be pushed back with a graceful hand. Charlesworth took one more look at the brassy gold of this lock of hair, and retired to a corner to conceal his mirth, while Bedd stolidly noted Mr. Cecil's name and address. "All very well for old Charles, giggling to hisself in the background and leaving me to get on with the job," thought Sergeant Bedd grimly; he wiped a grin from his face with a huge brown hand and announced that Mr. Cecil was now ready to be questioned.

There was a frightful silence. Charlesworth struggled to control himself and came forward to put a polite and restrained question; but his voice betrayed him and they all three jumped as he asked suddenly with a tremendous roar: "What did you do with the poison?"

The colour left Cecil's face, leaving two little patches of rouge high up on his cheekbones; his brown eyes stared at Charlesworth in stark terror and he said not a word. There was no temptation to giggle now. Charlesworth

38

pulled his chair in front of the other and sat down facing him. "Now then, quickly—what did you do with the poison?"

"I haven't got any poison! I never touched any poison!"

"Oh, look here, now. . . . Mr. Bevan's just told us that he asked you to get rid of a whole lot of oxalic acid crystals that had been spilt in the showroom. I want to know what you did with them."

"Oh, yes; well—I——" The moment had passed. Cecil's face cleared and he sat collecting his wits, looking down at his nervous hands. "I put it down the huh-hah," he declared at last in a shaking voice.

"The lavatory, sir," interpreted Bedd, without a smile.

"Yes, that's right," said Cecil, eagerly. "I went down with Mrs. Harris as soon as she had swept the powder up and I put it all down the huh-hah."

"You went straight down with her?" asked Charlesworth, and, receiving a nod in reply: "Have you any idea how much it was? A tablespoonful? A teaspoonful?"

"Not more than a teaspoonful, I don't think."

"Well, that disposes of that. You realize, of course, that Miss Doon died from taking a similar poison and we're trying to find out whether it can have been any of this lot."

"Oh, I don't think it can, Inspector. She couldn't have got any—it wasn't left lying about at all, at least I don't think so."

"You don't think she might have taken some on purpose, do you?"

The uneasy look crept back into the brown eyes; the colour began to ebb again. He said, with rising hysteria: "No, no, of course not. Why should she have wanted to kill herself? It's a dreadful idea."

"Or that she might have had it deliberately given to her by somebody else."

Cecil gave a girlish little scream at such a grisly thought and protested that it was more than unlikely: "She was not a very *nice* girl, Inspector, rather a *cruel* girl, but who could have wanted to kill her? Oh, I *don't* think that's quite

39

likely!" He fluttered his lashes and flapped his hands and finally bowed himself out. Charlesworth turned with an explosion of laughter to Bedd: "This is the rummiest case I ever was on in all my life; God bless our home, whatever are we coming to next! And for heaven's sake, Sergeant, explain to me if you can, why they should be so damn delighted when I suggest that the girl was murdered. There's something behind all this."

"It's a long way be'ind as far as I'm concerned, Mr. Charlesworth," said Sergeant Bedd, with a worried shake of his head.

### 3

The morning wore away and most of the afternoon, and Charlesworth thought that he had never before beheld such a galaxy of feminine beauty. Irene followed Cecil, a tiny brunette, agitated and in tears. She confirmed her part of the history of the luncheon hour; she had been with a customer from one to two, and then had rushed off with Cecil to the Ritz Hotel where a peeress was waiting impatiently for the famous grey model. She was terribly cross, said Irene, with a wealth of irrelevant detail; she had kept them pinning and ironing and fussing, although the model had only that moment been finished by the workroom, and they had not got back to Christophe's until after four o'clock. By that time poor Doon had been taken off to hospital; it was all too awful, sobbed Irene, and crept away to summon Rachel.

Rachel looked white and strained, but was under a stern control. She gave her name and address composedly; she was married and had one child; she was in the process of divorcing her husband, having obtained her *decree nisi* three months previously, with the custody of her daughter. She was twenty-nine. "Anything else you want to know?" her attitude seemed to demand, contemptuously. Charlesworth made it clear that there was.

Rachel described her part in the purchase of the poison and in the events of the morning. Doon had been taken ill about three o'clock. Yes, of course she had been surprised. Mr. Bevan had sent her to the hospital after Doon, and the doctor there had asked her whether it was possible for Doon to have taken any corrosive poison; she had told him about the oxalic acid, of course, but she didn't see how Doon could have taken any of that. She had reported it to Mr. Bevan and Mr. Bevan had made all sorts of inquiries as to whether it had been left lying about. After they left the shop at six o'clock she and Mrs. David, Victoria David, had gone to the hospital and stayed there till Doon was dead. She went off to fetch Victoria.

Mr. Charlesworth's susceptible heart did three somersaults and landed at Victoria's feet. Vivid and eager, exquisitely fragile with her pale-gold hair and shining eyes, she seemed like an April breeze in the stuffy little room. In a sort of a daze he heard her give her name and address, and then, conscious of a silence, started to put feverish questions. Was it correct that she had bought some oxalic acid with Mrs. Gay? "Oh, yes," said Victoria. Could she think of any way in which Miss Doon might have accidentally taken a dose of it? "Oh, no," said Victoria. Was it correct that she had gone down to the kitchen while the lunch was being served out? Well, yes, but only for a moment, to tell Irene that she was wanted upstairs. She herself and Mrs. Gay had spent half the night in the hospital till poor Doon died. "We were both rather fond of her," added Victoria, sadly.

"Let me get this straight: you and Rachel Gay and Irene Best are the salesladies in the showroom, is that right?"

"Yes."

"And Miss—er—Miss Aileen Wheeler," said Charlesworth, consulting a list, "Miss Wheeler and Miss Judy Carol are the mannequins?"

"Yes, they don't sell, they just walk around in the models and show the customers what they are going to look like in the dresses—perhaps!" said Victoria, explaining to mere man. She added casually, "Judy's not here to-day."

"Not here?"

"No, she rang up this morning to say that she wasn't well." Victoria looked vaguely troubled.

"Nobody's told me this."

"Mr. Bevan's been so worried and upset that I don't believe he's realized. Gregory knows. I suppose you could go and see Judy at her home; can I ring her up and say you're coming?"

"No, I'll have to arrange about that later. Where were we? Oh, yes, you were telling me about the shop. Now, Miss Doon? What was she?"

"She kept the stock and things; she was the sort of link between the *salon* and the workroom upstairs. Miss Gregory is Mr. Bevan's secretary and glorified general factotum. She dances attendance on him with a very stately measure."

"And what about this Mr. Cecil?"

"Oh, well, Christophe's was really built round him; he does the designs and copes with most of the important customers, and so on. Mr. Bevan owns the shop and he's got another one in Paris and he's opening a branch in Deauville; but Cissie's really the most important part of it—he's marvellous in his own sphere."

"Cissie?"

"I'm sorry; we always call him that and I forgot. When you see him, you'll understand."

"I've seen him," said Charlesworth.

"Oh, then you do understand," said Victoria, smiling faintly.

Encouraged by the smile, Charlesworth cast about for further questions. "Did you know Miss Doon well? Did you see anything of her outside her work?"

"Yes, a bit. She used to come to our flat sometimes. My husband's a painter, you see, and she sat to him for one or two nudes. He was terribly thrilled with her."

A cloud passed over her face, but Charlesworth was quite unable to make out whether it might be attributed to jealousy or resentment, or merely to the tragic thought that the lovely body now lay cold and quiet in a mortuary. He let her go.

Aileen came next, a goddess, draping herself with languid grace across the arm of a chair, and answering his questions in accents of the utmost gentility, but with an intonation that rang like a tocsin in his ears. "Did you ever see Miss Doon outside the shop?" asked Charlesworth, having taken her over the events of the previous day. "Did you know her personally apart from your work?"

"No, I did not."

"Were you on friendly terms with her in the shop?"

"The mannequins saw hardly anything of her in the shop; I've never even spoken to her outside."

"I suppose you haven't any idea as to how she might have come to take a dose of this oxalic acid?"

"Not a sausage," said Aileen automatically, and took her departure.

Even Bedd's equable pulse had been stirred by the vision of her wild-rose face and burnished hair, but he shook his head sadly after the retreating form. "Beautiful, but dumb," said Bedd.

"Pity she isn't," replied Charlesworth, and mentally crossed Aileen off his books.

Mrs. 'Arris provided a savoury in this feast of sweetness. A stout, red-cheeked woman, who looked as though she wore a life-belt fastened under her worn woollen cardigan, she marched into the office and, planting her feet wide apart, demanded: "Wot's this? Perlice?"

"That's right. We——"

"Well, I never done it."

"Nobody has suggested——"

"I never done nothink. It's all 'er lies."

"Now, please be quiet, Mrs. Harris——"

"A bit of fish, maybe, and a few cold potatoes, no good to anybody, but nothing more I *won't* allow. I've always bin known as a good, 'ard-workin' woman, and without my 'usband's sent for, nothing else will I say."

"I don't know what you're talking about, Mrs. Harris. Now please be quiet and let me put a few simple questions to you."

"Sending for the perlice, just for a bit a fish."

"This has nothing to do with fish. A young lady, Miss Doon, has died, and I'm simply here to find out what she died from. I believe the staff here have lunch in the basement and that you're generally down there helping with the serving out and so on; and I want you to tell me whether you think it's possible that Miss Doon had anything to eat, or any tea, between lunch-time and the time she was taken ill."

"Not without she 'ad some sweets or somethink in 'er office, she didn't. Tea she did not 'ave, that I do know. She was took bad before it went round."

"But she ate her lunch all right?"

"No, she did not, never being a one for curried rabbit and complaining Monday it was worse than ever."

"What was wrong with it?"

"Nothink that I could see, but she was always one to make a fuss. 'I can't eat this 'ere,' she says, 'worse than usual it is,' she says. 'What's for sweet, Mrs. 'Arris?' she says. 'Jelly, Miss,' I says. 'Good lord,' she says, 'what are we comin' to? Well, bring me mine, Mrs. 'Arris,' she says, 'and take this muck away.'"

"And did you give her a jelly?"

"Yes, cook give me a jelly through the 'atch, and I takes and gives it to Miss Doon. 'There you are, Miss,' I says. 'And cook says you can 'ave another 'elping if you want it, being as 'ow Miss Gregory's out and won't want 'ers.'"

"What happened to the rest of her meat?"

"Well, there wasn't much left. After all 'er grumbling she seemed to 'ave got through most of it. Put it all in the dustbin, I did. D'you think it was orf?"

"Well, something did upset Miss Doon, didn't it? I suppose the dustbins have been emptied long ago?"

"Yes, the sergeant arst me that first thing this morning. Emptied before I got 'ere they was. I wonder if there was somethink wrong with that rabbit? Come to think of it, I 'ad terrible pains in the night, meself?"

"What, last night? After the rabbit?"

"That's right, chronic they were. I says to my 'usband, 'George,' I says, 'my stomach's terrible agen,' I says. . . ."

"Oh, then you've had these pains before? They weren't something new?"

"Bless you, no. I 'as them nearly every night. Wot I suffer nobody knows, not without it's my husband. 'George,' I says to 'im . . ."

"But under the circumstances, you don't think it need necessarily have been the rabbit?"

"Well, you never know, do you? Still, the other young ladies 'asn't complained, not without it was Miss Rose from the workroom, but that was a needle what she got in 'er finger from the sewing-machine. . . ."

"Thank you, thanks awfully, Mrs. Harris. You see it was all nothing to worry about, was it? And you've been very helpful."

"Well, it was the brooch, atcherly, sir, that I 'ad at the back of me mind. Miss Doon she lorst 'er brooch, see? and Miss Gregory she would 'ave it that I'd got something to do with it, and they kept on going at me, and worriting that poor little Macaroni about it too, and 'er as innercent as the babe unborn, and that fond of Miss Doon she would do nothink to 'arm 'er, let alone steal 'er brooch. Then all the time it turns up in the lining of Miss Doon's coat when she was being took. That Gregory I'd like to scrag 'er. You won't take no notice of anythink she tells you, will you, sir?"

"Not as far as the brooch is concerned. Don't you worry, Mrs. Harris, that's all right with me; and the fish too. . . ."

Mrs. 'Arris thanked him with tears in her eyes and drifted out, still muttering.

If Mrs. 'Arris provided the savoury, Miss Gregory certainly started off as the sorbet. She greeted Charlesworth frigidly, and totally ignored the sergeant, who felt himself, most unreasonably, getting pink and uncomfortable. She was a tall, rather angular girl, growing a little heavy at the hips, and with a small oval lump, probably of

45

thyroid origin, prominent in her slender throat. She was dressed with meticulous care and made up heavily but with an inexpert hand. Charlesworth turned his head uneasily from the stare of her cold, grey eyes, but started off briskly enough with his questionnaire.

"Miss Gregory, I understand that you didn't go into the room where the young ladies were using this oxalic acid which is suspected of having killed Miss Doon?"

"No, I did not. I was standing behind Mr. Bevan, and I could see it lying on the floor. He picked some of it up in his hand and turned to show it to me, but he threw it down again and I sent the charwoman to brush it all up. It was perfectly disgraceful that the stuff should have been lying about the place. The salesgirls are very nice people and so on, but they are completely irresponsible. Mr. Bevan's always saying so to me."

"She means she's always saying so to Mr. Bevan," thought Charlesworth, disgusted. He asked the usual question as to her personal relations with the dead girl.

Gregory's expression grew guarded. "At one time I was rather friendly with her; I found I didn't like the sort of people she went about with and I stopped seeing her."

"About this luncheon business—we think she may possibly have taken some poison by accident then. You didn't help in the dishing out, I understand?"

"No, I did not. That's the charwoman's job and I consider that it's quite unnecessary that the girls should do it for her. It only spoils these people and they begin to take advantage of it . . . she should dish out the food and put the plates in the hot-cupboards and let the girls help themselves as they come down. However——"

"Anyway, you didn't assist."

"No, I was upstairs in Mr. Bevan's office. I came down after they were all at the table, to tell Miss Doon that her luncheon appointment with Mr. Bevan was off. He had been thinking of sending her to the new branch which he is opening in Deauville and he had arranged to take her out and discuss the matter and make arrangements and so on;

but that morning he came round to see me and told me he had decided to send me instead, so of course he had to cancel his date with her—or rather, I'm afraid, he forgot all about it, and he asked me to come out for a little celebration."

Charlesworth looked at her triumphant, gloating face and hated her. "This is the perfect poisoner," he thought. "She's cruel and treacherous and selfish as hell. I must check up on this female most carefully." He changed the course of his questions a little. "Mrs. Best was in the running for the job, I believe?"

"Irene Best? Did she tell you so? Well, that really is rather pathetic. There was a slight chance for her, I suppose, if Mr. Bevan hadn't been able to spare either Miss Doon or myself; and she had a certain amount of experience and had managed the showroom here—under Mr. Cecil—for quite a long time. But as I pointed out to Mr. Bevan, she was quite impossible for the post: I didn't like doing it, of course, but it was my duty to show him that she really wouldn't have done. Poor little thing, she has no personality, you see, and after all it is rather important in a position like that to have presence and a certain amount of *charm*, if you see what I mean, and after all, poor little Mrs. Best is even quite—well, you can see for yourself. . . ."

"What the devil is she gassing about?" thought Bedd, as Gregory's voice grew lower and more confidential. "I believe she's taken quite a fancy to our Charles. What a hope she's got, with all these daisies flying about! Better do some rescue work 'ere, I think. "Well, now, Mr. Charlesworth, sir," he announced, with much preliminary clearing of his throat, "there's one more witness for us to see, Miss Doon's seckerterry; and then we'll be finished, sir." " 'Igh time too," he added inwardly, glancing at his watch. "Does she think we've got all night to spend listening to 'er running down 'er girl friends?"

"Good work, stout Cortez," said Charlesworth, as soon as they were alone. "I was getting quite frightened. She came so close that I thought she was going to eat my face.

47

Ye gods, what's this?" he added, as Macaroni came wailing up the stairs.

Kindness, sternness, terrorism, nothing could abate Macaroni's sobs. Charlesworth was quite impressed by the magnitude of her grief. "To think that I should have carried the poison to her my*self*!" howled Macaroni, and would not be comforted. They gave it up at last and contented themselves with extracting their information through her tears.

"You took the packet from Mrs. Gay and put it in your pocket. What happened next?"

"Mr. Bevan came in," sobbed Macaroni, with a fresh outburst of weeping at the memory of this awful contretemps.

"And what did you do then?"

"I ran downstairs and I gave the powder to Miss Doon and she put it in the left-hand drawer of her desk, because she keeps that locked, you see, and then she locked the drawer and I don't know anything more about it."

The sergeant went down to fetch it. "Is this all there was?" asked Charlesworth, holding the packet out before her.

"Yes, that's all."

"Well, now, look carefully. We don't want any mistakes. Is this the way the paper was screwed up?"

Macaroni gazed at it with tearful eyes. "Yes, just like that."

"You don't think it's been touched since Miss Doon put it in her drawer?"

"I don't think so," said Macaroni, lugubriously.

Charlesworth opened the paper and displayed a small quantity of powdered crystals within. "Would you say that this was the exact amount you were given? Think very carefully before you answer."

This second admonition was too much for Macaroni. She burst into tears again and all that could be heard was that it was too, too dreadful to think that she should have been the means of poisoning her dear Miss Doon.

"But, my child, you say that none of the poison has

48

gone; so it can't have been any of the lot that you took
down to her."

"There might be a few grains less."

"A few grains less wouldn't make the slightest difference
as far as you're concerned. A few grains wouldn't kill a
person. What you mean is, not that you think there are a
few grains less, but that if there were, you couldn't be sure
of telling; isn't that right?"

"Well, yes."

"And you're quite certain that there isn't any sub-
stantial difference between the packet as you gave it to
her and as it is now?"

"Well, no."

"Then at least you needn't feel any blame, need you?
Now, could anyone have gone to the packet—could they,
perhaps, have taken some out and filled it up again?"

"But how *could* they? I had the key all the time."

"Well, that's just what I'm asking you. Could they
have? And you say, no. All right, then—does that
mean that you've had the key of the drawer ever since?"

"Yes. When poor Miss Doon—when they took her
away in the ambulance, she gave me all her keys and I—I
thought I'd better keep them like I keep my own,"
choked Macaroni, quite overcome by her memories.
"She always used to take them home with her at night."

"That was very wise of you," said Charlesworth,
kindly. "Now, do you think that there's any possibility
of there being another key?"

"Oh, no, because there were only two and I've got the
duplicate. It's quite a new desk. I used to take one lot
home with me and Miss Doon used to take the others and
then, you see, if she was late or didn't come in or was—
was ill, or anything—or if I was ill, then at least one of us
would be able to open the desk."

"This is very interesting, Bedd, isn't it?" said Charlesworth, leaning back in his chair, and forgetting Macaroni's presence entirely. "You see the child says that the
poison was untouched; and if she took the keys home with
her, Miss Doon's as well as her own, I don't see how anyone

49

else can have got at it. That's definitely the only supply of poison Doon can have got from upstairs; it does seem to cut out accident and suicide, doesn't it? It begins to look as if your something fishy was something very fishy after all. Equally, if this is a case of murder it must have been unpremeditated, because nobody can possibly have known that the stuff was going to be brought into the place—there were too many people concerned in the suggestion that it should be bought; and in that case there won't have been time to juggle about with extra keys and things to have got any out of the desk; you might check up on that, will you? and see that none have been lost or anything funny; but it looks to me as if we can leave out that one teaspoonful of poison altogether. They had about four times that amount, and I suppose they must have used at least one teaspoonful to clean the hat . . . that leaves two spoonsful unaccounted for, including what was spilt when they first brought it into the place, and what they spilt later on . . . oh, my poor little faggot," he cried, coming out of his reverie at the sound of Macaroni's accelerated weeping. "I'd entirely forgotten you. Now, don't upset yourself all over again! Murder and suicide are very ugly words, we know, but we want to find out all we can and prove that it wasn't either of them, but just a very sad accident. You trot back to your work, now, and try to forget all about it—and God grant that she does forget," he added piously, as Macaroni went wailing down the stairs again. "What an ass I was to blurt it all out in front of her. Fortunately, I don't think she's too bright in the upper storey, Bedd, do you? I shouldn't think she'll have taken much of it in."

### 4

They left the shop and went at once to Judy's address. Charlesworth was surprised to find it, in sharp contrast to Doon's lodgings, a tall, comfortable house in a fashionable square. A parlourmaid showed them into the drawing-room where, after a moment, Judy's mother joined them, a pretty, pleasant little woman, a tiny bit flustered at this intrusion of the law but still able to meet it with grace and charm. She gave an impression of trying to hide some pleasurable excitement beneath an appearance of suitable regret at their unhappy mission. He introduced himself and asked if it were possible to see her daughter.

"Oh, yes, of course—well, that is, I don't know. She's supposed to be ill; oh dear, I don't know—how can I explain . . . well, you see, the truth is, Inspector, that I didn't want my daughter to go to the shop this morning so I rang up and told Miss Gregory that she was not well."

"Isn't she ill at all, then?"

"Oh, Inspector, you won't say anything to Mr. Bevan, will you? Judy will be so cross with me if you do. The girls aren't very busy there just now, it being August and so forth, and I really didn't think it would matter for once if she didn't go; I ought to explain to you perhaps, Inspector, that my daughter doesn't really need to work; she likes to have a job and be what she imagines is independent, but it isn't as if it mattered very much to her, and I'm afraid, when anything else crops up—well, I do feel that she can take a day off if she wants to. . . ."

"And what cropped up to-day, Mrs. Carol, if you'll forgive my asking?"

She looked at him from beneath lowered lashes, and then said, laughing, that what had cropped up was a young man. "He used to be a great friend of my daughter's," she explained, "and now he's turned up again. She—she happened to ring him up last night, and as it was too late for him to call round then, he came along first thing this morning. He's a very great friend, Inspector, and though Judy was quite prepared to go off to work after she'd had a few words with him, I really couldn't bear that, and I took it upon myself to ring Miss Gregory. Judy was quite horrified at first, but she soon reconciled herself to the deception!" She laughed again.

"Is your daughter in? Can I see her now?"

"Yes, of course, if you won't be cross with her about the

not being well part of it. I'll tell her to come in here to you." She went off beaming.

Judy was Sergeant Bedd's favourite all through the case. He liked her frank, round face with its halo of deep-gold hair, her downright speech and her general air of health and cheerfulness. "Gimme a bit of a figger, sir," he would argue when Charlesworth raved about the ethereal charms of Victoria. "That Miss Judy's the one I like, a nice, straightforward English girl, comes from the North I shouldn't wonder . . . Yorkshire or something like that."

Judy shook hands with them both in her pleasant way: "I'm sorry to have dragged you round here. I ought to have gone to the shop but Mummy rang up and told Gregory some tarradiddles about me, so I thought I might as well stay at home."

"You were there yesterday?"

"Oh, yes. Yes, I was." She looked at them a little anxiously.

Once more Charlesworth outlined his mission. "You weren't concerned in bringing this oxalic acid into the shop, were you?"

"Well, no, I wasn't," said Judy, almost as though she would have liked to own up that she had been. "I went and talked to the girls while they were cleaning a hat with it, but I didn't actually have any of it."

"I believe that at lunch-time you went downstairs and helped to serve out the vegetables on to the different plates; is that so?"

"Yes, Inspector, I did, though I don't see what—well, anyway, I did do a few plates, because Rachel, Mrs. Gay, that is, was talking to Cissie, and we wanted to get on with our lunch."

"Were you very friendly with Miss Doon?"

"Good lord, no, I loathed her," said Judy, with a sort of cheerful abandon that was quite a relief after the guarded answers so many of the others had given. "I didn't see anything of her outside the shop, of course, and I never had anything to do with her while I was there, if I could possibly help it."

"Your staying away to-day had nothing to do with her death?"

"No, how could it?"

"It's rather a coincidence, isn't it?"

"Well, it isn't at all, actually. You see, last night, when Doon was so ill I thought—I thought a friend of hers ought to know, so I rang him up and told him about it in case he might want to go to the hospital or anything, especially as the doctor had made it pretty clear that Doon might be going to die. I thought this—this person that I rang up was still a great friend of Doon's, but, as it turned out, he wasn't any longer; well, then," said Judy, getting deeper and deeper into the mire, "he said—well, I ought to explain to you that he used to be a friend of *mine*—and he said he would come round and see me, but as it was a bit late then, my mother said he had better come to-day; well, his idea of to-day was before breakfast this morning, so you see my mother rang up Christophe's ... oh dear," cried Judy, breaking down completely and starting to laugh, "I suppose I'd better be done with it and tell you that this morning, at the unearthly hour of eight o'clock, I got engaged to him."

So that was the joy they were bubbling over with, she and her mother. They were rather charming, Charlesworth could not help thinking, so naïvely and unashamedly happy about the whole affair. It was quite an effort to drag the conversation back to Doon.

"You can't think of any way in which she might have taken any of this poison, can you?"

Now her face took on a wary look: he hated to see it there, so much in contrast with her open, generous manner. She insisted, more emphatically than he quite liked, that she couldn't imagine how Doon could possibly have taken any oxalic acid. She had never connected it with her death until Miss Gregory had told Mummy about it on the telephone this morning.

Charlesworth shook hands with her and he and the sergeant went slowly down to the car. Judy and Aileen, Irene, Rachel, Victoria—but not Victoria!—Gregory,

Bevan, Cecil, Mrs. 'Arris, Macaroni . . . was one of them a murderer? Could it have been suicide? Remembering those lovely faces and anxious eyes he could not help wishing that the sergeant's "something fishy" would turn out to be just an accident after all. But in his heart he knew that that was too much to hope.

# Three

### I

THAT night at nine-thirty, Charlesworth suddenly let out a wild yell and rushed to the telephone.

"Louise, my angel—this is too awful! I quite forgot about coming round to see you!"

"Were you supposed to be coming round to see me?"

"Well, darling, of *course*. I've got a damn great bunch of daisies here for you. I've been coming round ever since I left you last night."

"What stopped you, anyway?"

"I'm on a case, you see; rather a treat it is—it all takes place in a dress shop, a dozen women and two men and one of *them's* only half a man. . . ."

"I can't hear a word you're saying, Charles. Anyway, you can't start coming round now. The daisies must wait till to-morrow. Come early and have supper."

"Oh, my sweet, that's too marvellous of you. I will if I possibly can; may I leave it that I will if I *possibly* can? You see, there's a lot to do on this case, it might keep me late, but if I can manage to get away, of course I'll come."

"My Mr. Charlesworth is cooling off," said Miss Taylor to her mother as she replaced the receiver. "However, I believe three months is quite a record."

"Oh, I'm sorry," said Miss Taylor's mother. "Such a nice boy. Who is he transferring his affections to?"

"To a dozen women and one and a half men," said Miss Taylor, and gave a little sigh.

Charlesworth met the sergeant by appointment at the Yard. "Who would be a ruddy detective, Bedd? I sat up half the night with wet towels round my head and all I've got out of it is a stiff neck. Just the same, I've come to one conclusion—it looks mighty like murder."

"You really think that, Mr. Charlesworth, do you?"

"Yes, I do. The secretary child's perfectly clear; the packet she took downstairs hasn't been touched. Doon didn't take any more when she spoke to the girls at the table—her hands were too full even to take what they offered to her; and she definitely didn't go out during the day, so she couldn't have got any extra. Therefore it couldn't have been suicide and I honestly don't see where accident could have come in. The stuff that was spilled was all given to Cecil; three of the girls, at least, saw the charwoman hand it over to him. What he did with it afterwards, heaven only knows—he's obviously lying when he says he put it down the huh-hah! You don't suppose he can have left it about and the girl have picked it up accidentally? He might be afraid to say."

"She was shut in her office with Mr. Bevan and the seckerterry all the morning. After lunch she sat at the table talking to the other young ladies and then she went straight back into her office; Cecil he hadn't bin into her office so he couldn't 've left it there, and I don't see what other time there was for her to get hold of it. She couldn't have taken it except with her lunch, and that's a fact, Mr. Charlesworth; except it was given to her in her office before she came out to her lunch, and Mr. Bevan and the seckerterry they both alibis each other there."

Charlesworth reflected, twirling back and forth in his desk-chair. "Except for just a moment while Bevan left them and spoke to Cecil at the carving table and went upstairs. Macaroni came out directly afterwards, but she was alone with Doon for a minute or two."

"Well, it don't seem likely, do it, sir? How could she 'ave given the girl a teaspoonful of poison crystals in that short time? Miss Doon wouldn't have bin taking sweets or anythink of that sort just before lunch; and, anyway, there's the packet of poison intact in the drawer, and the other young ladies has agreed that it was just the same quantity as they gave the kid to take downstairs."

"You're preaching to the converted, Bedd. Personally, I think there's no doubt about it. Somebody pinched some of the crystals the girls were using upstairs and put it on the bunny they had at lunch-time; but the lord knows how we're going to find out who."

"They all seem to have been messing about down in the dining-room while it was being served out, don't they, sir? I think this is going to turn out to be a question of motive before we're done with it; find out who could 'ave done it and then choose the chap who had the best reason to do it; but it's always hard to get a conviction in them cases."

"Don't I know it! Who's your favourite so far, Bedd?"

"That Cecil, sir. He's not telling the truth and that means 'e's got somethink to 'ide."

"What we want is to have a look at his pockets; if he'd taken the powder straight to the huh-hah he'd have carried it there in his hand and not put it in his pocket at all; but if he didn't—and I'm certain he's lying about it—he'd have shoved it into his pocket and, being what it was, just a screw of paper twiddled up by the charlady, it will have left signs in the lining or I'm a Dutchman. I think we'll fuss off up to the shop and ask Cissie to take his coat off."

"Be careful 'e don't misunderstand you," said Bedd, with a grin.

Arrived at the silver doors the sergeant remained in the car. "I got another idea, sir. I won't say anythink about it at the moment, if you don't mind, but you won't be wanting me right away; will it do if I get back in 'alf an hour?"

"Yes, all right, if you feel that way about it. But I shan't start on Cecil till you come back—I need a chaperon!"

Toria came forward again across the parquet and

repeated her little joke. "Good God," thought Charlesworth, "I never saw such eyes in all my days!" Aloud he asked if Mr. Bevan were in.

"Not yet, I'm afraid. Will you wait for him?"

"Yes, I've got to meet my sergeant here. Can I come and talk to the lovelies, do you think?"

They gave him a chair in their little cubby-hole. Toria and Rachel shared a table in one corner, Irene's desk was in the other, with her back to them. They clustered round him in their turquoise overalls, two dark heads and one exquisitely fair.

"Is this where you were cleaning the hat?"

"Yes," said Rachel. "I wish we'd never tried."

"It ruined the hat too," said Victoria. As though ashamed of her flippancy she added: "It's terrible to think she's actually dead!"

"Did you *like* her?" he asked them all, collectively.

"She was a funny soul," said Victoria, slowly. "She was like oysters—you either loved her or you hàted her."

"I loved her," said Rachel in her warm, sweet voice "She was so gay and big-hearted and generous; there wa nothing mean or petty about Doon."

"I liked her too," said Toria. "You didn't though Rene, did you?"

"No, I didn't," said Irene. "I can't think how anyone can say she was kind. She said the most cruel things, sarcastic things, and she was always laughing at people and making fun of them. I don't like that sort of person."

, 'Macaroni adored her, and she should know, she worked for her."

"Yes, but it was just a goofy, silly sort of affection.' Victoria began to side with Irene. "She was often terribly rough and irritable to Macaroni, only Macaroni never saw when she was being sarcastic. Look at the way Doon treated her over that brooch affair; as if the ruddy kid would pinch a brooch. . . ."

"I thought the brooch was Mrs. 'Arris's bit of trouble," said Charlesworth.

"Oh, poor old Mother 'Arris got it too. Gregory

started it, of course, but Doon joined in. The trouble with Doon was that she never stopped to think; she just said or did the first thing that came into her head—that was the secret of her generosity, really; it wasn't a very deep quality—it was just that her first impulse was to give and she followed it without further to-do. In the same way, she'd have given the brooch to either of them, any day of the week; but if she loses it and Gregory says Mrs. 'Arris took it, she rushes off and accuses Mrs. 'Arris. I do think that was rotten of her and so did we all. Rachel was furious with her, weren't you, Ray?"

"Yes, I was," said Rachel, flushing at the memory of her own wrath. "It was most unjust and I told them so. . . ."

"Oh, she's a tiger when she's roused," said Victoria, laughing. "She looks so sweet and gentle, Mr. Charlesworth, but you can't trust her—she's a tiger when she's rou . . ." She broke off, looking rather uncomfortable at the implication of her words. Charlesworth changed the direction of the conversation.

"Was Miss Doon engaged or anything?"

There was a sudden silence. Rachel broke it, saying carelessly that she didn't think so. "We didn't know much about her outside Christophe et Cie." The others looked relieved.

"What are you trying to hide from me?"

Toria looked at him and laughed. "Nothing that you're not bound to find out for yourself very soon. We just don't want to be the first people to tell you. It's very mere, anyway."

"Isn't that your sergeant at the door?" said Rachel.

Charlesworth rose and went to meet him half-way across the showroom. "What have you been up to, Bedd?"

"Doing a little petty larceny, sir."

"I thought it was something of the sort. Well, what are the proceeds?"

" 'Alf a dozen grains of oxalic acid crystal out of the lining of a coat pocket, sir."

"Good lord, Bedd, you're a wonder. Where did you find the coat?"

" 'Angin' in a wardrobe of Mr. Cecil's flat."

"You figured that the elegant Cissie would wear his suits in strict rotation?"

"That's right, sir."

"And you burgled the blinking flat?"

"I 'ad to get the porter to let me go in and write a note to Mr. Cecil asking 'im to be there at seven o'clock to-night for an interview with you, sir," said Bedd, with a great display of offended virtue.

"What am I supposed to say to him at seven o'clock this evening, may I ask?"

"You might arst 'im what he done with the rest of the poison, I suppose, sir," suggested Sergeant Bedd, respectfully.

3

After an exhausting morning, Charlesworth had some lunch and, picking up the sergeant, headed the little car for Hampstead. "My brain's whizzing round and round like a propeller," he said. "Fresh air and solitude, that's what we need . . . and I don't want to set eyes on another woman for a month. Unless it's Victoria David," he amended, laughing, "or the adorable Mrs. Best or Rachel Gay, or even Judy, the Yorkshire lass, with her golden hair. I never saw so many lovelies as there are in that place in all my life. . . ." He rambled on happily until they came to the Vale of Health, and there, snuffing joyfully at the pleasant, clean air, he stopped the car and got down to business.

"Now, let's try and get this thing straight. I've been concentrating most of this morning on how the stuff was administered, and altogether here's what I've arrived at: it appears that the staff in this damn shop are paid so much, whatever their salaries are, inclusive of lunch on the premises; apparently quite a few of the big shops do it, and Bevan is very keen on it, the idea being that the girls have a good meal once a day at least, and don't save up for silk stockings and what not at the expense of their little tums. He says that the output of work is a

59

lot higher since he started this racket, especially, as a matter of interest, towards the end of the week, when it used to go down appreciably, for the simple reason that the kids had spent all their pennies and were living till Friday on buns and a cup of tea. Of course, it's done chiefly for the workroom—they have about fifty girls up there—but as the food is being cooked for them, the executive staff may as well benefit too. The workroom girls are fed upstairs in relays and don't come into this at all. Bevan has a tray sent up to his office and Cecil often has lunch with him there. Occasionally, however, he stays and eats with the girls and so it was on Monday."

"Feels more at 'ome, I dare say," suggested the sergeant, with a grin.

"I shouldn't be surprised. Also, on the rare occasions when the executives are indulged with a chicken or a duck or something like that, he presides over the fortunate fowl with a carving knife. I tell you this to explain that it was fairly normal for Cissie to have been messing about with the unmanly job of dishing out lunch for a pack of shop girls.

"As far as the kitchen's concerned, Bedd, you saw it for yourself, and I think we can wash that out as a possible source of infection. The meat and vegetables were handed out in bulk and a certain jelly was the only thing sent into the dining-room earmarked for Miss Doon. I think the crystals would have shown up on that, and anyway they would have tasted terribly bitter on such anæmic stuff as jelly. Apart from that, the cook and her little bottlewasher can give each other perfectly good alibis for the entire morning, and couldn't possibly have got hold of any of the poison; and even granting the possibility of collusion, they were never seen outside their kitchen during the whole day; don't you agree that the people in the kitchen and the workroom can be washed out entirely?"

"Yes, I do, sir. I think we can concentrate on the show-room, and, of course, Mrs. Harris and the seckerterry."

"Good. Well, then I think we can start off with ten

possibles and ten only. Mrs. Harris and Macaroni, as you say; Bevan, Cecil and Miss Gregory; the three salesgirls, Victoria, Rachel and Irene—I trust they'll excuse my using their Christian names but it makes life so much less complicated—and the mannequins, Aileen and Judy. There's a larger staff, actually, but a lot of them are away on their holidays, and I don't think we need count them at all. So there we are, ten little nigger boys; and the more I think about it the more I'm convinced that one of them couldn't resist the temptation of all that poison lying about, and that he or she deliberately and of malice aforethought pinched a little of it and sprinkled it on the poor girl's food; but who it was, I haven't the faintest idea!"

"She didn't eat anything else during the day, sir?"

"No, I've got that pretty well set. She took nothing except the meat and vegetables; and the jelly which I think is obviously an innocent party. If she'd taken oxalic before she got to the shop, the symptoms would have come on much earlier and anyway the coincidence would have been a bit too much, wouldn't it? She didn't have any tea because she had already been taken ill; and she didn't leave the place to get hold of any more poison outside; and, as far as I can make out, she didn't eat anything in her own office; so we're left with the meat and two veg."

"It was curry, sir, wasn't it?"

"Yes, curried rabbit and, of course, that was a gift to any poisoner, Bedd. It would absorb the crystals quite quickly, especially if they were rather fine as oxalic acid often is; and it would disguise the taste as much as anything could. It evidently didn't disguise it entirely, because, according to Mrs. 'Arris, the girl did complain; but she was always a bit fussy about her food and nobody took any notice of her."

"Bit of a coincidence, would you say, sir, having such a perfect dish to 'and, all ready for putting poison on? Couldn't 'ave been arranged, could it?"

"I don't think so. The cook makes up the menus and

it was all fixed before ever the poison was brought into the place; in fact, it was already cooking by then. No, I think it was just a bit of luck and the murderer took advantage of it. I look at it this way; the whole thing was done on the spur of the moment; there was the poison lying about and it suddenly occurred to somebody that if they got hold of a little of it, a chance might come for them to use it; then they discovered that there was curry for lunch, and there was their opportunity sooner than they could have hoped. What we want to find out is, who had that opportunity, and who, out of all the people who had the opportunity to obtain it, had the opportunity to administer it; and out of them who had the motive."

"Process of elimination, Mr. Charlesworth?"

"Well, I'm very fond of my process of elimination. I like to clear out the Might-have-done-its and the Would-have-done-its and the Look-as-if-they-done-its and get down to the *Could*-have-done-its; when I've done that I look for motive; and when I've got that, I look for proofs. I like to clear my decks for action. Unfortunately, in this case nearly every blighter in the cast seems to have been a Could-have-done-it."

"They'd have to have the two opportunities, sir. One to obtain and one to administer."

"Practically all of them had both."

"That's a pity, sir. Don't leave the decks quite so clear for action, do it?" said Bedd, with a twinkle.

Charlesworth acknowledged this thrust with rueful good-humour and proceeded to relate the history of the luncheon hour as he had gleaned it from Bevan on the previous morning. Bedd listened acutely and at the conclusion emitted a heavy groan. "Decks don't look too good now, sir! Wot a shambles!"

"You see what I meant? Every single soul went to the table or near the plate of food. Of course you can't say that everyone would actually have been able to put anything on to the plate, but, on the other hand, we can't be sure that any of them would not have been able to. Certainly no one saw anything funny, but that means exactly nothing."

They pondered in silence for a while. "Let's make a list," said Charlesworth at last.

"Three columns," agreed the sergeant. "Opportunity to Obtain, Opportunity to Administer, and Motive. How's that, sir?"

"Column number three's going to look a bit thin, but never mind, go ahead. Let's take Bevan first: he went up to the table when they were cleaning the hat; he even picked up some of the powder, though they say he threw it all down again . . . he might quite possibly have kept some in his hand, I suppose. As to putting it on the plate, he leant right across the table and spoke to Cecil—he could have dropped it on then."

"What about motive?"

"None that I know of, unless there was some lovey-dovey going on what we know nothing about. Shove him down $A + B - C$. What about Cecil?"

"He's very much plus A and B, sir. Only a matter of motive. He took charge of all the crystals that were swept up and, of course, he was dishing out before lunch."

"Yes, we must check up carefully on a motive for him. Who else? Rachel Gay?"

"She could have taken the oxalic from the showroom and she helped with the serving out. Motive again."

"The same applied to the two mannequins."

"And to Mrs. David."

"Not Victoria, sergeant!"

"She was cleaning the 'at, sir; in fact it was her that first brought the poison into the place, her and Rachel Gay. I don't say that was deliberate, because it all seems to have grown up too natural like; but she could have taken some of it easy enough, and she went right up to the table, by all accounts, and put her 'and over that very plate of food, when she said, 'I'll 'ave that bit.' "

"Yes, but Bedd, don't you *see*! She thought Miss Doon was going to be out to lunch; she couldn't have poisoned her because she didn't even know she was going to be there. The same goes for Mrs. Best, Irene Best. She didn't come downstairs at all after it had been decided that Miss Doon was staying in to lunch."

"Well, but Mrs. David did, sir. She came downstairs and went to the 'ot-cupboard and got her lunch, while Miss Gregory was with Miss Doon in her office."

"And put the poison on the other plate then? No, you don't, Sergeant. It would have been easy to do, I grant you, but Victoria didn't go to that hot-cupboard at all. The cupboards are divided, one on each side of the hatch, and Victoria's was in the one nearest to the table; the poisoned plate was in the other one."

"As you like, sir. Well then, Miss Gregory; she actually took the plate out of the far cupboard and gave it to Miss Doon; she'd 'ave to take the tin cover-thing off the top, and there'd be ample opportunity for her to put poison on it then."

"Yes, but no motive; she had the job they all wanted, and she had the luncheon party and from all accounts she was highly pleased with herself; what's even more to the point, I don't see how she could have got hold of any of the stuff. When she came in with Bevan she stayed outside the girls' room where they were cleaning the hat and everybody agrees that she didn't touch the crystals at all. She went straight downstairs and told the charwoman to go and clear up the mess. Then she went into the cloak room in the basement."

"There's no possibility of collusion, I suppose, with Mr. Cecil? He couldn't have given her any of what he took?"

"No, he went downstairs with Mrs. 'Arris and out to the huh-hah, where I suppose he just put the stuff in his pocket and came back; anyway, he went straight upstairs again, and didn't see Miss Gregory at all; Mrs. 'Arris was in the kitchen all the time. After that he was in the showroom holding an indignation meeting with the girls about the way Mr. Bevan had spoken to him."

"Miss Gregory couldn't have got hold of any from Mrs. Harris?"

"Mrs. 'Arris says she never set eyes on her the whole

morning, except when the Gregory came down and told her to go and brush the stuff off the showroom floor. Besides, Bedd, have a heart; they were in the midst of an unholy row about the missing brooch; it wasn't likely that Miss Gregory was going to approach the old girl and beg for the loan of a little poison for murderous purposes."

"The brooch business might have been a put-up job."

"You've got a bee in your bonnet about Gregory; how could it have been a put-up job when they can't possibly have known that the poison was coming into the place?"

"Well, all right, sir. Miss Gregory's out and the two young ladies is out; Victoria David and Irene Best. What about this 'ere Macaroni?"

"I believe she's out too. She took the stuff she was given straight down to Miss Doon and handed it over to her, as she says she did; because Bevan told me that Doon mentioned it to him afterwards. And there it is now, just as the girls say they gave it to her; packet screwed up the same way and approximately the same amount of poison."

"She might have picked some up in the scramble, after she dropped the lot they were cleaning the hat with."

"No. Everyone agrees that she gave one yelp when she saw Bevan in the showroom and legged it downstairs as fast as she could lick. She certainly had opportunity to put poison on the plate, because it was she that put the plate in the hot-cupboard; and I supposed there may have been a motive mixed up in this business of the brooch, though I think most of the suspicion had shifted to Mrs. 'Arris; but she couldn't have got any poison, I'm practically sure."

"Well, then, she's —A+B+C. Then there's Mrs. 'Arris herself."

"And she's got everything, Bedd. Motive, ready-made; opportunity to obtain and ample opportunity to administer."

"I don't like to think it of the old girl, Mr. Charlesworth, straight I don't."

"Neither do I, poor old faggot. All the same, I'm afraid she's Suspect No. 1. Let's see how the list looks now."

The sergeant licked a stub of pencil and made a laborious table. "Minus A for Irene," pointed out Charlesworth, looking over his shoulder. "She was nowhere near the table where they were cleaning the hat; she couldn't have had any poison."

"She was in the room, sir."

"Yes, but she never touched the crystals, Bedd. Everyone says that. She is supposed to have picked a few up off the floor, but Mrs. Gay says there was hardly any there, and she herself only got a few of the bigger grains; the rest you couldn't get hold of . . . they were swept up with a vacuum cleaner next morning."

"Anyway, it 'ardly matters, sir, as she's minus B as well. 'Ere you are, Mr. Charlesworth, in order of suspicion."

He presented the list with pride and Charlesworth gazed at it hopefully.

| | Opportunity to Obtain | | Opportunity to Administer | | Motive | |
|---|---|---|---|---|---|---|
| Mrs. Harris | + | A | + | B | + | C |
| Mr. Cecil | + | A | + | B | + | ?C |
| Mr. Bevan | + | A | + | B | + | ?C |
| Rachel | + | A | + | B | − | C |
| Aileen | + | A | + | B | − | C |
| Judy | + | A | + | B | − | C |
| Gregory | − | A | + | B | − | C |
| Macaroni | − | A | + | B | + | C |
| Victoria | − | A | − | B | − | C |
| Irene | − | A | − | B | − | C |

Probable: Mrs. Harris, Mr. Cecil, Mr. Bevan
Possible: Rachel, Aileen, Judy
Impossible: Gregory, Macaroni, Victoria, Irene

"So what?" said Sergeant Bedd at last, having recently been to the pictures.

### 4

Cecil lived in a block of flats in Bayswater, not one of those great rabbit-warrens but a little nest of bijou service flats for bachelors. There was a good deal of pseudo-Tudor furniture in the hall and the lift was panelled and decorated to correspond. It worked, however, with twentieth-century efficiency and Charlesworth rang the bell of number 9 on the second floor.

Cecil appeared in a dressing-gown whose sickly yellow served only to heighten the extraordinary pallor of his face. The lock of hair fell more limply than ever over his furrowed brow and he frequently, during the conversation that followed, forgot all about tossing it back. His flat was in a state of chaotic disorder; nails and tin-tacks were naked upon the walls as though innumerable pictures and draperies had been recently torn from them; a solitary photograph stuck out here and there, the book-shelves were empty and half a dozen occasional tables did nothing but take up room. Charlesworth sat down gingerly in a Victorian rocking-chair and, motioning away the gros-point footstool which Cissie solicitously placed beneath his feet, proceeded to open fire.

"Mr. Cecil, I must explain that I wasn't entirely satis-fied with what you told me yesterday about your disposal of that oxalic acid. I want you to repeat to me exactly what you did after Mr. Bevan asked you to have it swept up."

"I put it down the huh-hah, Inspector, as I said."

"Begin at the beginning, will you? Mrs. Harris swept it up and gave it to you? All of it?"

"Oh, yes, Inspector; she swept it right into her dustpan and then tipped it out on to a piece of white paper; there wasn't any left in the pan or on the floor."

"You're quite sure of that?"

"Oh, yes, I am, and you can ask the girls; they were there too . . . naughty things, they should never have brought it in."

"Did Mrs. Best help to pick it up?"

"Nobody touched it, Inspector; I was standing there watching it until Mrs. Harris came upstairs, and Irene was sitting in her corner all the time."

"And then you carried it straight down to the lavatory in the area?"

"Yes."

"Did you see anyone on the way?"

"On the way? Of course not, Inspector, there was no one to see."

"You didn't speak to Miss Gregory?"

"No, I didn't even see her."

"So that nobody can say whether or not you had the poison in your hand?"

"Mrs. Harris may have noticed it; she followed me down the stairs."

"And she would have seen you come back with it in your pocket?"

"Yes, she was in the . . . no, I mean, of course not. I didn't have it in my pocket."

"There are traces of it in the lining."

Cecil regarded him with terrified brown eyes. "There can't be! There aren't. . . ."

"Oh, yes, there are."

For a moment he thought that Cecil was going to faint; but after a long silence a cunning look crept over the pallid face and he suggested, like a child trying out a story which it hardly hopes will be believed: "Perhaps I put the hand holding the poison into my pocket as I went downstairs. I may easily have done that. . . in fact, now I come to think of it, I do believe that I unconsciously . . ."

From this bright suggestion he would not be budged.


# *Four*

## I

BEFORE the shop opened next morning, Charlesworth was on the threshold of Christophe et Cie. Judy came forward, still in her outdoor coat, and opened the silver door. "You're a bit early, Mr. Charlesworth! We haven't started the day yet."

"I'm in rather a hurry this morning, but I wanted to see Mr. Bevan for a minute. Is he in?"

"I shouldn't think so, but I've only just got here myself. Would you like to go over to his office and see; you know the way by now, I should imagine."

She ran downstairs. Charlesworth walked quickly across the heavy carpet and lifted his hand to knock at the door of Bevan's room; he dropped it again as a voice came from within, speaking low and tenderly: "Haven't you got a kind word for me this morning, after I've taken all the trouble to get here early so as to talk to you? Not even a little kiss?"

"Not a sausage," said a nasal voice, and there was a gurgle of soft laughter.

Charlesworth strolled back to the door. Aileen! Aileen and Bevan! The key was still in the silver lock and he turned it and went out to the car. After a moment's thought he cancelled his original plans and headed for Bevan's flat.

Maryland Mansions was a block of flats larger but not less pretentious than Cecil's bijou nest. It took a good deal of time to sort out the night-watchman on Bevan's stair-way from an army of porters, remarkable rather for the splendour of their uniform than for their physique; but at last Charlesworth ran him to earth, breakfasting in a dingy room next to the boiler-house; and, once discovered, he was delighted to air his views.

"Come right in, sir, and sit down. It's a bit 'ot in 'ere, account of the furnaces next door, but you get used to it. Excuse me going on with me meal, but I just got off duty, see; bit of excitement we've 'ad with this 'ere murder in Mr. Bevan's shop. Reporter, is it?"

"Police," said Charlesworth, briefly.

"Oh, p'lice. That's different. I don't mind telling you I wouldn't 've said much if you was from the Press," said the night-watchman hurriedly; "you 'as to be careful in a thing like this. Libel and such. Not but what you can't be libelled for telling the truth and the truth is 'e's been at 'ome both nights and all night since the murder was done. For murder it was, sir, mark my words; tired of 'er, that's what it was, and 'aving a bit of a lull now, before takin' up with 'is new paramore."

"Are you suggesting that Mr. Bevan made away with Miss Doon?"

The watchman looked a little frightened. "Did I ever say so, sir? No, no, I'm suggestin' nothink; but a man wot plays about as 'e plays about . . ."

"Do Mr. Bevan's lady friends come here to his flat?" asked Charlesworth, at a venture.

"Well, not to say all of them, they don't. She come 'ere a bit, and there was another used to be 'ere a lot but not lately. Red 'ead, she was; she was terrible."

"Terrible in what way?"

"Made up she was, and was she fresh? I took 'er up in the lift one night and 'I 'ope you're not bashful, porter,' she says, and ups 'er skirt and starts fixin' 'er suspender. Give me quite a turn!"

"I should think so, indeed," said Charlesworth, sympathetically.

"Miss Wheeler, that was, but she 'asn't been for a long time now. There was another girl came from the shop, I reckernised 'er photo in the papers, a tall, dark girl; and there's another one, a sour-faced b—— young lady, but she mostly comes of a morning; I think she must be a secretary or somethink of that."

Charlesworth went over to a heap of newspapers in the corner of the room. "Would this be the dark one?"

"That's 'er; Mrs. Rachel Gay, but I 'aven't seen 'er often and not for a long time. I don't see the other gel 'ere."

"And this would be the one that comes in the mornings?" asked Charlesworth, indicating a very bad photograph of Gregory. "The one you think's a secretary. . . ."

"I can't rightly say, sir, she's got 'er 'and over 'er face, 'asn't she?" He passed over Victoria's photograph and Judy's. "Never seen 'em."

"Nor this one—Irene Best?"

"Never set eyes on 'er."

After much thought and not without a little financial persuasion he contrived to remember certain dates on which Bevan had definitely spent the night away from home. Armed with these, Charlesworth went round to the address which Aileen had given him. A motherly landlady opened the door and her mouth at the same time.

"Are you from the Press? Come in, my dear, and sit yerself down. 'Ave a cup of tea, do. I was just going to 'ave one meself. We 'ad two young chaps 'ere this morning, already. Quite on the front page, we are."

She led him into her private sitting-room, threading her bulk with miraculous dexterity through a multitude of rickety bamboo tables on which were knick-knacks and photographs in almost unbelievable profusion. Charlesworth's long legs made havoc among presents from Hove and shell-covered boxes, but at last he found himself wedged securely into an ancient plush-covered chair, and Aileen's landlady made formal introductions.

"Simpson, my name is, Mrs. Simpson. My 'usband made a rare joke of that when the Duke of Windsor got married—God bless 'im," she added, making a small ducking movement towards a picture of George VI and his family which hung over the mantelpiece, presumably to show that no offence need be taken where none intended. "I used to be a Miss King, see? and my 'usband 'e says, 'Not the first time a Simpson's married a King,' 'e says. Not bad, was it? You can put that in your paper, young man."

Charlesworth indicated solemnly that his editor would be delirious with joy, even though it seemed probable that similar permission had been extended to the two young chaps who had already preceded him. "Now, could you give me some information for a little article about Miss Aileen? 'Life of a Mannequin,' that kind of thing. 'Her Friends,' and so on."

"Well, as to friends, she don't 'ave many these days not with that sloppy Arthur of 'ers 'anging around. I reckon she must be potty on 'im to let 'im boss 'er about the way 'e does: can't see what she sees in 'im, meself. 'E ain't got tuppence to bless 'imself with but 'e puts on the airs of a lord!"

"Doesn't Mr. Bevan come to visit her? You've seen his picture in the papers, I expect?"

"Oh, yes, I seen 'im in the papers, but I don't think 'e's ever bin 'ere or I'd 've remembered 'im. She 'ad enough chaps before Arthur come along, though always well be'aved, but since she took up with 'im she don't 'ardly seem to go out at all."

"Not what you'd expect in a girl of her looks," said Charlesworth. "They have a gay time, most of them."

"Yes, but wot does it lead to?" Mrs. Simpson gulped her tea and nodded darkly. "Murder, that's wot. I don't say young Aileen, but these painted 'ussies—one of them done that Miss Doon in, pore girl, and she as nice and pleasant-spoken a young lady as you could wish to meet, even if she did dress a bit odd."

"Miss Doon? Did you know her?"

"Well, not to say *know*," admitted Mrs. Simpson reluctantly. "But I remember 'er coming 'ere once to see Aileen, and she spoke ever so pleasant when I let 'er in at the front door. Quite upset she was when I told 'er I thought Aileen was out. 'But I must see 'er,' she says, 'it's most urgent,' she says. Then she looks at me, ever so nice, and 'Do try and find 'er for me,' she says. Matter of fact, she was in, after all. She was a 'andsome girl, Miss Doon—and where is she now? Lying there in the mortuary, stark and stiff, dead and murdered."

"Beastly, isn't it?" agreed Charlesworth, absently.

"The perlice arst young Aileen about it and, like a silly girl, she lorst 'er 'ead and said Miss Doon never come 'ere, and she never saw 'er outside of the shop. She told me not to say nothink about it, if they come ferreting round 'ere, and I shan't. Nothink to do with them, is it? She only come the once and Aileen 'aving denied it in the 'eat of the moment like, it would look a bit funny if they found out about it now, wouldn't it?"

"Very funny indeed," said Charlesworth, grimly.

"So don't put it in your paper, will you now? because I wouldn't like to get young Aileen into trouble; she's got enough coming to 'er with that Arthur of 'ers, the sloppy thing. By the way, what is your paper?"

"The *Evening Light*," said Charlesworth, at a venture.

"The *Evening Light?* Lor', you are thorough! I told all this once to the chap what come round before you."

"Don't say someone's been here from the *Light* already!" cried Charlesworth, leaping to his feet. "Good heavens, I have been wasting your time. What a shame; they must have sent two of us out on the same job. Anyway, it's been awfully interesting, Mrs. Simpson, and I for one don't feel that I've wasted my time at all. *Very* pleased to have met you."

"Same to you, I'm shore," said Mrs. Simpson, to his huge delight.

He drove westwards, and, on an impulse, stopped at Rachel's unpretentious door. A refined edition of Mrs. Simpson answered the bell. "Excuse me, but I'm from the Press. . . ."

"Well, I have nothing to say to the Press." She shut the door in his face.

Charlesworth drove on, unruffled. Before his mind's eye was Aileen's lovely, expressionless face, and ringing in his ears Aileen's unhurried voice.

"Did you know her personally apart from your work?"

"No, I did not."

"Were you on friendly terms with her in the shop?"

"The mannequins hardly saw anything of her in the shop; I've never even spoken to her outside."

Not much of the 'eat of the moment about *that*.

## 2

Bedd was waiting in Charlesworth's office and received an invitation to lunch. Over their chops and beer they compared notes. The sergeant had renewed acquaintance with Miss Doon's landlady, who, her memory refreshed by the Press photographs, was able to confirm that Bevan had been a frequent visitor. There was a gentleman in the habit of staying very late, but she could not swear that it was he. Delicate handling elicited the admission that by very late the landlady meant all night . . . with a hurried qualification that the young lady paid her weekly for the flat and it was no business of hers what she done in it.

"Did you get any dates?" said Charlesworth.

"No, sir, she began to regret having said so much and she shut up after that."

"Well, damn it, couldn't you have had a shot, Bedd? Here I've got all the nights that Bevan has been out lately and we could have done a beautiful bit of dove-tailing."

"Very sorry, sir."

"I'm a better blinking sleuth than you are, Bedd, that's what it is. I've discovered that young Aileen has been lying like a trooper about not knowing the Doon girl in her private life; and what's more, that she has an illicit intrigue going on with Bevan, presumably without the knowledge of her Arthur, of whom you are also about to hear. She was closeted with Bevan in his office at half-past nine this morning. . . ."

"But . . ."

"Hang on a minute, just let me say my piece, and then you can but away as much as you like. Now, here's how I see it, Bedd: we have Aileen, a regular peach, one has to admit, and Bevan has an eye on her. But at the same time he has an eye on Doon—and Doon begins to get the upper hand, so that Aileen is obliged to stake her all on Arthur. But Bevan turns dog-in-the-manger, and he starts to chase Aileen again. Doon isn't having any and she tries a little moral blackmail—'You lay off my Bevan,' she says, 'or I'll tell your Arthur.' So Doon dies; and Aileen and Bevan are busy necking in his office at a most ungodly hour this morning, and no one to breathe a word to Aileen's Arthur; incidentally, perhaps now that Aileen's got Bevan all to herself again, she won't worry so much in the future about poor Arthur."

Bedd made no comment. Charlesworth glanced at him in surprise, and then penitently. "Come, now, Sergeant, no ill-feeling. I had to wag my tail a little about my great discoveries. What have you got to say about them?"

Bedd took a swig of beer and with much deliberation

wiped the froth from his lips. He folded his handkerchief and returned it to his pocket and, leaning back in his chair, regarded the great detective with a twinkling eye.

"I'm sorry about the dates, sir," he said, ponderously.

"That's all right, Bedd, that's quite all right, old man. I do realize that if anyone could possibly have got the dates you would have. Now, what do you think of all this business about Aileen?"

" 'Arf past nine this morning, sir? In Mr. Bevan's office?"

"Yes, what do you think of that?"

"Only," said Sergeant Bedd, happily, "that at 'arf-past nine this morning, Miss Aileen was walking along Oxford Street as fast as 'er legs could carry 'er. Because I 'appened to see 'er."

Charlesworth rushed round to Christophe et Cie. "Aileen," he said, encountering her at the door, "you're a very naughty girl; you were late for work this morning."

"You police know everything," said Aileen, laughing. "But don't tell Mr. Bevan."

They walked over to where the salesgirls sat. Victoria drew him like a magnet and he went and stood beside her and joined in their easy conversation. A customer came in, fussy and self-important, and Rachel went to her. "A two-piece, madam? Yes, of course. We have a little silk one that would suit you terribly well. Aileen, put on that 'July' model for madam, will you, please . . . didn't you have a green one, madam, just before the summer? This is rather the same in style and I'm sure you'll like it. . . ."

The customer hated it. "Well, never mind, madam, there's lots more for you to choose from. Mr. Cecil has some drawings for a new one, in a slightly heavier ma·erial . . . would you like to see those? . . ."

Cissie appeared from Bevan's office and Irene went to speak to him. "Mr. Cecil, Lady Mary's coming in at four o'clock; she isn't satisfied with the hat, that blue felt you know—isn't it a bother? . . ."

Charlesworth, left alone with Victoria, found himself,

for once in his life, tongue-tied and self-conscious. She caught his embarrassment, though she was innocent of the cause of it, and, for something to say, commented on his silk handkerchief. He pulled it out of his pocket and she rubbed the thick silk between her fingers and said lightly, "Oh, lovely—how rich and luxurious you must be!"

"You can have it if you like," he said, foolishly.

"Don't be silly," cried Toria. "I didn't mean it that way at all." She laughed a soft little laugh, and it rang in his heart like a knell for he thought he knew when he had heard it before.

He picked up the handkerchief and deliberately laid a trap for her. "What will you give me for it?" he said, and she answered as he had known she would, "Not a sausage!" and laughed again.

So it wasn't Aileen who had been in Bevan's office; but someone who used Aileen's absurd phrase and imitated Aileen's absurd accent and laughed at her own imitation. Victoria! He thrust the handkerchief into his pocket and marched blindly out of the shop.

### 3

Rachel, released from her customer, came back to the cubby-hole. "I've been wanting to talk to you, Toria. What the hell shall I do about Bevan? He's getting terribly amorous again."

"Smack his beastly face," said Victoria, viciously.

"He'd give me the sack if I did. I have to keep in with him, that's the trouble. I can't afford to be out of a job."

"I know, darling. But you shouldn't be so attractive—wherever you go it'll be the same thing."

"I must say, it generally is," said Rachel, mournfully. "It's this beastly sex-appeal; I wish I didn't have it. It was awful when I was on the stage; you know what people are like there."

"Couldn't be worse than Bevan. What's he been doing now?"

"Well, he got here at dawn this morning, and made me go into his office and started worrying me again. I'm so petrified my husband will find out about that wretched evening. I tried to make Bevan promise to be a bit more discreet. . . ."

"That won't do any good, my dear."

"Not a sausage," agreed Rachel, laughing ruefully.

Irene appeared in the doorway. "You sounded just like Aileen when you said that. You two shouldn't copy her so much; I can't tell you apart now, and you soon won't be able to speak the King's English yourselves."

"Come and sit down, Irene darling, and tell Rachel what she's to do about Bevan. He's been pestering her again."

"You should never have gone to his flat that evening, dear. We told you so at the time."

"Well, he was very nice in those days, Rene, and I must say he behaved terribly well up to then."

"I think he was really been on her for a bit," said Victoria, judicially.

"Would you have married him, Rachel?"

"I might have," said Rachel. "He was rather attractive, you know, and he must have pots of money; it would have been nice for Jessica to have had a rich stepfather and I'm a bit sick of scraping along at four pounds ten a week. But since the flat episode—no, thank you."

"You shouldn't have stayed so late, dear."

"I know, Irene. It was asking for trouble. Anyway, it put an end to my girlish illusions, so it may have been a good thing, in the end."

"It's easy for us to talk, Rene," said Toria. "Bevan's never cast his lecherous eye in our direction. I wonder why," she added with genuine interest.

"Well, you're too heavily married, dear, and as for me— I've been with Christophe's so long that he looks on me as part of the fixtures and fittings. Awkward when the detective asked us about Doon being engaged, wasn't it? You were very good then, Rachel, putting him off. We didn't want to get mixed up in all those revelations, did we?"

"We didn't put him off very much," said Victoria, thoughtfully. "He's an odd young man. He's just offered to give me his silk hankie, because I said I liked it; and when I wouldn't take it he rushed out of the place like a madman."

"Victoria! You don't mean to say that he's fallen for you?"

"God forbid," said Victoria, piously.

"Why do all the free men get keen on Toria?" asked Rachel, with mock petulance. "Only the dirty old men go for you and me, Irene."

"*I* don't want them, bond or free," said Victoria. "I've got Bobby Dazzler and he's all I can do with. Anyway, you can hardly call Bevan a dirty old man, Rachel!"

They fell into a discussion of Bevan's attributes: but Charlesworth, doggedly determined to put the detective before the man, was closeted in his little office, with the notes of the case spread around him, trying to find some connection between Doon's murder and an affair between Bevan and Victoria. Pushed out of sight in a drawer was a blue silk handkerchief.

4

To Gregory a murder in the shop was no excuse for slackening efficiency. She cheerfully shouldered Doon's work as well as her own and filed from morning till night and calculated with unabated enthusiasm, until the luckless Macaroni almost cried for mercy. On the Thursday morning, three days after Doon's death, the work was completely up to date and she dismissed the snivelling secretary to her own dungeon and sat complacently in Bevan's office, reviewing her handiwork. Bevan came in and threw himself into a chair.

"Oh, Frank, I'm so glad you've come. I've been wanting to ask you . . ."

"For God's sake don't call me Frank in business hours," said Bevan, roughly. "How many times have I told you that? Can't you be more careful?"

78

It was the first time she had ever made such a slip and he had certainly never mentioned it before. Her eyes filled with tears and she sat silent, gazing at the neat papers before her.

"Well, what is it?" he asked, and as she made no reply, "What's the matter? Why don't you say what you were going to say?"

"Never mind now; I'll ask you another time."

"What the devil's the matter with you, these days?" said Bevan in a savage undertone. "What are you always weeping and moping about?"

"Don't you think I've got something to weep and mope about?"

"That's just the damn silly kind of thing a woman always says; what sort of a reply do you expect me to make to such a remark as that?"

"Well, I think a few kind words wouldn't be a bad reply," said Gregory, sadly. "They'd be the first you'd spoken to me for a very long time."

"My dear girl, you don't want me to make love to you before the whole shop, do you? Do pull yourself together and keep that sort of thing for out-of-business hours."

"I never see you now in out-of-business hours."

"I like that—only last Monday I spent most of the morning at your flat."

"And talked business all the time!" said Gregory, bitterly.

"Good lord, woman, what did you expect, directly after breakfast?"

"But you've just quoted it as—well, never mind. . . ." Gregory gave it up as hopeless. "I was only going to ask what you are doing about Deauville. Monsieur Georges is agitating and we can't put it off much longer. Besides, we shall have to think about getting somebody else here."

"I've decided to send Mrs. Best."

"You're not going to send me, after all?"

"How can I, and leave myself here without a stock-keeper and without you?" said Bevan, impatiently. "You'll have to carry on with Miss Doon's work as well as your own and we must train somebody to replace her. Irene Best can go to the new branch—you'll have to run through the work very carefully with her, but she knows quite enough about it—and Rachel Gay can pick up her showroom routine easily enough."

"Rachel *Gay*—to have charge of the showroom!"

"Yes, why not?"

She looked at him oddly. "Nothing. Only I should have thought that Victoria ought to have had it. Won't it look rather like favouritism?"

"Rachel Gay is a favourite with everybody," said Bevan, curtly. "Even in a crowd of catty women I don't believe there's a soul who'd grudge her promotion—Victoria David least of all."

"It was only that Victoria came a little before Rachel; but still—you know best. Will you get someone to replace Irene?"

"Not till the summer's over. We're slack enough as it is, goodness knows, and we shall probably go bust with the Press screaming their heads off over this wretched affair."

"I don't think we shall," said Gregory, shrewdly. "Clients don't mind publicity of this sort—not our kind of clients, anyway. They're keeping off now, till Doon's buried and so on—they couldn't very well do anything else; but if you ask me, as soon as the inquest's over they'll start pouring in, trying to get the girls to talk and tell them tit-bits; if we handle it carefully it may not be a bad thing for us in the end. Of course it's very dreadful about Doon and I'm very sorry," she added perfunctorily, "but one can't help recognizing that a bit of a fillip is just what we need, right in the middle of August; and that's what her death may give us."

Bevan gave her his sideways glance and smiled into her hard grey eyes. "You're a strange girl," he said; "in some ways you're as sentimental as a schoolgirl and in others you're as hard as nails—but you certainly are a help to a man at a time like this. I don't know what the devil I should have done without you. Now, look here: you must tell the girls what you've just been saying to me. . .

80

go out and see them now. Afterwards, send Mrs. Best in here, and I shall want to see Rachel after that—don't say what about. But first of all get them together and have a word with them; tell them that this publicity must be turned to advantage if they don't want to ruin the shop—and find themselves all out of jobs. Arrange with them how to deal with questions—try to fix up an atmosphere of regret, and so on, without too much of the funereal. The whole thing is ghastly and depressing, of course, but there's no point in our making it worse. Personally, I'm afraid it will kill us, for this season, anyway, but you may be right. I hope to God you are!"

Here was a mission after Gregory's own heart and she held court at one end of the empty *salon*, under a crystal chandelier. To divest the interview of too much air of authority which she knew would be bitterly resented, she seated herself on a small gilt table and swung her legs in quite a jolly schoolgirl fashion; but alas! the sight of the scraggy ankles above her tight, neat shoes inspired nothing but a nervy revulsion, and the long neck with its prominent lump in the centre seemed to the girls to twist and turn like a snake; the unsmiling eyes above the joyless smile looked into faces that responded with neither eyes nor lips and she told her story in an atmosphere of growing and almost deliberate misunderstanding. Judy was the first to reply and she did so with an outburst of scornful anger that took all of them aback.

"Do you mean that you want us to gas and gabble about poor old Doon to any morbid female that comes in here seeking for sensation?. . . I'm damned if *I* will."

"I don't mean that, of course, Judy, dear, and you know it, don't you now?"

Judy wrenched herself free of Gregory's deprecatory hand. "I don't know anything except that you want us to make capital for this beastly shop out of Doon's death. I never heard anything so filthy and indecent in my life."

"That's nonsense, my dear. I simply want to prevent the business from coming to unnecessary harm."

"The business! You'd sell your soul for this bloody

business, Gregory, I really believe you would. I believe you're capable of murdering Doon yourself," cried Judy, hysterically, "just to get publicity for Christophe et Cie."

There was a horrible silence. "Don't be an idiot, Judy," said Rachel at last. "The publicity's much more likely to harm Christophe's than to do it good, and you know it. Gregory's only trying to do her best to save it—though I must say, Gregory, I don't think much of your way of going about it."

But Gregory was staring at Judy, speechless with fury. "Since when have *you* been so much up in arms for Doon's sake?" she burst out, disregarding Rachel's efforts for peace. "Before you accuse other people of murder, you'd better examine your own conscience. What about Doon and your young man? Doon took him away from you, didn't she? *You* didn't particularly love her, did you?"

Judy walked away without a word, but after a moment she came back. "I shouldn't have said that," she said, deliberately, honesty struggling with her angry pride. "I didn't mean it when I said that you killed Doon: I happen to know that you didn't. As for my young man as you call him, you're on the wrong tack there; it's true that Doon took him away, and I hated her for it; I hated her like hell, and I don't care who knows it—but if I *had* killed her, I wouldn't have poisoned her; and I'm not going to gossip about her now that she's dead." She walked away again.

Rachel stood irresolute. "Have you finished your speech, Gregory? Because, if so . . ."

"Leave her alone, dear; she'll get over it. I'm afraid we're all unstrung and say things we don't mean," said Gregory, apologizing a little for her own behaviour. They were indeed all of them nervy and on edge. Doon's last hour in their midst had not been beautiful and her death was a terrible shock; moreover, among them moved a murderer—a murderer might even be one of the little group in which they stood. Aileen said, evidently following this train of thought: "Arthur wants me to leave."

"Oh, Aileen, don't do that," cried Rachel, impulsively affectionate. "Let's all stick together and get through it somehow. Whatever should we do without our redhead?"

Aileen looked at her in mild surprise and Rachel felt a little abashed at her own eagerness; but Gregory fell upon the embryo of emotionalism and proceeded to develop the theme of a united sisterhood until the original perpetrator could have sunk through the floor with shame, and Victoria felt cold slugs of embarrassment crawling down her spine. Irene, never averse to a little sentimentality, remained in earnest discussion with Gregory, half enjoying it, half hypnotized by the staring eyes; but Rachel and Victoria crept away and hid themselves in their little room, propping their aching foreheads upon their hands.

"Things are getting terrible, Rachel, aren't they?" said Victoria, miserably. "Fancy Judy flying off the handle like that. Heaven knows, she never was one to mince her words, as Mrs. Harris would say, but to go all hysterical and practically accuse Gregory of murdering Doon! . . ."

"But she took it back very handsomely. She sounded very certain, Toria; why should she have said that she *knew* Gregory didn't do it?"

"You don't think there can be any truth in what Gregory said—I mean about Judy's Bill, and all that?"

"Oh, my dear, no! Not Judy. Judy might have hit Doon over the head or something, but it was true when she said she wouldn't have poisoned her. Anyway, all that fuss was ages ago—it was when Gregory was so thick with Doon; I suppose that's how she knew—and Judy's engaged again now."

"Yes, but Rachel, only since Doon's death! Judy rang Bill up that night Doon was ill. . . of course, as soon as they started talking, she began to undestand that he'd fallen out of love with Doon long ago, and was only waiting and praying for the chance to come back to her. . . it didn't come until Doon was dead."

"I suppose she *might* have seen the poison lying about. . . ."

83

"Rachel, this is ghastly, isn't it? How can we be saying such things and about dear little Judy of all people? But it's all so dark and beastly—I shall start suspecting myself next. Thank God I've got you, Ray," she added, soberly. "I can say with absolute faith that I know you didn't do it, and I know *I* didn't do it, so that does make two of us at least. And Rene, of course," she added, hurriedly.

"Toria, you haven't noticed anything funny about Rene? She's been terribly queer since this affair, hasn't she?"

"She's upset about Doon, that's all. She's a tender-hearted little thing."

"Yes, but, Toria, she did want to go to Deauville most *terribly*. . . ."

"But Doon wasn't going to Deauville, Rachel. Gregory was."

"Gregory won't go now. Bevan can't possibly spare her. It means that Irene will go—it comes to the same thing."

"But, my dear, nobody would kill anyone for such a round-about reason as that; it's fantastic! And, anyway, Irene, of all people; she's terribly sentimental—she wouldn't kill a mouse."

"There's a lot of difference between sentiment and sentimentality," said Rachel, slowly. "Irene's sentimental, and lots of sentimental people have a very hard streak in them. She wouldn't kill a mouse, it's true; but she'd set a trap for one, and if it got caught by its leg and squeaked and struggled, she'd go away somewhere where she wouldn't hear it—but she'd leave it to die. *I'd* set a trap for it myself; but if it wasn't killed outright I'd—I'd release the trap and let it go or at least put it out of its pain."

"And I'm so sentimental that I wouldn't even set the trap," said Victoria, smiling. "But Rachel, don't worry about Irene. I did, too, but it's all right, I'm sure it is. After all, she couldn't have had any of the oxalic acid. . . ."

"She did pick up a few grains off the floor," said Rachel, "but it was awfully little, because I saw it. And she was right in her corner when Macaroni spilt it; she never moved at all. . . ."

84

"And also," began Victoria, but the words froze on her lips; she looked up and saw that Rachel had gone very white—they stared into each other's eyes, and at that moment Irene came out of Bevan's room and Bevan himself, standing at the door, called out pleasantly: "Mrs. Gay, come over here, will you? I want to have a word with you."

Irene looked excited, but not entirely happy. Gregory, still in the glow of their recent confabulation, caught her hand and poured out congratulations on her getting the post at Deauville; but Irene released herself coldly and, with a brief word to Victoria, took her handbag and went downstairs to the cloakroom. A clock struck six. The doors were locked, frocks and hats removed from their stands and carefully put away in cupboards, and all but the window lights extinguished one by one. Blue satin overalls were hitched on to pegs, silk-stockinged legs twinkled up the area steps: the traffic of London held out its greedy arms.

Left to herself, Gregory walked home in an agony of self-examination. She knew that she was unpopular. Everywhere she went, she met with the same spirit of distrust and frustration. "I can't understand it," she thought, drearily, stepping along in her sharp, business-like way, leaning forward a little from the hips, grasping her uncompromising handbag by its handle; "can it really be only because they're silly and shallow and not worth while? Look at Aileen: a brainless little idiot and not even a lady; and yet Rachel is quite upset at the idea of losing her. Rachel herself—she's as generous and warm and good-natured as a child; but she closes up her heart when I come near. Victoria's voice changes and they all stop laughing and talking; and then when I move away everything's free and natural and friendly again." She began to pray to some half-forgotten personal gods of her childhood: "What can I do to make them like me more? Is it because they recognize that I'm, perhaps, in a different class from them, that I've got a better brain, more—more *depth* . . . maybe if I pretended to be just as

85

silly and aimless and easy-going . . . oh, God! I really believe I'd do that, if I could feel that they would be friends with me, be fond of me . . . if only I needn't walk through the world so utterly, and unbearably, alone. . . ."

Her heart was humble and her eyes full of tears as she put her key in the latch and opened the door of her room. Over a biscuit-box peeped two pointed ears and a pair of startled eyes. She caught up a heavy slipper and, holding it by the heel, gave chase.

## *Five*

### I

CHARLESWORTH, with a sigh of relief, abandoned all thoughts of a Bevan-Victoria alliance. After all, he told himself, the laughing voice in the office had given no indication of consent; and, whatever lay behind that little mystery, there was a minus B registered against Victoria's name in the list of suspects: she had not known that Doon was going to be in to lunch, so she could not possibly be guilty of murdering her. Moreover, he could think of no conceivable reason that she might have had; the job at Deauville had not been remotely within reach, nor on account of her marriage could she have accepted it. Her husband's work had hitherto proved meritorious rather than profitable, but she lived with him on terms of extravagant devotion and was apparently perfectly happy to continue with her job until the day when his genius should burst upon an astonished and undeserving world. . . . Jealousy? It was true that Doon had sat to him and that he had "been terribly thrilled with her," but Charlesworth had the sense to know that admiration of his model is by no means invariably a cause of disruption in a painter's home. Besides, if she were interested in Bevan—but Charlesworth fought against that.

No, he could confine his attentions to the six suspects

who had all had the two famous Opportunities: Cecil, Bevan, Rachel; Judy, Aileen, Mrs. Harris. Despairing of discrimination he shut his eyes tightly and applied a pin. The lot fell upon Cecil and, without wasting time on needless speculation, Charlesworth drove himself round to the bijou service flats to begin his battle anew.

Cecil was out and was not expected back that night. Charlesworth proceeded to pump the servants, but without result; he was turning away when the housekeeper, disappointed at having been of so little assistance, casually added that it was a pity they couldn't have asked Mr. Cecil's friend about it, as he had been ever such a friend of that Miss Doon; but that he, of course, had disappeared.

"Disappeared!"

"That's right, sir, and neither Mr. Cecil nor anyone else knows where he is."

"Why didn't you tell me this before?" asked Charlesworth, heatedly.

"You never asked, sir; and I'm sure I couldn't know there was any connection, or I'd 've told you at once. Tuesday night, it was; the night after the pore young lady died."

Mr. Cecil and Mr. Elliot, they'd been as devoted as could be. Fair sloppy, was the housekeeper's private opinion, but this she did not communicate to the gentleman. Never a cross word, however, it was *not* too much to say; never a cross word until the terrible week-end, when high voices had been heard from behind the communal door; high voices and angry words and the terrible, embarrassing sound of a man in tears.

"On the Monday Mr. Cecil went off to the shop, sir, as gloomy as could be; as soon as 'e'd gone, Mr. Elliot came downstairs and the porter saw 'im go off with his little suitcase, and no one's set eyes on him since. None of us 'ere, that's to say; though 'e came back that evening and had supper with Mr. Cecil, I believe. They didn't eat much, I can tell you; and next morning all his things had been packed away and there were his suitcases and a big, old-fashioned trunk in the 'all of the flat."

"Didn't anyone see him leave after supper?"

"No, sir. I went up to the flat in the morning as Mr. Cecil didn't ring for 'is breakfast—we looks after our gentlemen very careful 'ere, sir, and I thought they might 'ave overslept. Mr. Elliot wasn't there and his bed hadn't been slept in, as I found afterwards. Mr. Cecil came to the door looking 'orrible ill; 'e was just going off to the shop without 'is breakfast, saying 'e didn't want none. Ill all night 'e'd been, 'im or Mr. Elliot, and the mess in the bathroom was somethink awful, sir, if you'll forgive me mentioning it; Mr. Cecil 'e looked as if 'e'd seen a ghost. He come 'ome early and took the suitcases and the trunk in a taxi and . . ." At this second mention of the trunk, realization suddenly dawned upon Mrs. Boot and she was took so faint as to be of no further assistance.

The porter, a smart young Welshman with his wits about him, corroborated this story. He remembered showing Mr. Charlesworth up to the flat on the previous evening; Cecil had then only half an hour returned from his expedition with the luggage, but of course he had not thought of mentioning it.

"Did he take a cab off the rank?"

"No, sir, it was a passin' one 'e called."

"I suppose you didn't hear what address he gave?"

"No, sir, indeed; I'm verry sorry, but I couldn't know it was important, could I? I'm verry sorry indeed, sir."

"No, no, of course you couldn't know; possibly it wasn't important, after all. Isn't it odd that you didn't see Mr. Elliot leave on the Tuesday night, after he'd had supper with Mr. Cecil?"

"Well, I dunno, sir. We 'aven't got a lot of porters 'ere, only me, bein' a small block; you see; and of course I'm not in the 'all the whole time. 'E might 'ave gone out without my seein' 'im, sir."

"You're sure he came, I suppose?"

"I dunno, indeed, sir. I didn't see 'im, but Mr. Cecil ordered dinner for two, and Mrs. Boot was sure it was for Mr. Elliot because Mr. Cecil ordered a duck, sir; Mr. Elliot was very fond of duck, but Mr. Cecil didn't like it at all, accordin' to Mrs. Boot; you see 'ow it is, sir, we can't say for certain."

To Charlesworth it was certain enough. "I must get hold of that trunk," he thought. Aloud he said to the porter, "Did you bring the luggage down from the flat?"

"Yes, I did, sir. I 'ad to get the valet to 'elp me with the trunk; Mr. Cecil would never put 'is 'and to a thing like that; 'e just stood and looked on . . . indeed, I never saw a man look so ill! 'It's very heavy!' 'e said."

"They always say that," thought Charlesworth, joyfully. He climbed into his car and, sitting stationary at the wheel, gave himself up to a good deal of anxious thought.

There was a certain young man at the Yard who, by his smug efficiency, had earned for himself the deadly loathing of all his colleagues; he had recently added to his laurels by unearthing, in a murder case, not only the murderer but a haul of long-missing jewelry. Charlesworth had a vision of this gentleman's face when he, Charlesworth, should appear at the Chief's office for congratulation and approval on his single-handed apprehension of a totally unsuspected trunk murderer, over and above the little matter in hand; and he straightway determined that, for the remainder of that day, at least, he would see it through alone.

He put himself mentally into the position of a trunk murderer, with a body to hide. In this case, he thought, the gruesome baggage would have been deposited at a large railway station as far as possible from the scene of the crime, and he headed the car for Liverpool Street. Here, however, he drew a blank and, after a heated and infuriating half-hour, found himself once more obliged to assume the mental outlook of a man with a load of mischief; by eight o'clock that evening he had decided that his mind and Cecil's must work along totally different lines; and at nine, somewhat belatedly, he rang up Scotland Yard. It was agreed that a search should be made for the taxi-driver and investigations carried out at all likely baggage depositories. "Good work," said the authority, to whom he gave his own somewhat prejudiced version of the affair. "Quite a feather in your cap,

Charlesworth." Charlesworth, glowing with modest satisfaction, returned to his muttons.

He had developed a passionate desire to discover the nature of the week-end row between Cecil and Elliot. He rang Bevan's number but there was no reply, and with a pleasant excitement he tried Victoria's. A voice, presumably that of the detestable painter, explained that Victoria was out, and mumbling an apology, he rang off. Rachel, however, answered his call, and after a rambling explanation he embarked upon his questionnaire. Rachel adopted the feminine attitude, all too familiar to Scotland Yard, of reluctance to say anything that might incriminate anybody, guilty or otherwise; but she could see no possible connection between Cissie's friend Elliot and the murder of Doon, and she readily admitted that Doon had frequently enlarged to them, with much humorous detail, upon the attentions of that aesthetic young man.

"But you don't think Cissie would have killed Doon, just because she wouldn't be kind to his boy friend?" she asked, half-laughing, down the 'phone.

"More likely to have killed the boy friend," suggested Charlesworth, lightly.

"Oh, Mr. Charlesworth, have a heart! Poor Cissie— he'd faint at the sight of blood."

Charlesworth had a vision of Cecil appearing white and distraught at the door of a bedroom where someone had been 'orrible ill all night; of the trunk in the tiny hall and of Cissie remarking that it was "very heavy" and driving off with it in a taxi, heaven only knew where. A subdued mutter at the other end of the line roused him from these reflections and Rachel announced: "Victoria says that, anyway, Cissie's boy friend has left him and disappeared."

"Oh, is Mrs. David there?"

"Hallo, Mr. Charlesworth," said Victoria's voice. "If you want to know about Elliot it's no good because he's hopped off. Cissie told me so himself on Tuesday, when he came to the shop; he was in a terrible state about it— didn't you notice how ill he looked?"

"I put it down to the upset about Miss Doon's

death. Was he very fond of this chap, or something?"

"Well, Mr. Charlesworth, you know what these people are. He was always getting violent friendships and they never lasted more than about six months. It came very expensive because the whole flat always had to be done up to suit the artistic peculiarities of the new soul-mate. Last year it was ultra-modern, but Elliot went all Edwardian and you couldn't see the place for plush-framed photographs and china cats."

"They're all gone now," said Charlesworth. "His belongings have been packed up and moved; as a matter of fact, I've been hunting them all over London."

"Whatever for?"

"There's a sort of a—well, a sort of a paper which I want to see; I can't explain, but it's very important to the case."

Mumble-mumble-mumble went the telephone; Rachel came back on the line. "Did you say you'd been looking for Elliot's trunks and things?"

"I've spent the last three hours doing nothing else."

"Oh. What a pity you didn't ring us sooner," said Rachel, casually. "Because they're all at Christophe's."

"What!" yelled Charlesworth, leaping several feet into the air.

"Oi, don't deafen me. Yes, Cissie brought them along on Wednesday evening just as we were shutting up the shop . . . what, Victoria?" . . . mumble-mumble . . . "oh, well, Victoria says to tell you that Cecil said he couldn't bear to have them in the flat any more . . . what, darling? Well, don't tell me while I'm trying to tell *him*. . . . Well, Mr. Charlesworth, Victoria says to explain to you that it's nothing, because he always does this every time he breaks with anyone; he just stuck them in the basement until Elliot should come back for them."

"Good God," said Charlesworth, wiping a clammy brow. "How could I get hold of them, right away?"

"What, now, to-night?"

"Yes, it's absolutely—I mean, this paper thing's terribly important."

An orgy of mumbling followed, at the end of which Rachel said doubtfully, "Toria says that as it's so frightfully important and mysterious, we could let you in with one of our keys."

Charlesworth picked them up at Rachel's flat, two excited figures in summer frocks and swinging big straw hats; Victoria's blue eyes were shining, her pale hair glinted in the light of the street lamps—she looked like a dryad, strayed from a woodland into the London streets. She wriggled into the seat beside Charlesworth, and her hair brushed his cheek as she turned to speak to Rachel, behind them. His heart melted within him; the determined young detective gave way to the love-lorn young man. "This is hell," he thought. . . . "I never knew it could be so bad as this. . . ."

It was eleven o'clock as, with a word to the patrolling policeman, they opened the showroom door and crept down to the darkened basement. The time-switch operated as they were on the stairs and even the window lights went out. "Hell," said Rachel, laughing out of the pitchy dark. "I shall never find the switch . . . ah, here it is. . . ." With a click, light flooded the room; below the stairs Charlesworth could see two suitcases and an ominous big black hump.

"There they are, Mr. Charlesworth. Shall we stand by and hold up the lid for you?"

"No, no," said Charlesworth, shuddering at the very idea. He looked round desperately. "Here, you go in here, will you, please; I don't want you to move out of this room." He pushed them into Doon's office and returned to his task. "I wish to heavens I'd thought of bringing the bobby with me," he thought, as he gingerly tried the catch. "This is the most unpleasant job I've taken on for many a long day." The trunk was unlocked and he clicked back the latches and lifted the heavy lid.

Rachel and Victoria waited in Doon's little office. "It's sad to think that this is the last place she ever saw," said Rachel, sombrely. "She was such a bright sort of a soul, one can hardly realize she's dead. You have to sort of laugh and make jokes and things to keep yourself going, don't you, Toria? But it's pretty good hell, really, knowing that poor Doon was killed and wondering who on earth could have done it. What do you think this peculiar young man is doing fussing about with Elliot's trunks?—there can't be any clue in them; it's simply fantastic." She broke off suddenly: "Good lord, Mr. Charlesworth, what on earth is the matter? How ghastly you look!"

"Where's the telephone?" gasped Charlesworth, white to the gills.

"Well, here it is, bang under your nose. Shall I get a number for you?"

Charlesworth grabbed at the instrument and dialled with shaking hands. "Charlesworth here. Put me through to Roberts. I say, sir," said Charlesworth to the gentleman who had contributed the feather, "you can call off the search for that taxi-driver; and don't bother any more about the luggage depositories. I've found the trunk."

"All right, take it easy, man. What's in it?" said the great man, reaching out a hand to put into motion the machinery for dealing with bodies in trunks.

"A whole lot of plush-framed photographs," said Charlesworth, with a groan, "and a couple of china cats." He put down the receiver and wiped his perspiring face.

Victoria, staring at him, suddenly began to laugh. "Mr. Charlesworth, you didn't think—you couldn't have thought—oh, Rachel! Oh, Mr. Charlesworth! he thought poor Cissie had bundled up the boy friend—oh, God! don't let me laugh any more, it's making my face ache all down the sides. Mr. Charlesworth, confess that you did think it was poor Mr. Elliot, all rolled up like a whiting, in the bottom of the trunk!"

But Rachel did not laugh. She took two paces forward and suddenly pulled aside the heavy curtains that framed the mock-window of the little office; and Macaroni stumbled forward into the room.

Macaroni's devotion to Doon had not been without a very solid foundation. A foolish and inexperienced girl, she had celebrated her seventeenth birthday with several port-and-lemons in the company of a young gentleman called Ginger Marks; and with Ginger she had subsequently gone to the greyhound races. Flushed with port-and-lemon, and an initial easy win of seven and threepence, she had staked and finally lost her whole week's salary. "What a pity," said Ginger Marks, sympathetically. "You could 'a got the 'ole lot back on this next race."

"I don't see 'ow you make that out," said Macaroni, sniffing resentfully.

"Well, it's Cambrian Hopeful, see? The one I got a tip for. I told you to keep something back; this one's a cert. 'Ere," said Ginger nobly, in the certainty of victory, "I could lend you a couple a bob."

"How much will I get if it wins?" asked Macaroni, regarding her empty purse with growing dismay.

Mr. Marks embarked upon a complicated series of calculations, squinting at the board and affecting an intelligent interest in the tic-tac men. Unable to spin it out any further, he finally announced that she stood to win seventeen bob.

"Seventeen shillings!" cried Macaroni, dissolving into tears again, "but that isn't nearly enough. I've lost all me salary, two pound ten, and three shillings over from last week, and I have to give me mother thirty shillings and I don't know what she'll say if she finds out I've lost it at the dogs. . . ." She peered desperately into the recesses of her handbag in the hopes of finding even a lurking sixpence to swell the stake; and her eyes alighted upon a little square envelope. Mrs. 'Arris's pay.

Behind the glittering façades, beneath the clockwork precision, it is still the everyday human heart that pumps the blood through the stream of commercial life. If Mrs. 'Arris were not present to receive her pay packet, no shining robot automatically diverted it into an appointed place. Miss Doon picked it up carelessly off Bevan's desk and said that she would see that the old girl got it to-morrow; and passed it on to Macaroni with instructions to put it in a drawer of the desk and remind her about it in the morning. Macaroni, in the excitement of being seventeen and having a date with Ginger Marks, forgot about putting it in the drawer and left it in the pocket of her overall; and, changing hurriedly into her best for the evening's dissipation, transferred it to her handbag and thought she would leave it in the office on her way out. Now, at the greyhound races, with nothing but the loan of two bob between herself and disaster, she took out the little square packet and weighed it in her hand.

Half-way round the course, Cambrian Hopeful sat down and indulged in a good, long scratch.

Macaroni, in most pitiable remorse and terror, sought out Doon the next morning and told her the dreadful story. It was not in Doon's character to refuse assistance to any creature in need; she procured a new square envelope and handed over Mrs. 'Arris's pay intact; she made good the thirty shillings for Macaroni's mother, and even furnished an excuse for its delay; and finally she advanced five shillings for current expenses, and, highly amused at her new role, read Macaroni a lecture upon the evils of gambling, drink, and theft. Macaroni, bathed in tears, wrote out an IOU, stating the circumstances under which she had become indebted to Miss Doon, and her earnest intention of paying her back at the rate of six shillings a week.

"I shall keep this till you've paid it all back," said Doon, severely, tearing up the IOU under cover of her desk, and throwing the pieces into the wastepaper-basket. "And if I ever again find that you have been losing more money than you've got, at the dogs, I shall show it to Mr. Bevan, and tell him the whole story." She had already told Mr. Bevan the whole story in the sanctity of his office, and had borrowed the money to make good Macaroni's depredations; but it would be best for the child to have some tangible threat held over her foolish head, and she solemnly locked up nothing in a small wall safe, to which there was no duplicate key. It was this non-existent note which, with her devoted friend Lydia, Macaroni had come to find.

Lydia crept forth from under the desk when Macaroni was so dramatically discovered, a short, stout girl, with pronounced Jewish features and handsomely rounded legs, who immediately joined her fellow conspirator in a chorus of tears. Charlesworth packed the four girls into his car and, dropping Rachel and Victoria at their respective doors, proceeded with his prizes to Scotland Yard. There he marched them into an unprepossessing room, sat them down upon two hard wooden chairs, and sent for a sergeant. Bedd had long ago gone home to his garden city, but Sergeant Tubb obliged with a notebook and stub of pencil, and, after the customary explanations and warnings which the felons were much too tearful to comprehend or appreciate, Charlesworth perched himself on one corner of the wooden table and opened fire.

"Now, then, Mac—er—Miss McEnery, I want to know what you were doing at the shop at such an unearthly hour, and I'm afraid you won't be able to leave here until I've found out."

Macaroni and Lydia immediately burst into tears again, but assured him that they were doing "nothing."

"Now, that's just nonsense, isn't it? You didn't go there in the middle of the night just for the fun of the thing. Why *did* you go?"

"Dulcie wanted to get somethink of hers," admitted Lydia at last, perceiving through her tears that prevarication would only lengthen proceedings.

"What did you want to get?"

More tears. "For heaven's sake be quiet!" cried Charlesworth, exasperated. "All this howling won't help you at all. I shall throw you into prison and let you howl there, and no one will hear you. Now, what was this something you wanted to get?"

"It was somethink out of the little safe," sobbed Macaroni, appalled by this terrible threat.

"Which safe? The one in Mr. Bevan's office?"

"Oh, no, not that one!" cried Macaroni, shocked into coherency. "Mr. Bevan would never have given me the key of that one. It was the little safe in Miss Doon's office; we only keep the old designs and the receipts and things in there."

"Why couldn't you have gone to it during the day?"

"Well, Mr. Bevan had the keys, you see," explained Lydia, taking the initiative into her own hands. "Dulcie arst him for it this morning, but he just went to the safe himself—she pretended she wanted some things about the office, you see, but he got them out and gave them to her. Then this evening he gave her one of the duplicate keys because he'd forgotten to give it to Miss Gregory before she went home and she might want it; so he told Dulcie to give it to Miss Gregory in the morning, you see, because he's going to the inquest and she'll be in charge of the shop, or something, isn't it, Dulcie?"

"That's right, and then he said he'd be working late, to-night, you see, so I couldn't go to the safe while he was there, and he said he might come in early to-morrow morning if he didn't get the work finished, and do it before he went to the inquest, so I couldn't leave it till then in case he got here before me, and then if I had to give the key to Miss Gregory and she went to the safe . . . and found . . ." words failed Macaroni at the very thought of this catastrophe.

"Do you mean to say that you and—and Lydia have been hanging about all this evening waiting for Mr. Bevan to leave the shop? . . ."

"We just waited till he went; he was a terrible long time, and he went over to the pub, in the middle, and brought in some beer and sangwidges or something, so Dulcie and I went to Lyons and had an ice-cream-sundae each," elaborated Lydia. "Dulcie paid, because it was because of her that we were doing it; then we went back; and after a long time Mr. Bevan came out and went off up Regent Street, and we let ourselves in with Dulcie's basement key, but we couldn't put on any lights or anything in case they showed; we'd just finished looking in the safe when we heard you coming, and we were so frightened that we hid. It was very uncomfortable under the table," she added, candidly, rubbing her pudgy calves, "and anyway, we didn't find it in the safe."

"And what was it that you didn't find?"

Lydia looked doubtfully at Macaroni. "Look here," said Charlesworth, encouragingly, "don't you think you'd better be sensible girls and tell me the whole thing? You've told me so much and it hasn't done you any harm, has it? As far as that's concerned, you can go right home and think no more about it ; I shan't say a word to Mr. Bevan and you can ask Mrs. David and Mrs. Gay to keep quiet about it . . . say that I ask them to. Don't you think you might just as well tell me what you wanted to find and be done with it? . . ."

Tears once more. "Now do stop crying and be sensible. What was it—a paper, wasn't it?"

"It was nothink to do with the shop," exclaimed Lydia, trying to be helpful.

"Did it belong to Miss McEnery?"

"Oh, yes!"

"Was it of any value—any value to anyone else, I mean?"

"Oh, no!"

"Was it a letter?"

"Oh, yes."

"What the devil *is* this—Animal, Vegetable, and Mineral?" thought Sergeant Tubb, stifling a yawn. "The ruddy kid got 'erself in the family way, and the Doon girl got 'old of the birth suttificit and was 'olding it over 'er 'ead. Why don't 'e get on with it?"

Half an hour later Charlesworth was delighted with his own perspicacity at coming to approximately the same conclusion. He promised to make an official inspection of the safes and locked drawers on the following morning, and to remove anything that might tarnish Macaroni's good name; and sent the girls away blissfully unconscious of the interpretation that had been put on their ghastly secret.

The sergeant departed, yawning pointedly; and he himself went wearily home to bed. He was anxious and dejected, and miserably in love, and all night long he dreamt that Victoria was trying to present him with a plush-framed photograph of her husband, who kept on turning into a large blue china cat.

## Six

### I

THE inquest was a formal affair of identification and adjournment. Bevan had been instructed to attend and thought it proper to be accompanied by one or two of his staff. Victoria and Irene, present by his instructions, had co-opted an unwilling Bobby Dazzler to protect them from the over-exuberant attentions of the Press.

Charlesworth, obliged to submit to an introduction to Victoria's husband, thought he had never beheld a more revolting specimen. The famous Dazzler was a tallish, thin young man, with an admirable forehead and sleepy brown eyes, and was considered by less prejudiced observers to be both personable and agreeable, though he concealed his excellent brain behind a manner often bordering upon imbecility. He gravely related to Charlesworth the full history of Victoria's awakening to the realization of his beauty and the subsequent christening, while Toria buzzed around him like an affectionate fly.

Charlesworth, unable to determine whether or not he were being laughed at, replied guardedly that it must make things somewhat awkward; and added with polite jocularity that he didn't believe the young ladies at Christophe's knew that Mr. David had any other name.

"Oh, I think they do," said the Dazzler, perfectly seriously. "Before we were married, in other words, before Victoria was in a position to behold me in my early morning glory, she used to call me her darling Pingo. That was

99

awkward, if you like. I could hear them yelling it all over the place, when I went to call for her at the shop: "Tell Victoria her darling Pingo's here." Even Mr. Cecil used to refer to me as Darling Pingo and it made me feel very uncomfortable. Mrs. 'Arris calls me Mr. Pingo to this day; she hasn't cottoned on to Bobby Dazzler yet and I believe she has dark suspicions that Toria is leading a sort of double life. I say," he continued, without the slightest change of tone as Victoria moved away to speak to Irene, "I hope you're getting to the bottom of this business, are you? because the girls will be demented if you don't very soon."

"I'm doing my best," said Charlesworth, humbly, "but it's a tricky business."

"Is it? I thought it must be. All the same, the position is pretty beastly, isn't it? I don't like to think of Toria working at that place with somebody running loose who has already done one person in. I've tried to get her to chuck it, but she doesn't want to leave Rachel, and Rachel can't afford to lose her job; and, of course, we do need the money," added the Dazzler with disarming candour.

"Oh, I think they're fairly safe, if that's what you mean," said Charlesworth, who had not previously considered this side of the affair. "The murder was an unpremeditated one, of that I'm pretty sure, and the only danger would be to anyone who knew too much. As long as the killer is safe from discovery, I think the others will be safe too . . ."

"Of course we're perfectly safe," said Victoria, who had strolled back to them; "don't listen to him, Mr. Charlesworth. He thinks Bevan's a sort of Bluebeard who will do for us, one by one, systematically. . . ." She wandered away again.

"Well, I do think Bevan's the dirty dog," admitted Bobby Dazzler, with quite a show of enthusiasm. "He's the most awful bounder and he's always messing around with one or other of the girls. I don't know how he went about it, but a man who can muck about on his own doorstep in such an undesirable fashion, is likely to get into some sort of trouble sooner or later and to have to take a dramatic way out."

"I realized, of course, that Mr. Bevan was more than an uncle to Miss Doon," said Charlesworth, interested; he did not mention Aileen; but he remembered the voices in the little office, and went on doggedly: "Do you suggest that Miss Doon wasn't the only attraction on the staff?"

"Good heavens, no, of course she wasn't. He's a man who can't keep his hands off any female; that's obvious, isn't it? Loathsome chap, to my mind. He made a few passes at Victoria once, before we were married, but I went and had a few words with him and, without stating anything in open court, we came to a mutual understanding that if there was any more of it, I would knock his bloody block off. Rachel's had an awful time and of course that woman Gregory is in it up to the neck."

"Miss Gregory!"

"Well, my dear chap, surely that's plain to see, I mean a woman like that—sex-starved and what not—all I can say is, I wouldn't be shut up alone with her for all the tea in China; and Bevan isn't the sort of man that needs asking twice."

"I did inquire about her, though not from this point of view; but the porter at Bevan's flats told me that she never went there except in the mornings, presumably in a secretarial capacity."

"Ah, well, 'a secretarial capacity' covers a multitude of sins; besides, she has a nice quiet flat of her own. Personally, I think he got tied up between the lot of them and did poor Doon in; a little spiritual blackmail going on perhaps, or something of the kind. She was a nice thing, too—I painted her once or twice and she had the best hips I ever saw on a woman."

"Didn't Mrs. David object to that?" asked Charlesworth fatuously, but before he could stop himself.

The Dazzler looked at him quickly, and then dropped his heavy lids again: "My dear chap, if Toria thought twice about every model I rave over, the place would be littered with foaming corpses. At least, I suppose they would foam, because she would obviously murder them with arsenic extracted from my green paints; do people foam when they die of arsenic?"

Charlesworth left the court, and after a hasty snack at the nearest pub went round to Doon's flat. The place had been combed for possible clues to her death, but he thought that, in the light of his more recently acquired knowledge, he might come upon something that would give him a lead.

The landlady, very much frightened, appeared at the door. "There's a gentleman there already, sir."

"Nobody except the police has any right in the flat."

"'E forced 'is way in, sir. 'E's got 'is own key and it wasn't for me to stop 'im." A ten-shilling note still clasped in her hand told the rest of her story.

He pushed the door open abruptly and marched into the flat. Bending over a desk in one corner was Bevan.

Charlesworth hailed him politely. "I expect we're looking for the same thing," he suggested. "Perhaps I can help you?"

Bevan was disconcerted but gave no sign of alarm. "I'm looking for my letters," he said, and calmly returned to the search.

Charlesworth seated himself on the arm of a chair and swung his leg. After five minutes during which Bevan went methodically through the papers in the desk, he asked pleasantly, "Why the act? You've got them in your pocket all the time."

Bevan could hardly refrain from laughing. "How the devil did you know?"

"I can see the bulge in your breast pocket; it wasn't there when you were in court, because I happened to be struck all over again at the super-excellent fit of your suit; and you must have come straight here to have got in before me; you'd better let me take charge of them, will you?"

"My dear fellow, spare my blushes! You only want them as evidence of the affair, and I'll give you all you need. This kind of correspondence looks so ghastly, read by a third party, and I wanted to spare the poor girl now that she's dead. Of course, you were bound to find out;

she's been my mistress for about eight or nine months, and a damned attractive creature she was too. Here's my latchkey, the badge of iniquity, and I've no doubt Mother Whatsisname in the basement will confirm all you want to know."

"Were you—er—associating with Miss Doon right up to the end?"

"I was in very close—er—association with her two days before she died," said Bevan, mockingly.

"Did she come often to your flat?"

"Once or twice but not more often than I could help. I believe in keeping my wires apart."

"Do you mind my asking whether you have many 'wires' at the moment?"

"At the moment, no. She was a very attractive young woman, and I had actually settled down to a sort of un-blessed monogamy with her."

"There was no question of her having a rival in your affections?"

Bevan looked uneasy but answered boldly enough: "Certainly not."

"What about Miss Gregory?" asked Charlesworth at a venture.

"Miss Gregory? Do you know all about that, too?"

"I know that Miss Doon replaced her. . . ."

"Well, hardly; the Gregory was never anything more than an interlude, if that . . . in fact, the damn woman's a perfect nuisance, and was already getting too hot to handle before I ever took up with the other one; Magda Doon didn't give tuppence for *her*, if that's what you're getting at."

"But you did dismiss at least one young lady in Miss Doon's favour?"

"Ah, yes, but she was different."

"That would be the redhead?" suggested Charlesworth, remembering the porter's description.

"The redhead," agreed Bevan, mildly surprised.

"Miss Wheeler?"

"Miss Wheeler, yes."

"Did she 'go quietly,' as they say?"

"She did, thank goodness; there was very little sentimentality about that affair and she found all she wanted: somebody to take my place. Filthy Lucre are, I regret to say, Miss Wheeler's first and second names."

Charlesworth reflected that Aileen's Arthur did not appear, from all accounts, to represent Filthy Lucre to any great degree; marriage and respectability, however, might have still stronger charms. He switched the conversation from the living to the dead.

"In spite of her attractions, you had almost decided to send Miss Doon to France?"

Bevan reflected for a moment. "I'll tell you how it was, Inspector," he said at last, with every appearance of candour. "If the girl went to Deauville I could do what I liked about her; I could see a lot of her or I need hardly see her at all. To be absolutely frank, she was becoming just a little bit of a bore, though I assure you that there was no question of a rival as you so refreshingly put it. She was very anxious to go, not realizing, of course, that it might be going to be her swan song; and I decided that I'd send her. In the meantime, however, Miss Gregory was becoming even more of a bore, and I decided that of the two I could better deal with Miss Doon. . . ."

"A somewhat dangerous business?" suggested Charlesworth, smoothly.

"Well, there are infinite advantages in having your women beholden to you for their bread and butter; it's tricky, of course, but it's the spice of life, and if they're liable to land themselves out of a job, they're more likely to 'go quietly'—again, as you put it."

"Miss Doon didn't go very quietly."

"My dear man, I've told you all this to show you how entirely unconnected Miss Doon's death is with any of my affairs. When I first talked to you, you suggested suicide, and I admit that I got the wind up, in case she should have done away with herself, and that a scandal should come out which would be bad for the business; then I realized how unlikely it was—she hadn't the faintest idea that I was cooling off her, and although she couldn't go to the new place, she was having quite a leg up in the business and would be seeing a good deal more of me; as for the two others, Miss Gregory had got the job she wanted, so *she* was quite happy, and the Wheeler girl had got a new love, so there was no cause for ill-feeling there; what the reason of the murder may have been I don't pretend to know; but it certainly wasn't in any way connected with me."

"Why did you come for the letters, then?"

"For the reasons I've already given you. I knew that she kept them in a comic little drawer in her desk—your people would never spot it if they weren't looking for it; and she had a whole lot of her own notes to me which she took back one day when she was round at my flat. I'm not the sort of man who commits himself on paper to a woman, but those made pretty warm reading, and I couldn't quite remember what I might have written myself; I was all against the desk being sold or disposed of, with these incriminating documents still in it."

Charlesworth got to his feet. "Well, I'll have them now." He held out his hand.

"For God's sake——" said Bevan, impatiently.

"I must have them, I'm afraid, Mr. Bevan. Come on, quickly, please, you're not in a position to argue. Clear out now, will you . . . and, murder or no murder, " he added viciously behind Bevan's retreating back, "hanging's too good for you!"

A further search of the desk failed to produce anything of the slightest interest, and driving back to the Yard, he asked himself whether his visit had really been very productive, except as a proof, if any were needed, as to Bevan's relations with the dead girl and with her colleagues. Bedd, however, hearing the story, put his finger on an important point. "I don't see that we need look any further for a motive for that Miss Aileen, sir. She may have gone a lot less quietly than he thinks, Arthur or no Arthur. A woman scorned, Mr. Charlesworth, that's when the poison gets flying around."

"You may be right, Bedd. I must have a word with

Aileen Wheeler. What a mess it all is—I never was so muddled up with a case in all my life. I'm having dinner with the Chief to-night, and what on earth I'm going to say to him . . ."

2

"You're unusually silent to-night, my boy," said the great man, as they lit their after-dinner cigarettes. "What am I to tell your father when I see him on Saturday? That we're knocking the stuffing out of you in the department?"

"Don't say that, sir, or mother will be round at all hours with antidotes to night starvation!"

"And how's the love affair going—let's see, it isn't Miss Humphreys any more. What was the new one's name?"

Charlesworth looked silly. "I expect you're thinking of Louise, sir. She was a jolly sweet girl, Louise was, but, of course, it wasn't serious, sir, and as a matter of fact this—er—this case has rather put her out of my head. . . ."

"Ah, yes, the case. I was going to ask you about that. You're getting along all right, Charlesworth, are you? because—this is unofficial, you know—Sir George was asking me yesterday how things were going. He thinks you're a bit young to be handling an affair which is so much in the public eye. Don't take it to heart, my dear boy," he added at the sight of Charlesworth's clouded face. "We aren't going to snatch it away from you without a word of warning; but, of course, when you took it on we had no idea that it was going to turn into such a terrific affair. I thought I would have you along to-night and just have a quiet chat with you so that I shall know what line to take with Sir George in the morning."

Charlesworth looked miserably round the quiet club room, with its shaded lights, its well-polished mahogany and its velvet hangings. The waiters moved softly among the damask-covered tables, the diners golloped their soup or sipped their port, solid, contented, respectable. "Silly old buffers," he thought, irritably. "Just like Sir George,

106

with his walrus moustache and pink eyes; they're all Sir Georges—everything must go like clockwork or they begin wanting to know why. As if I can't manage my own job in my own way. . . ." He fished out a pencil and made a large black blob on a menu card. "Of course, it *is* rather complicated, sir," he admitted slowly. "All the same, I don't see that anyone could have done more than I have in the time. When I started we had no idea whether it was murder or suicide or accident; I've been able to rule out accident and suicide. I've boiled it down to a list of ten suspects and I've already gone a long way towards establishing motives—though I must say," he added, ruefully, "that all the wrong ones seem to have motives. But it isn't a simple business of two and two make four and whoever you put on the job, I don't see how they could make it so."

He made a second large blob beside the first and added four long spikes. "This is only the fourth day," he went on, scribbling away gloomily, "and out of my ten possibles I've got it down to five probables, and out of my five probables I've got two very-likelies. . . . I don't think it's too bad, sir. I don't see why Sir George . . ."

"Now, hold your horses, Charlesworth. Nobody's accusing you of mishandling the case. I think you've done very well so far, and so does Sir George. He had a look through your notes and he thought they were extremely clear and very much to the point."

"Oh, Bedd does those," said Charlesworth airily and quite inaccurately, his good-humour entirely restored. "He's a treasure, is old Bedd. Between us, we can cope with things, sir, if you'll give me the chance. Of course, I'd like to talk it over with you, very much. I'm in a bit of a fog at the moment, I must confess, but my point is that so would anybody else be. It's the manager fellow, Bevan, that did it, only I can't prove it, and I can't quite see the motive. In any case, I don't see how we're ever going to get a conviction, whoever it is; what makes it so difficult is that it was obviously done on the spur of the moment and because the poison was available; especially as a good many people were there to share the suspicion by having access to the girl's food."

"Sir George and I were playing with a theory that someone might have come, either out of the shop through the back door of Bevan's office or from somewhere else altogether, gone down the area steps and done the deed at some unspecified time."

"Oh, I considered that, but it won't wash, sir. Bevan went straight to Miss Doon's office, after he had ordered the poison to be swept up, and he stayed there, with the door shut, until he came out again and spoke to Cecil on his way upstairs. The little secretary was with them in the office the whole time. Besides, Mrs. Harris was standing at her sink washing up from the moment that she came downstairs from brushing the stuff up; she was keeping an eye out for a knife-grinder and she had a full view of the area steps; no one could have come down them without being seen by her, and nobody did. Nobody passed through the kitchen, in fact, nobody came into the kitchen at all, until Mrs. Best came down at twelve o'clock to have her own lunch and afterwards to help serve out for the one o'clock lunch; the girls from the workroom have theirs sent upstairs."

"But later on Mrs. Harris was serving the lunch?"

"Yes, but still with an eye out for the knife-grinder; anyway, by that time Cecil was standing at the head of the service table, very close to the area door which is just under the stairs, and at least one or two of the girls were with him all the time. Nobody could have come in then."

"Could anyone have come down the area steps during the few minutes in which the woman was upstairs sweeping up the crystals?"

"I suppose they could have, sir, but the food wasn't out of the kitchen then, and nobody had had time to get hold of any of the poison; in any event, nobody left the showroom except Miss Gregory, who came down to tell Mrs. Harris to take her dustpan and brush upstairs."

"What happened to her?"

"Well, she says that she went off into the ladies'

cloakroom, which is also in the basement; there's no proof of that; but, anyway, she had no poison, that's as certain as can be. Bevan and the secretary were giving each other alibis in the little office; I think we must definitely cut out any time for administration of the poison, except for the twenty minutes between the time Cecil and Mrs. Best started to serve out the curry and the time the girl sat down to eat it."

"Anyway, that's getting somewhere. Who have you got on your very-probable list besides Mr. Bevan?"

"Well, there's Cecil and there's the char. There's something very peculiar about this chap Cecil, but I hope I can clear it up pretty soon. That friend of his, Elliot, is missing, and he's in a terrible state and obviously has something to hide . . . though not in a trunk," added Charlesworth, grinning foolishly. "The friend appears to have had a crush on Miss Doon and I've been wondering since last night whether Cecil can have murdered her for the benefit of the other man. I must say I think that that's stretching the claims of friendship rather far; a better explanation would be that he murdered her in a fit of jealousy because the other fellow was keen on her. He's an unbalanced, hysterical sort of creature; one of these Oedipus complexes, by all accounts. If he did kill the girl he'll be the easiest to convict because he'll give himself away. The odd thing, though, is this; during my first interview with him, and with Bevan, both the sergeant and I noticed that when I mentioned the possibility of murder, each of them seemed relieved. Bevan's explained his since—he was afraid the girl had committed suicide; but I can't see why it should have been in Cecil's case."

The blobs had become a head and a body, and the spikes were now four knobby legs. A most outrageous camel was emerging from Charlesworth's unconscious pencil. He began to decorate it with small dots as he went on, frowning with concentration. "The other very-likely is the charwoman, Mrs. Harris. She had both opportunities and a cut-and-dried motive; if she did it, we're sunk, because we shall never prove it. Then there are the four possibles: there's Aileen Wheeler, the mannequin (she's almost a very-likely, really, because she had quite a respectable motive—or rather a motive that was the reverse of respectable—besides the two opportunities); Judy, the other mannequin, who makes no secret of the fact that she detested Doon, and who seems to have benefited by her death to the extent of one fiancé, returned to the fold—she had both opportunities; and Rachel Gay, but so far I haven't traced any motive for her. Anyway, she seems a very unlikely person to commit a murder of this kind—or else she's a very good actress."

"Not a *very* good actress," said the superintendent, coolly, "but an actress. I've seen her on the stage."

"No!"

"Yes, I have. I never forget a name. A big, dark girl?"

"That's the one. Where did you see her?"

"I don't remember at all. It must have been several years ago and I have an idea that it was in the provinces somewhere, but I really couldn't say. Only I remember the name and I remember the girl."

"Well, that's the most extraordinary thing, sir. However, I don't know that it helps us very much, when one comes to examine it. There doesn't seem to be the ghost of a motive. Still, I wonder . . ."

A tremendous forest grew up around Charlesworth's camel while he wondered. His chief repressed a desire to point out the improbability of such a background, and inquired after the remaining four suspects. "Well, they're hardly suspects at all," said Charlesworth, scribbling busily. "They're the ones who are in a way involved, but who had only one of the two opportunities. There's the secretary; she could have poisoned the food, and she had the most excellent reasons for wanting to do away with Doon, who was apparently in possession of a letter which contained proof of the kid's having gone off the rails at some time—I imagine she was holding it over Macaroni's head for some reason of her own, though not, I imagine, for money. However, I still think she's innocent; she only had a certain quantity of the poison and that much was found in the drawer where Miss Doon put it; moreover, Bevan gives the child an alibi for the whole period between the time she came downstairs and the time she went to the kitchen to give the message about the lunch; she had no time to go out and get more oxalic and that's certain."

"She couldn't have administered it in some way during the few minutes after Bevan left the office?"

"Well, but where could she have got it from, sir?"

"All right, have it your own way; but there seems to me to be a flaw there somewhere, Charlesworth, only I can't put my finger on it. Think it over. Now, who's next?"

"Only three more, sir. Irene Best, Miss Gregory, Victoria David. Gregory may have had a motive because she is supposed to have been in love with Bevan and he, of course, was living with Miss Doon; however, though she might have administered poison, she couldn't have got hold of it, so that lets her out. Irene Best had no motive that I can see, neither had Mrs. David; in any event, at the time when they might have used the opportunity to poison the food, they were each under the impression that Miss Doon was going to be out to lunch: in fact, Mrs. Best really is out of it altogether because she had no motive and neither of the two famous opportunities."

Charlesworth finished his forest and added a dot to a minute space on the camel's back. "No, Bevan's my favourite, sir. He's the villain."

"But when could he have administered it?" asked the superintendent, gazing at him rather blankly.

"Ye gods, these old buffers!" thought Charlesworth, regarding his chief (who had just turned fifty) with a despairing though tolerant eye. "He hauls me over the coals about the case and he hasn't even read the damn notes." "You'll have noticed in my interview with him, sir," he explained patiently, "that Bevan admitted that after he came out of Miss Doon's office he walked straight up to the table and leant across it to speak in a low voice to Mr. Cecil. He could easily have dropped the poison on to the plate while he did that."

The superintendent continued to gaze at him. "Good lord!" he thought, "these boys! They make the most excellent and accurate notes on a case and never even notice the significance of them." He had observed the poor-old-gentleman note in the young man's voice and he could not keep a trace of asperity out of his own as he pointed out: "Hasn't it dawned on you that Bevan couldn't have known which was Miss Doon's plate?"

Very pink in the face, Charlesworth fished out his own rough notebook and scanned it anxiously. "You're perfectly right, sir. I'm very sorry. . . . I thought I'd caught you napping then," he added, with an apologetic grin.

"It hadn't occurred to me that you'd missed that—why did you think I'd tried to work out a theory of his coming down the area steps at a different time?"

Charlesworth, who had privately thought that the dear old geyser had been talking through his hat, made no reply except to bemoan the erasure of Bevan from his list of probables. "He did seem so perfect for the part."

"Have you any proof of this supposed affair with the dead girl?"

"Oh, yes, I've got a whole bunch of letters. I've still got them on me, as a matter of fact; I hadn't time to read them at the Yard, so I thought I'd run through them while I changed. Pretty pornographic, most of them!" He produced them from his pocket and idly sorted them through. "Hallo, I didn't see this one; it's in a different handwriting. . . ." He unfolded a single sheet of notepaper, and as he read its contents he suddenly went stiff and rather cold. His mind flew back to the half-hour he had spent with the lovelies in their little cubbyhole; he heard again Rachel's warm voice, saying, "I loved her!" and Victoria's laughter, trailing off into silence: "She looks so sweet and kind, Mr. Charlesworth, but you can't trust her; Rachel's a tiger when she's roused!"

He handed the letter across the table; in a large, round, feminine scrawl, punctuated only by dashes and obviously written in haste, it read: "Please make an opportunity for me to talk to you at the shop to-morrow—it's more vital than ever that nothing shall come out about—you know what—you're the only person in the world who can give me away and if you do, my God, I'll kill you." The last words were heavily underlined. If he had not recognized the handwriting, the signature was clear for all the world to see: "Rachel Gay."

## *Seven*

### I

RACHEL was dressing to go to Doon's funeral—struggling into a long-sleeved grey frock, polishing patent leather shoes, ripping the gay green feathers off a hat. A pair of black suede gloves lay upon the dressing-table; she thrust them suddenly out of sight and went to the telephone.

"Hallo, is that you, Judy? My dear, have you got an extra pair of black gloves, because I can't find mine, and I thought you might be able to lend me some. Oh, thank you, darling. What? Well, if they don't I shall just have to carry them scrunched up in my hand. I'd better call for you in my taxi and collect them, and then we can go on together."

"I was supposed to be taking Macaroni," said Judy.

"Oh, never mind that. I'll ring up Aileen and tell her to call for Macaroni on her way through Camden Town. She'll have to pass quite near."

"Well, I'm taking Mrs. 'Arris, anyway."

"Nonsense, Judy, you can't do that."

"I've promised to let her come with me and I'm jolly well going to," said Judy, a trifle irritated at having her plans so summarily disarranged. "Bevan told her to stay away, I know, but the poor old thing would be broken-hearted if she didn't go. She loathed Doon while she was alive, of course, but she's all against missing a funeral."

"I don't think you ought to take her if Bevan doesn't want her there."

"It isn't Bevan's funeral," said Judy, "and I'm taking her, so that's all there is to it. Anyway, you'd better get a move on, Rachel, if you're calling for me. It's twenty past already."

Rachel, having rung up Aileen, returned to her dressing. A seam had given way in one of her thin silk stockings and she stitched it up, rapidly but with infinite care. A clean handkerchief, powder-puff, lipstick, a couple of ten-shilling notes and some small change were transferred to her black handbag; she put on her hat, carefully brushed the shoulders of her frock, and ran down the stairs.

"Going off to the funeral of that pore young lady," said the first charlady to the second charlady as she passed them in the hall. "Looks fair 'eartbroke, don't she?"

The second charlady was unsentimental. "She don't look 'eartbroke to me, Mrs. Spong," she said, frowning heavily after the elegant figure. "I tell you what she looks to me: cross as two sticks, that's what she looks to me!"

The arrangements for the funeral had been a nightmare to Bevan. Doon's parents had cabled expenses, but, of necessity, left all arrangements in his hands. It had been decided to close the shop for the day—it was a Saturday, anyway, and decency demanded little less; but the problem of the attendance at the graveside was fraught with embarrassment. The Press would certainly miss no detail of the affair, and the absence of all or any of the dead girl's colleagues might be taken amiss. On the other hand, the whole of England was by this time aware that, by a process of elimination, the murderer must be one of the staff of Christophe et Cie, and Bevan pictured with a shudder headlines blaring forth that the killer had walked with bowed head behind the victim's coffin and placed hypocritical flowers upon her grave. He decided at last that most of the staff must be present, but that one or two absentees would, at least, leave an element of doubt for the public mind to seize upon, and he accordingly chose, at random, Irene and Mrs. 'Arris and instructed them to stay away. Mrs. 'Arris's reaction was typical; lose her job she might, but miss the funeral she would *not*! Irene, only too glad of the excuse to be absent, assented willingly and the Press was informed that she was too unwell to attend. But alas for excellent intentions! That night headlines screamed that she alone had stayed away, and all over the country men and women took up malicious pens.

Gregory had been in favour of hiring several large cars, one for Bevan, one for Cecil and herself, and one for the girls, but, "No, thanks," said Bevan, grimly. "I should only need a fat cigar to look like a theatrical manager arriving with the season's bunch of sweeties, fresh from their triumphs at Monte Carlo. Let them all come along in ones and twos in the best-looking taxis they can find, and I'll pay their fares; and tell them not to send individual wreaths and things. We don't want the papers printing the inscriptions and heading them, 'Farewell Message of a Murderer?'"

"They couldn't," said Gregory, literally. "It would be libel."

"Libel or no libel, I don't want the girls sending flowers privately, do you hear? I shall order a large wreath from myself and one from them all collectively. Cecil had better send something, too."

"Won't that look rather mean—only three wreaths?"

"Will it? *I* don't know. What a hell of a business this all is. Well, let the workroom send one, and perhaps we could divide up the showroom and send one from the mannequins and one from the salesgirls and yourself. You arrange it somehow—I can't think any more about it. Do your best for me, like a good girl; if I don't stop going over and over the thing, I shall be off my head. Damn this bloody publicity—whatever we do will be wrong."

Mrs. 'Arris was sitting on a chair in Mrs. Carol's elegant hall when Rachel arrived to call for Judy. "Ow, Miss Rachel, you are late. We thought you was never coming."

"There's plenty of time," said Rachel, coldly. "I've got my taxi waiting, Judy."

They sat down side by side in the cab and Mrs. 'Arris perched herself on one of the small front seats. "Here's a pair of Mummy's gloves," said Judy, handing them over. "She says not to return them—they're quite old ones."

Their taxi joined the line of cars waiting at the appointed spot, and then started on the long, slow drive through the London streets. In front of them went Toria and the Dazzler in their small and shabby car; behind them Macaroni sobbed and snivelled and Aileen regarded her with dispassionate disgust. Mrs. 'Arris applied a large black-bordered handkerchief to such tears as she could squeeze out, and Rachel leant back in her corner and closed her eyes. After half an hour, when they had very little further to go, she said suddenly in a low, but perfectly audible voice, "Mrs. 'Arris."

Mrs. 'Arris continued to stare out of the window with her handkerchief to her nose. She knew that tone of voice very well. There's none so deaf as them that wants to 'ear what won't be said in front of them if they *ain't* deaf, thought Mrs. 'Arris, and many a tit-bit had she learnt at the shop through this purely imaginary failing of hers. "Mrs. 'Arris," the young ladies would say softly. "Can you 'ear what we're saying?" was what they meant; she would go on quietly with her work and out would come their secrets—oh, she'd picked up a lot that way, and now what was coming? She gave a tremendous sniff and gazed blankly upon the passing scene.

Rachel looked at her sharply. "I've got something to say to you, Judy, and I don't want another soul to hear it—it's perfect hell her being here at all, but I can't wait, so thank goodness she's deaf."

"How mysterious you are, Rachel! Do you mean to say that all this business about the gloves was just an excuse?"

"Yes, of course. I've got a perfectly good pair at home, but I suddenly realized something this morning while I was dressing and I had to get hold of you at once before you made any—mistakes."

"What on earth about?"

"About Doon's death. Judy—you know who killed her, don't you?".

"Yes," said Judy, suddenly very still.

"How do you know?"

"I saw you picking up the poison, Rachel, off the floor."

"I thought you did," said Rachel, indifferently. "I remember now, looking up and seeing you standing at the door of your room. Now, Judy, what I want to say to you is this. Mr. Charlesworth told the Dazzler something yesterday that was very much to the point: he said that everybody at Christophe's was safe *until they knew too much*. And you do know too much. So I wanted to warn you, Judy—just as long as there's a chance of your telling what you know, your own life is in danger. You haven't got proof, you know, and *I* haven't admitted anything, have I? Mr. Charlesworth would have to find out a lot more than you can tell him, before he acted—and in the meantime anything could happen to you, couldn't it, Judy? You hated Doon—I believe sometimes you'd have killed her yourself, if you could. Why should you bother about who actually did? If it's going to be found out, Charlesworth will find it without any help from you—meanwhile, you do nothing—and I'll do nothing. Will you promise?"

"I can't promise," said Judy, white and shaking. "I wasn't going to say anything, anyway, but I can't promise. I'll think it over."

"You must promise, Judy. You must swear to do nothing and you must promise never to breathe a word to anyone about what I've said to you to-day. Otherwise—you don't want to die, do you, Judy? As it happens, neither do I. Look, we're coming to the gates—promise me, swear to me, that you'll keep quiet; promise me!"

Mrs. 'Arris sniffed and gazed and listened with all her might. Judy promised.

2

It was a dismal day for August, cold and sunless and inclined to rain, but a crowd of sightseers had gathered in the cemetery and the girls had to push their way past them and into the tiny chapel. Charlesworth, from a quiet corner, watched them coming slowly up the path towards him. Rachel and Judy walked stiffly beside each other, in troubled silence; Mrs. 'Arris waddled after them, her best black winter coat belted about her for the occasion, a velvet toque, cast out from Christophe's, perched back-to-front on her head. Toria looked pale and sad, but her hair was like candlelight under her big black hat. Cecil swept back his forelock with a shaking hand, and minced along with a look of self-conscious grief on his pallid face; Bevan was nervous and ill-at-ease, Macaroni bathed in tears. Only Aileen walked nonchalantly up the path, and might have been a debutante at a garden party, obliged to wear grey on the death of her cousin, the Duke. She caught sight of Charlesworth in his corner and bestowed upon him a gracious, fleeting smile.

The coffin was borne slowly in and placed on its trestles before the marble altar. A clergyman embarked upon a series of singularly inappropriate prayers. The girls stood together in a little group, their lovely heads bent, tears in their eyes; Bevan looked cross, Cecil sniffed and fidgeted, Gregory stared at something she did not see. "She looks pretty grim," thought Charlesworth, watching her haggard face and the bitter line of her mouth. "What a strange woman she is: I never saw anyone who so obviously took trouble with her clothes, and then looked so damned awful when she had them on." His attention was caught by a movement at the door of the chapel: "Hallo, who have we here? Pals of Doon's, I suppose. Snappy-looking piece with the henna and the silver fox; where have I seen her before? What frightful-looking bounders the chaps are; they must be Doon's old flames. I wish this fellow would stop gassing and let us get out of here."

"Doon would have laughed like hell if she could have seen all this," whispered the Dazzler to Victoria, as they filed out to the graveside. "She must be enjoying it like anything, wherever she is. She had a great sense of the ridiculous, hadn't she? and I'm sure she'd be tickled to death (not a very happy metaphor, my dear!) to see all these chaps making faces at each other across the pews and Cissie's eye-black running with his emotion."

"Oh, darling, I'm so glad you suggested that! I've been so depressed thinking it was all ghastly and not a bit like Doon; but, of course, you're quite right—she would simply have loved it! If only it wouldn't rain; and how muddy and dreadful it is. Rachel looks awful—she was so fond of Doon and I think she's more upset than she lets on. Talk to me some more, Bobby, I'm sure I shall howl very soon."

"Don't do that, for goodness' sake. That's just what Charlesworth's waiting for. One tear and he'll clap you into prison, without further argument. He's gazing at Bevan as if he expects him to yell out a confession at any moment."

"Oh, darling, you don't really think that's why he's here?"

"Of course, why else? He wouldn't sweat all this way out and risk getting his feet wet and catching pneumonia just out of respect for the dear departed. No, my dear, he's waiting for someone to get the heebie-jeebies and give themselves away, and by the look on some of these faces I should think he may be lucky."

A cordon of police kept the crowd at a respectful distance. They threaded their dismal way between marble angels and granite slabs, sad little wooden crosses and fresh mounds of earth, and came to a halt at a yawning square hole, surrounded by wooden boards. The solemn words were spoken and a handful of earth scattered into the grave after the coffin was lowered slowly into the ground. Charlesworth anxiously scanned the faces around him; Victoria, Rachel, and Judy stood together, quiet and still; Gregory was between Bevan and Cecil, all with white faces and downcast eyes; Macaroni and Mrs. 'Arris sobbed in unison. But none of them moved. Only Aileen, standing elegantly aloof at the foot of the grave, grew suddenly pale and sinking to her knees, toppled slowly, gracefully, languid as ever, on to the very edge of the pit, and lay there motionless, with her lovely hair in the mud.

# Eight

IT certainly was uncompromisingly dull, being companion to old Mrs. Prout. Holly thought she never could have stuck it, if it hadn't been for the Society people who sometimes came down with Mr. Cecil on Saturday or Sunday afternoons. It was true that they only raved a bit about the garden and made foolish noises at the budgerigars, and went away again, and it always meant a lot more work and fuss; still, it did make a change and one saw all sorts of people— "ladies" and duchesses and sometimes even an actress. Holly went all goofy at the thought of the actress who had once actually laid a hand on her arm and called her Pretty Poppet. The actress called her dog Pretty Poppet and her maid Pretty Poppet, and even her husband Pretty Poppet, on the rare occasions when she spoke to him, but Holly was not to know that, and it had quite altered her ideas about giving notice to Mrs. Prout the very moment the guests had gone. She had flown on the wings of joy to fetch the actress's handbag—which was what the actress had asked her Pretty Poppet to fetch; and now here was Saturday again, and Mr. Cecil would be down this afternoon and would tell them all about the murder. At least he would tell his mother, Mrs. Prout, about the murder, but it came to very much the same thing since Holly had found out that, by applying her ear to the floor of her bedroom, she could catch every word that was spoken in the sitting-room below. She had made this discovery on the first terrible afternoon when she had heard Mr. Cecil weeping and it had become so absolutely imperative to know what he was weeping about. It was nothing at all really, and she had since realized that Mr. Cecil was always weeping. He wept when a dress went wrong, or when a client was displeased, or when one of his friends let him down; and every time he wept his mother petted him and comforted him and praised him into happiness again. More like a girl, Mr. Cecil; it was his mother's fault, really, thought Holly, who had never heard of the Oedipus complex and was ignorant of the name of Freud. His father had died during Cecil's childhood, having, during the eight years of their married life, been such a husband as Mrs. Prout despaired of replacing; and she had settled down in the country to find solace in the constant company of her only child. Mr. Cecil —his name was Mr. Prout, of course, but one could see that that would never have done—lived in a flat in London, so as to be near his work; but he had recently established his mother in the prettiest little eighteenth-century cottage imaginable, and he spent his week-ends with her there. Sometimes one of the boy friends came down with him and there would be skippings about in the garden and discussions about the flowers and re-namings of the budgerigars. When he was devoid of other employment, Mr. Cecil always rechristened the budgerigars, and during the short time that Holly had been at Trianon they had already been called "Sweet and Lovely," "Louis and 'Toinette," and, best of all to Cecil's mind, "Sacred and Profane." "Let me introduce the love-birds—Sacred and Profane Love," he would say, and the duchesses and the actresses and the "ladies" thought it delicious. "Petit Trianon" was the name of the eighteenth-century cottage; and if the villagers called it, oafishly, the "little 'ouse," even more simply, "Prout's," Cecil was above such petty considerations as the preferences of the local bourgeoisie.

Holly had, of course, read all about the murder in the papers. It only showed how right she had been to stay with Mrs. Prout, where there was the chance of inside information as to such terrific goings-on. She spent a happy afternoon with her ear glued to the bedroom carpet, and nothing but the fact that it was Myrna Loy at the local cinema could have dragged her away from the house. At six o'clock, however, she rose stiffly to her feet and, going down to the kitchen, begged for a surreptitious cup of tea.

"Coo, Miss Holly, I thought you was 'aving your afternoon out!"

"Yes, I am; well, I mean, you know what I mean. Mrs. Prout thinks I am."

"Yes, she does, and a rare old time her and Mr. Cissel is 'aving in the droring-room. Talking and 'owling and arguing—you ought to 'ave 'eard it."

"I did," thought Holly, smiling to herself.

"I couldn't get 'old of a word, though I don't mind admitting that I listened for a bit outside the door; I wanted to find out about this 'ere murder, but they didn't seem to be saying nothink about that—a lot of nonsense about that Mr. Elliot; seems 'e's gorn orf or somethink. I wish I could 'ave 'eard it."

"You shouldn't listen at doors, Gladys, it's very wrong indeed," said Holly piously, and trotted off down the drive.

A young man of astonishing good looks was bending over a car just outside the gate. He raised his hat as Holly appeared and, straightening himself, said, with a pleasant smile, "Good evening, miss. Would you mind me asking you if you live in that house?"

"Well, as a matter of fact, I do," replied Holly, all of a flutter. "Why?"

"Because I seem to have run out of water and the car's boiling a bit. Do you think you could possibly let me have a jugful?"

"Yes, of course. I'll come back with you and get the maid to give you some."

Gladys obliged with a large enamel jug, filled at the kitchen sink, and with this the young man replenished his radiator. The accelerator responded to his touch and he was just about to drive off when he appeared to be struck with a sudden idea.

"I suppose I couldn't give you a lift anywhere?" he suggested.

Holly hesitated. All men were beasts and a fate sometimes overtook young women which, according to her mother's teaching, was worse than death itself. On the other hand, there was an air of impeccable respectability about the young man with the little car and, what was very much more to the point, a distinct look of Robert Taylor; there was not much adventure for a young lady of nineteen, stuck away in a Kentish village with an old lady and a young man enmeshed in his mother's apron-strings. "Do or die," thought Holly, and tilting her chin in imitation of Myrna Loy, she scrambled into the car.

It transpired from her rather feverish chatter that she was not alone at Trianon. She lived there with an elderly lady whose son had just come down for the week-end. He was staying till Monday morning.

"How do you know *that*?" said the young man, with a bovine humour rather surprising in one hitherto so well conducted. "He may be going to run off to-night and when you get back he'll be gorn."

"Oh, no, he won't," said Holly, essaying such coyness as was evidently expected of her. "He distinctly told his mother that he would be staying till Monday. He generally goes back on Sunday night, but he isn't this time."

Detective Officer Tomlinson heaved a sigh of relief. That meant that he could take a room at the local pub and at least have a decent night. Meanwhile, he might as well cultivate the companion and see if he couldn't dig any information out of her. He inquired as to her plans for the evening.

"Well, I was going to the flicks, as a matter of fact," replied Holly, who found it necessary to qualify a great many of her statements with this, frequently meaningless, phrase.

"Oh, don't do that. It's far too lovely a night to spend in a stuffy cinema. Why don't you let me take you for a run and perhaps have a bite and a cup of coffee some-where?"

Here was adventure with a vengeance. Supposing that he should stop the car and suddenly produce a tin of black-lead and cover her with it from head to foot! Holly had heard of such incomprehensible occurrences and even worse, and for a moment her heart failed her. A sideways glance at the young man's face, however, showed such an indubitable resemblance to Robert Taylor as caused caution to be thrown to the winds. She settled herself more comfortably in the seat beside him and, tilting the chin until it ached, cried with a pronounced American accent: "Drive on, big boy!"

The rain that had made a muddy heap of poor Doon's grave had brought out the sweet scent of the Kentish orchards, where the fruit hung ripely upon the boughs and the whitened stems of the trees were gentle ghosts in the twilight. There was a magic over the rolling countryside and the boy felt guilty and a little ashamed at the game he was playing with this foolish girl. However, duty was duty and he could not go back to Mr. Charlesworth with a tale that the summer evening had gone to his head; he plied her with innocent questions, and she, flattered and fluttering, poured out her story of small woes and delights; of petty triumphs and trifling heartaches and still-childish longings. The actress who had called her Pretty Poppet; the "ladies" who came down from Town; the doting old mother and sloppy young man, and the overwhelming excitement of the murder in the very shop that Mr. Cecil worked for.

Mr. Tomlinson had heard of the murder, of course, and was thrilled to meet someone in close contact with so famous an affaire. Not that Holly could tell him much, she admitted. She had expected Mr. Cecil to be full of it, but instead he had kept talking about his own affairs—as usual, just like him! and something or other which he had done, something rather awful—he wouldn't even tell his mother what it was.

"Whatever could it have been?" asked Mr. Tomlinson, no longer obliged to show more interest than he felt.

"I can't imagine. Something awful, anyway. He kept saying that she would never forgive him if she knew, which was perfectly silly because she would forgive him whatever he did. They spend their lives forgiving each other."

"Perhaps he did the murder himself?"

"Good gracious, no. He'd faint at the sight of blood."

"There wasn't any blood,'' pointed out the young man, laughing. "It was done by poisoning."

"I meant it metterphorically," said Holly, with much dignity. "Anyway, it was nothing to do with that; I think he must have been to a fortune-teller or something. He kept talking about crystals."

The young man stopped the car so suddenly that Holly expected the blackleading to begin at any moment, and a half-pleasurable excitement rose within her at the thought that she might be about to find out at last what was worse than death. However, Mr. Tomlinson's interest seemed to be confined to Mr. Cecil and his stupid maternal confidences. He ran the car gently down a little grass slope at the edge of the road and, putting his arm along the back of the seat behind her shoulders, asked, in a strangely excited voice: "What about the crystals?"

"It's all nothing," said Holly, piqued. "He told Mrs. Prout that somebody had given him some crystals or a crystal, I couldn't hear that part very well; and that he had done something dreadful with them, or it. It must have been it because nobody could possibly want more than one crystal."

"Did he say who he'd given it to?"

"He didn't say he'd given it to anybody. He said he'd done something dreadful with them or with it, and that his mother would never forgive him if she knew. Then he got all sloppy and asked her if she'd mind if he left her for ever, which was simply fishing, because he knows perfectly well that the old girl would die without him; but, of course, she got frightfully het up and said that he mustn't say such dreadful things."

"Did he mean that he might be going away—abroad, perhaps?"

"Oh, no, it sounded more as if he might die or be killed or something. It was all mixed up with Mr. Elliot in some way."

"Not with Miss Doon?"

"Yes, it was something to do with her, too. He was telling his mother that it was all Miss Doon's fault that

Mr. Elliot had left him; he said that Elliot had told him that he was in love with Miss Doon and was going to ask her to marry him. I'm sure she wouldn't have, because she seems to have been rather a bright sort of a person and he was nearly as girlish and silly as Cecil himself. He tried to squeeze my hand once, when he came down here, and Cecil saw him and got quite worked up about it; Elliot told him that he ought to make friends with some girls himself, and Mrs. Prout was furious and said that her darling was much better without a lot of designing women, and Cecil cried and said that his Faerie was the only woman in the world he needed; he always calls her Faerie, isn't it sick-making? It's out of Shakespeare, I think."

"Did Mr. Cecil seem to be angry with Miss Doon for taking Mr. Elliot away from him?"

"Well, I know he was, as a matter of fact, because last Saturday he was down here, and he was in a terrible flap about it. He kept on saying that he would die if Elliot broke up their friendship, or that he would kill Elliot sooner than see him married to that cruel girl, or that he would kill Miss Doon. I say," cried Holly, as the import of her own rapid gabble burst upon her, "I never thought of that—I wonder if he could have killed her, after all."

"If he was saying only the day before that he would like to—it does seem funny, don't it?"

"Yes, but he couldn't—I mean, he would pass out at the sight of—at the thought of poison; besides, he's always saying wild things like that; I don't think it really means anything. You don't honestly believe that he could have done it?"

"Well, it does seem funny, don't it?"

"I wish he wouldn't keep on saying that," thought Holly. "It goes give him away a bit. He isn't a gent at all, really. What Mother would say if she could see me now, a parson's daughter, with a strange young man who can't even talk the King's English, sitting in a car and arguing about a murder." "I tell you what," she exclaimed aloud, the King's English eluding even the parsonage

126

upbringing in the intensity of her sudden excitement, "I tell you what—I believe you're right; because now I come to think of it, at one time he started to blub and say that he would never have done it if he'd known she would die like that, and it was a terrible thing to take life and a lot of intense stuff like that, and about the spark of life and put out the light and then put out the light, which comes out of *Hamlet*, I think, and a lot more tripe like that. The old lady was nearly as keen to find out what he was talking about as I was, and she kept calling him my boy, my boy, and saying that he mustn't upset himself and that she knew he had nothing to reproach himself with, and so on; and he blubbed more and more and said, 'Ah, Faerie, you don't know what I've done!' Fancy calling her Faerie—it's *too* revolting, isn't it?"

Mr. Tomlinson led her skilfully back to the "crystal," but nothing more definite was forthcoming. He decided that it would be best and safest, for all parties, to allay her fears, and accordingly made out a very good case for Cecil's innocence in the murder. This he found not difficult, for, on analysis, his evidence to the contrary proved extremely vague. Holly allowed herself to be comforted, and after the promised bite and cup of coffee, was deposited back at the gate without even a smell of blacklead. She wandered disconsolately up to bed; the evening post had brought a reply from "Margot" about her spots, but she threw it aside and went to the window, where she could catch the last faint phut-phut-phut of the departing car. Voices came from below and once more she crouched, bottom up, with her ear to the ground; they were still at it, or if they had stopped they had started all over again; this time it was Mrs. Prout who was in tears and she was saying over and over again: "Of course your old mother understands, my precious; of course she understands. But oh!—it's dreadful to think of the risks you ran—and even now, what are we to do? Supposing the police find out? How could you have done such a thing, Cecil, my darling? The descriptions of what the poor girl suffered were terrible—terrible. I can't bear to think of it: it was a dreadful thing to do, a dreadful, dreadful . . ."

Here was confirmation beyond her wildest dreams. Holly leapt up and rushed to the window. But the phut-phut-phut of the car had died away.

## *Nine*

### I

TEN people read their post on Monday morning in stricken silence, for even the black heart of the murderer quailed at the things the anonymous letters had to say about Irene Best. Bevan was beside himself with remorse; he had chosen her to be absent from the funeral for no other reason than that she had been at hand when he had made his decision; if only that old fool Mrs. 'Arris had obeyed him, there would have been at least two objects for the public's suspicion, if they must take it in this way. He was bound to admit that it did look rather peculiar for one single person to have absented herself on a feeble excuse of ill-health, and he cursed the hour in which he had made his ill-fated arrangements and brought down this horrible attack upon her gentle head. Victoria, distraught, rushed round to Irene's little room with the Dazzler, unshaven and protesting, at her side. To her surprise, she found Aileen already there, roused to something approaching energy by her disgust at the cowardly attacks, holding Irene's hand and beseeching her not to allow herself to be upset. "*I* wouldn't," avowed Aileen, which was probably true, since no one in the memory of Christophe et Cie had seen her moved from her indifferent calm.

Irene looked terrible. Her face seemed to have shrunk to a tiny point and her eyes under their heavy lids were dark with despair. "Don't let yourself be upset by it Irene, my darling," implored Toria, joining her hopeless plea with Aileen's. "It's all too vile and cruel and wicked; but why should you care what such cheap and cowardly people think or say? We know you didn't—didn't kill Doon so as to enjoy her suffering, and—and all these revolting things . . . I mean, Irene, all your friends believe that you didn't murder her; why should you care what these horrible, unbalanced creatures write?"

"Have they sent letters about me to everybody?" asked Irene, dully.

"I don't know, darling. They sent one to me, and I suppose you got one, Aileen, did you? They must have got our addresses from the papers. But still, what does it matter if they have?"

"Everyone at Christophe's knows that you're the last person in the world that would have killed her, Rene," said Aileen, kindly. "Not a soul will take any notice of what a lot of mad people say; we all know that it was Bevan who told you to stay away, and why he told you. He said the same to Mrs. 'Arris, and if only that silly idiot Judy hadn't let her come, there wouldn't have been all this beastliness."

"Poor old Mrs. 'Arris would have got them too," said Irene, miserably. "You don't know how awful it is—how can I go to work to-day, with all the people in the streets thinking I stayed away from Doon's funeral because I killed her? I wouldn't—I wouldn't have killed Doon for anything. . . . I was very fond of her—at least, if I wasn't fond of her, I did quite like her; she'd never done me any harm . . . she was the last person I'd want to kill. . . ." She burst into tears.

"She'd better not come to the shop to-day," said Aileen, across the weeping head.

"Oh, Aileen, she must. It's the only thing to do. If she doesn't it will only give a worse handle to people to say things against her. Rene, darling, you must pull yourself together and come to Christophe's as if nothing had happened; Bobby Dazzler will take us all down in the car—he's waiting outside; once you're at the shop, there won't be anyone to see you who doesn't believe you're innocent. You must come, darling; if you don't, it will only give those ghastly people something much more to go upon. Be brave, my pet, and make up your mind to it; let's have a go at your face and get rid of the tear marks; and put on a good big hat that'll cover up your poor little mug and the fresh air will soon make it all right. You should see the Dazzler," prattled Victoria, vigorously applying a sponge; "he came out without shaving or anything," and he looks too awful—nobody could be dazzled by him to-day. You see how much Bobby thinks of you, Rene, darling. He's willing to imperil his reputation for beauty in my eyes and in the eyes of the world. There, that's better, isn't it, Aileen? It doesn't show a thing now, does it?"

"Not a sausage," said Aileen, warmly.

"You really think I'm doing the right thing?" asked Irene, doubtfully.

"Of course you are. Toria's quite right. It would give a completely wrong impression if you stayed away. Don't be worried, Rene; you're only going among people that believe in you—and are fond of you," added Aileen, with unparalleled enthusiasm, "isn't she, Victoria?"

"Of course she is," said Toria.

"Do you two really believe I'm innocent?" said Irene, looking wistfully into their eyes.

"Of course we do," repeated Aileen, as they came up to the car. "Don't we, Toria?"

"Of *course* we do," said Victoria, and turned away her head.

2

At the shop an indignation meeting was in full swing. All of the staff had received letters and another batch had been addressed to Christophe's. Bevan had, however, taken charge of these, and most of them were destroyed before they met other eyes. The morning papers had rehashed the news of Saturday's funeral and promised the customary early arrest. One or two of them had taken up the cudgels in Irene's favour, but their defence was, of necessity, as veiled as the attacks of the opposition, and little comfort could be derived from even the most favourable of them. Charlesworth had given out a carefully worded explanation which did something to appease the public mind; and he was working feverishly for some explanation of the ghastly muddle in which he found himself. Sir George was agitating, the Chief uncertain, and his colleagues full of good-natured derision. Only Bedd remained, solid and level-headed as ever, and to him the distracted young man turned for consolation.

"Unless I can get something definite by this evening, Bedd, I shall ask the superintendent for assistance. I can't bear to do it, but I mustn't go on mucking about like this . . . we really aren't any nearer a solution than we were when we started. We've got a good motive against Macaroni, and that's about all, except for this note from Rachel Gay, and I've sweated all the week-end and can't establish any further connection between her and the dead girl. Do you think I ought to question her? I don't want to put her on her guard."

"I should leave it for the moment, sir. There's this report to consider from Tomlinson. What about interviewing Cecil? Not but what it's difficult to see what we've got to go on."

"I'm much more inclined to think that it was all something to do with this other fellow, Elliot. Jenkins has been trying to trace him the whole week-end, but from the moment he left the flat there doesn't seem to be a sign of him. Cecil's story is that Elliot said on the Monday night that he was going to leave; they didn't see each other the following morning, and when Cecil got back from work in the evening, he'd gone. Cecil hoped he'd come back and he ordered dinner for him, but he never turned up; and Cecil accordingly packed up his possessions and deposited them in the basement at the shop. Certainly nobody saw Elliot return to the flat that evening, but that doesn't mean very much; there's only one porter, and he could easily miss anybody going in or out. If Cecil did do the fellow in, what's happened to the body? All we know for certain is that it wasn't taken away in a trunk!"

"It isn't really your worry, sir, what may have happened to Elliot."

"Well, it is, in a way, because till I can prove that the conversation Cecil had with his mother was about Elliot, I can't prove that it wasn't about Doon. I wonder if the trunks would help us in any way. I can't see why they should, but we might have a look—it would give us something to do," he added, bitterly.

Cecil had not yet returned from Kent so that elaboration was unnecessary. Bevan carelessly assented to their request and returned to an eager confabulation with his publicity agents. With small hope of results, they marched down to the basement and looked into the dark recess beneath the stairs.

The trunks had gone.

"Wasn't this place watched during the week-end?" yelled Charlesworth, when he had recovered the use of speech.

"I'm afraid not, sir. There was nothing to watch."

"They wasn't there when I got 'ere this morning," said Mrs. 'Arris, who was an interested spectator.

Bedd ignored her and addressed himself to Charlesworth. "You'd seen all there was to see, Mr. Charlesworth, sir; there was no clues or anythink to be mucked up; I spoke to the constable on night duty and asked him to keep an eye on the place, but other than that there was nothink necessary; that's really so, sir, isn't it?"

"I suppose so, I suppose so. How can we get hold of this bobby?"

The unfortunate policeman was located and dragged out of bed to come to the telephone. He had seen nothing untoward during his rounds, but he had since heard that P.C. Henson had put in a report that a man had removed some luggage from the basement in the course of the Saturday afternoon. As far as he knew, P.C. Henson would be on the same beat now. He returned, resentfully, to his bed.

P.C. Henson was discovered marching with all majesty down Regent Street. He had certainly reported to the Yard that the luggage had been taken. "I suppose no one thought of telling *me*!" cried Charlesworth, almost in tears. "I'm only the detective on this blasted job. A little thing like that couldn't be expected to interest *me*! Well, never mind, Henson, it isn't your fault, if you made your report all right; you did all you had to do. Tell me about this man."

"He had a key to the front door of the shop, sir. He told me that some luggage of his had been deposited there and that he had come to fetch it. I asked him what was in the boxes and had a look, just to make sure; I'd heard from—er—from the talk at the Yard that there was nothing of importance in the boxes, sir; and since he had the key and I hadn't had no instructions to the contrary, sir, I couldn't stop him taking them. He put them in a taxi and drove off. I took the number of the taxi, and he gave me the address—they're both in my report."

"It couldn't have been Cecil," said Charlesworth to Bedd. "Tomlinson says he didn't leave the country the whole week-end. What was this chap like, Henson? He wasn't a pale, fair young man, very pansy-looking?"

"Oh, no, sir. He was a big feller, fattish and had dark hair. Pansy-looking he certainly was, Mr. Charlesworth, but it wasn't Mr. Cecil. He said his name was Elliot."

3

Elliot was surprised and grieved that the police had been to any trouble about him. A call at his innocuous South Kensington hotel brought him out of bed, a flabby, dark man, a little below middle-age, clad in a pair of livery-looking yellow pyjamas and a satin dressing-gown of a very lovely green. They sat down in the small, square hotel bedroom, taken up almost entirely by the brass bedstead and shiny, modern washbasin; and Elliot, having carefully excluded every breath of air, curled himself on the edge of the bed and burst into a flurry of explanations.

"Can we have this from the beginning?" suggested Charlesworth, after some minutes. "You left Mr. Cecil's flat—when?"

"I left on the Monday morning. I just took a weeny suitcase with me and jumped on to a bus and came along here. I didn't want to see Cecil again, I didn't, really, after the rather beastly things he said to me on Sunday; he called Magda the most dreadful names . . . oh, it was *terrible*, my dear. . . ."

"Miss Magda Doon, is that?"

"Well, of *course*—I was madly in love with her—didn't you know? I met her at Christophe's and from that moment . . . she was so *strong*, you know, and vital, and then she was so *cruel* to me—my dear, she was as cruel as hell, that girl, and, I don't know, but there's something fascinating about it. . . ."

"Didn't you see her death reported in the papers?"

"But of *course*, and it was the most dreadful shock. I wanted to go to her funeral; I adore funerals, don't you? They're so entrancingly Victorian; all the lovely black horses and wavy plumes and the hideous wreaths and all the little individual studies of weeping women and the men striking unconscious attitudes of despair. . . . I so seldom get the chance of going to one where I know the actors, as it were—but there it was, I couldn't, very well; I didn't want to see Cecil, you see; I felt I just couldn't *face* a scene all over again, and besides, what with the move and the shock and everything I seemed to have caught a rather nasty little chill, and I've hardly been able to move out of this place ever since. I just crawled out and ordered a wreath, but there again, I didn't want Cecil to know it was from me, so I didn't put my name on it, just a message that she would understand, wherever she is . . . though I'm afraid there's no doubt about that, such a deliciously cruel creature as she was could never have settled down in what we understand by heaven. It was rather a lovely thing, the wreath, orchids crawling, as it were, up a simple wooden cross; a sort of symbol of death in the midst of sophistication: the triumph of nature over civilization. . . ."

"Yes, I saw it," said Charlesworth, shortly.

"It *was* rather lovely, didn't you think? I had a second one made for myself, and there it is now, hanging over my bed; the orchids are drooping a little, you see, and it seems sort of in keeping, doesn't it? She was so like an orchid herself."

"How did you know that Cecil had left your things at the shop?" asked Charlesworth, revolted by all this crawly symbolism.

"Oh, but one knew he always did," said Elliot, blushing faintly. "When he told Bunny that I was coming to live with him——Bunny was the boy who shared the flat with him before me——Bunny walked out in a pet and then Cecil couldn't bear to see all those familiar things all over the place and he took them all to Regent Street and put them in the basement of the shop. I helped him, so of course I knew. He told me he had done the same before Bunny came: he had a horrid fellow staying with him then, he was mad on the Chinese and filled the place with lacquer cabinets, too utterly banal for words; but the incense made Cecil feel sick. Bunny soon changed all that, but he did it up in the so-called modern style, and though it was extraordinarily well done, it was a trifle behind the times."

"Is there anything more I ought to ask this chap?" murmured Charlesworth to the sergeant, losing interest in the décor of Cecil's flat.

"No use saying anythink about the oxalic acid, I suppose, sir?"

"I don't think so; he had left the flat before it had even been brought into the shop. All right, Mr. Elliot," said Charlesworth, aloud. "I don't think there's anything else I want at the moment . . . you'll remain at this address, will you?"

"Yes, I shall be here till the end of the week, anyway," said Elliot. "But, officer—you won't say anything to Cecil, will you? I really couldn't stand another emotional scene just now, and after the shock and with my teeny chill . . ." They left him to it.

Charlesworth sent Bedd to the shop to fetch Cecil, and

himself returned to his office at Scotland Yard. There P.C. Henson's report confronted him from beneath some papers on his own chaotic desk; P.C. Jenkins was still looking all over London for the elusive Elliot. "Let him look," said Charlesworth savagely; but on hearing that he was even now on the other end of the telephone: "Put him through to me."

"Very sorry, sir," said Jenkins, when an opportunity at last occurred. "I don't see what more I could've done, sir. I suppose he was trying to 'ide from Mr. Cecil where 'e'd gorn; having only a small case 'e could 'ave 'opped on to a bus, and there's a lot of young gentlemen carrying suit-cases 'ops on to buses, sir. As for the 'otel, I'd 've come to it sooner or later, I suppose, but it means a lot of routine, Mr. Charlesworth, and I couldn't've done it in the time . . . not without a lot of luck, I couldn't. Very sorry, sir. I 'ope you won't 'old it against me, sir," said P.C. Jenkins, his aitches deserting him entirely in the stress of the moment.

"I never 'old things like this against people, Jenkins, you ought to know that by now," said Charlesworth, catching the infection. "Don't do it again, that's all. You needn't worry any more about it; I've got it off my chest and it's over. How's the missus?" he added, in a praiseworthy effort to make amends. P.C. Jenkins replied that his wife passed away some years ago.

Cecil, arriving at Christophe's with the faithful Mr. Tomlinson still in unobtrusive attendance, was met by Bedd with a polite request that he should go to the Yard, as Mr. Charlesworth would like to have a few words with him. "You're quite within your rights if you care to refuse, sir," explained the sergeant, as Cecil showed signs of rebellion, "but Mr. Charlesworth would be glad if you could make it convenient to come along with me."

"Yes, go along, Cecil, go along," said Bevan, to whom the sight of uniforms at the shop gave little pleasure. "Go and see what the inspector wants. They can't kill you, man," Cecil shuddered visibly, "and if you don't go willingly they'll get you there anyway."

At the Yard Charlesworth, uncertain of his ground, essayed an impression of sternness and much mystery. "Sit down, will you, Mr. Cecil. I have some questions of great gravity I want to ask you and I thought it would be more—more comfortable, shall I say, if I put them to you here."

"I'm sure I can't imagine what you can want to ask me, Inspector," said Cecil, frightened to death.

"Well, it's—er—it's come to my knowledge lately, Mr. Cecil, that during the week-end you had a quarrel with your friend, Mr. Elliot, and that, as a result of this quarrel, you were—er—were put to a serious temptation; on the Monday you found these oxalic acid crystals lying about, and you were tempted by this pure chance to take a very terrible course. Isn't this correct, Mr. Cecil?"

"I don't see what you can know about it," cried Cecil, staring at him with terrified eyes.

Charlesworth's air of importance strengthened enormously. There was little, it seemed to say, that the police did not know; but wouldn't it be better that they should hear it from Cecil's own lips? . . .

Cecil, about to have recourse to tears, changed his mind and asked with confounding simplicity what Charlesworth knew and how he knew it. Charlesworth, increasingly mysterious as he became increasingly out of his depth, replied that the police had ways and means. Cecil looked uncomfortable, but stuck to his guns and repeated with maddening monotony, "Well, what *do* you know?"

"We know that you kept the oxalic acid that was given over to you by the charwoman at Christophe's and used it for purposes of your own—very terrible purposes."

"Oh, no," cried Cecil, but his voice went into a thin wail.

"Oh, yes! And it places you in a position where you may find yourself in the hands of the law upon a very grave charge."

"Oh, no," wailed Cecil.

"Oh, yes! You're afraid for your life, aren't you, Mr. Cecil" (My God, I believe he's going to own up to it! thought Charlesworth).

But half an hour later they were still at it—question and answer, question and answer, question and answer. "I don't want to charge him," said Charlesworth to Bedd, taking a short respite at twelve-thirty. "I can't quite fathom what it's all about, can you? and we don't want to make any false steps. I'll give him another half-hour, and if he doesn't cough up we shall have to let him go for a bit . . . now then, Mr. Cecil . . ."

Question and answer, question and answer, question and answer. At one o'clock precisely Cecil put his head in his hands and confessed.


## Ten

### I

GREGORY had been right about the customers. The funeral decently over, they flocked into the showroom like elegant birds of prey and the staff, miserable and disgusted, were forced to answer their impertinent questions and satisfy their craving for sensation. The girls, despite their reception of Gregory's speech, were sufficiently hard-headed to realize that they must meet this situation in as willing a spirit as possible, and they accordingly agreed a hundred times a day that Doon had been terribly nice, that it was all terribly sad, that it was a terribly mysterious thing to have happened. Sales went up by leaps and bounds; clients, anxious to exhibit their connection with the now famous *salon*, introduced their friends; life-long customers of the other great dress-houses suddenly decided upon a change of style; the brides of the moment would hardly have felt married without at least something in their trousseaux from Christophe et Cie. By six o'clock on the Monday evening Bevan had twice 'phoned the Labour Exchange for new workroom hands and the three salesgirls and the mannequins had collapsed, worn out with the strain of the day, in the little room where, only a week ago, they had so light-heartedly cleaned the panama hat. Even Gregory came to join them there, looking tired and nervy, and raised her voice with theirs in protest against the clientele of Christophe et Cie. "I knew it would happen," she said, unable to keep the smugness out of her voice. "I told Mr. Bevan last week that this would happen; but I had no idea it would be so flagrant. Lady Crabb actually asked me if I thought it could be one of the showroom girls who had done it; and Mrs. Piggot wanted me to give her something of Doon's—could you believe that people could be so awful?"

"That's funny, Gregory, because Lady Crabb asked me if I thought it could be you!" said Aileen, smiling wanly.

"I had an awful old woman who wanted to know if we'd all go to a party at her house," said Rachel. "It's just incredible. She said she would pay for every one of us to have a new frock, designed by Cecil, if we would have it in black and wear it at her party; she ordered a black velvet copy of Cissie's old green model—you know, the one with the horrid little bitty frills all over it. I suppose it was to be a sort of mourning party. It nearly made me sick. The only consolation was Cissie's face when I asked him to copy the green model in black velvet!"

"Aren't there any nice, normal people left in the world?" said Victoria.

"I haven't come across any to-day," said Irene, bitterly. "They looked at me as if I had been in a freak show."

"Oh, darling, you imagine it!"

"No, I don't have to," said Irene, sadly, "because it's true. And a lot more letters came this afternoon; Bevan took them and tore them all up, but I saw them. I suppose there'll be hundreds at home and those horrible women from the next flat will come knocking at my door as soon as I get in, poking and prying and asking inquisitive questions. It seems funny to think that only a week ago, the worst I had against them was that they left a dirty ring round the bath. I wouldn't be surprised if it was them that sent the letter I got last night."

"You can't go home to that, Rene," said Victoria, firmly. "You must come back and sleep on the sofa in the flat. Oh, no, you can't, though, because the Dazzler's sister is having it to-night. Damn! What can we do now?"

"She could come with me," said Aileen, "if she doesn't mind sharing a bed."

Victoria knew that the fastidious Irene would mind very much. Rachel made the same offer in a rather doubtful tone of voice and Judy confessed that the house was full up with her lousy relations and she didn't think they could squeeze another person in anywhere. "But you have sort of guest-rooms at your flats, haven't you, Gregory? Couldn't Irene take one of those for to-night, and then perhaps to-morrow she could go to Toria's; or I might make Mummy see reason and turn out one of the aunts."

"Yes, of course, that's a marvellous idea," said Gregory. "They're nice little rooms, Irene, on the ground floor, with private bathrooms—like tiny flats, really. I can lend you pyjamas and things and—er—I'll have it put down on my rent, dear, so don't worry about that part of it." She spoke with genuine kindness and Irene, who was indeed overcome with depression at the idea of going back to her solitary, haunted little room, accepted gratefully.

"And come and have supper with me in my flat," added Gregory, the milk of human kindness overflowing.

This was rather more than Irene could bear; she cast an appealing look at Victoria, who rose most nobly to the occasion.

"No, I've got a brilliant idea," she cried, before Gregory could press her point. "Let's have a party at Rene's one-night flat. Bobby can take his sister out to dinner and I'll bring a bottle of sherry from home, and anything else I can find; Gregory, you needn't produce anything, as you're standing Irene her room for the night; Rachel can bring some fruit or some cake or something, and Aileen something else, and Judy something else—don't you think that's a good idea? We've all had rather a grisly day and we'll make a vow not to mention poor Doon or the shop the whole evening. Whoever does will have to pay a penny, and we'll put the proceeds towards a fund for keeping Irene in luxury guest-rooms for the rest of her days."

They broke up, laughing and refreshed. Irene and Gregory went ahead to book a room in the great block of flats where Gregory had her expensive one-room flatlet; Victoria flew home to abstract a bottle of the Dazzler's precious sherry and to raid her refrigerator for butter, cheese, and lettuces, and the remaining three girls dashed off to the shops for chocolates, fruit, and cake. "We only need a tin of cocoa and some Nestlé's milk to be back at school," said Rachel, half laughing, half cross. "What an ass Toria is, to let us in for this! We shall be all girls-together with Gregory before we know where we are, indulging in midnight feasts in this riotous fashion!"

Bevan, alone in his office, looked through the order book for the day. A heap of letters was pushed through the slit in the door; he glanced at them and all those addressed to Irene he tossed into the wastepaper-basket. Business was booming, right in the middle of the out-of-season, and nothing worried Bevan any more.

The party was not an unqualified success. Gregory and Irene had decided that the temporary flat was not large enough to accommodate them all, so a message had been left with the porter that the young ladies were to come straight upstairs, and it was held in Gregory's room. They studiously avoided all reference to the cloud that hung so darkly over them; but Irene could not forget the shock of that terrible morning's post nor the morbid scrutiny of the customers; and at nine o'clock she announced that, sweet and kind though they had all been, her nerves were at breaking point and she thought she would go to bed. Rachel, looking at the dark lines under her eyes, suggested aspirin and a hot drink; no aspirins were forthcoming, but Gregory had some sleeping powders, and though they were a prescription specially made up for her, she didn't think they would harm anybody, and suggested that Irene should try one. "I'll warm up some milk for you," she said, "and we can mix a powder into that and you can take it and go straight down to bed. The powders are in a little black box, Victoria, in the bathroom cupboard; you get them, will you, and I'll hot up the milk."

Gregory was enjoying herself enormously. Her consideration for Irene had thawed the coldness towards her of the other girls, and she could not do enough to show her eagerness or prove her worthiness to stay within the magic circle. She produced a beaker of foaming milk ("You just beat it up with a whisk, dear; people always ask me, but it's perfectly simple really"), and Victoria, having found the black box, carefully mixed in the contents of one of the tiny white packets. "I'll come down and see you into bed, Rene," she said, as Irene gratefully drank her hot milk. "Come on, Gregory, you and I'll go down with her and the others can wait here for us." The three of them took the lift to the ground floor.

At the door of Irene's room a small contretemps arose. The room had been taken in Gregory's name and the porter had handed the keys to her; she had, unthinkingly, put them straight into her handbag, and had now forgotten to bring them down with her. As she returned to the lift, however, a porter hove in sight and opened the door for them with his master-key and Irene led the way inside.

"I'll leave a glass of water near you," said Gregory, anxious to think of everything, "and I'll put the box of powders beside it, and if you don't sleep within half an hour or so, you can take another one. I've never had to yet, but the doctor told me I could if they didn't work within reasonable time."

"I shouldn't come into Christophe's till late to-morrow morning," said Victoria, proceeding vigorously with the tucking-in. "Bevan will understand. We'll tell him that you weren't well this evening. Gregory can pop in on her way to work and see how you are. She's got a key, so she needn't disturb you."

"I *was* an idiot to leave them upstairs," said Gregory. "You'll have to have one in the morning, Irene, so Toria had better drop it in through the letter-box on her way down to-night. Good night now, dear, and sleep well and forget all your worries." To Irene's horror she bent down and gave her a peck on the cheek.

"Bless you, darling," said Victoria, sparing her further demonstrations of affection. I'll put out the light; shall I? Bless you."

"Bless you, darling," said Irene, and they went quietly out.

Victoria stayed talking to Gregory after the others had gone. She was worried about Judy, who, unaccustomed to guarded speech and utterly opposed to anything bordering upon insincerity, was something of a bombshell to be loosed among inquisitive customers. "She told you that she wouldn't be polite to them, Gregory," said Victoria, taking advantage of the evening's friendliness to press her point, "and although she is trying for all our sakes, she won't be able to keep it up much longer. Can't you get Bevan to make some sort of new arrangement for the mannequins, so that they don't have to speak to the clients? The less Aileen says the better, she's such an idiot, bless her heart; and Judy will let fly one of these days as sure as eggs is eggs. They could just come in and show the frocks and buzz off again, instead of standing about; lots of houses do it like that in the ordinary way, and the models never speak to the customers at all. . . ."

When, soon after ten, she left the flat, she felt that she had never known Gregory so well, or liked her so much. She bade her an almost affectionate good-night, and shot down in the lift to the ground floor.

2

Charlesworth, meanwhile, had had a depressing day. After Cecil's collapse he had sought an interview with his chief and, in an agony of humiliation, confessed that he was no nearer a solution of the case and thought that he should hand it over to one of his seniors. "I've done my best, sir," he said, miserably, "but I don't seem to have got any forrader and I'm afraid that I may be wasting precious time. I'll hand over all the information to whoever you say, and see if he can do any better with it."

The superintendent was relieved of considerable embarrassment. He knew that a set-back of this kind would be extremely disheartening to an ordinarily capable and reliable officer and he had hitherto hesitated before insisting upon interference. Now that the suggestion had come from Charlesworth himself, however, his path was made considerably easier and he handed out comfort and encouragement on the one hand, while on the other he painlessly removed a large share of responsibility from the young man's shoulders. Contemporary with Charlesworth was that gentleman whom he had sought to confound in the matter of Cecil and the big black trunk; all unaware of the mutual detestation between these young men, the Chief suggested that, while Charlesworth retained his original status in charge of the case, Inspector Smithers should be put to work on it with him, and see if he could shed further light on what was certainly a most bewildering affair. Charlesworth, stifling his disgust, humbly acquiesced and sought out his pet aversion at the Yard.

Smithers was a pale, stout, puffy youth, with an unhealthy back to his neck and a general air of street urchin which inspired in all comers a longing to take a large handkerchief and wipe his blameless nose. He had, moreover, the guttersnipe type of brain, sharp, showy and nimble, but without depth or understanding. Rapid promotion had not added to his modesty. He leant back in his chair, twiddling his thumbs and listening with an air of insufferable efficiency to the outline of the case.

"That's the whole story," said Charlesworth, as he finished it. "The only thing which we have for fairly certain is that I think Cecil can be counted out of it. His explanation hangs together very nicely. His friend was walking out on him with the avowed (though rather optimistic) intention of getting married to someone that Cecil didn't like; and you have to know the two of them to appreciate what a how-d'you-do they could make of that simple fact. Suddenly, out of the blue, Cecil is given a surprise packet of poison, and it comes all over him that he will take it home and have some sort of an emotional scene with Elliot, scheduled to end in tears and reconciliation. Instead, he finds that the bird really has flown; he orders dinner for two, choosing all Elliot's special favourites, and sits down to wait for the footsteps that never come, feeling more and more like a film hero—or, if you like, heroine—as the time goes by. Finally, he eats a feeble meal, and because he's afraid of the servants talking, he does what he can to hide the fact that Elliot has never turned up; then he wanders about the flat packing up the beloved possessions, with all the accompanying pangs and trimmings; and when at the witching hour he realizes that Elliot really isn't coming back, he can bear it no longer and resolves to put an end to his miserable existence by taking the poison himself. If you know the type, you won't want to be told that he takes jolly good care that the end won't be a final one, and all he gets is a nasty pain, a violent headache, and a lot of very unromantic vomiting. He arrives at the shop the next morning to find that Doon has died overnight, after a pretty ghastly time—you remember he was out at the Ritz with Mrs. Best when the girl was taken ill—and the very thought of what he nearly let himself in for is a nightmare. He blenches at the mention of suicide—I couldn't think why he seemed so pleased at the idea that Doon was murdered, but it wasn't that—he was only registering relief when I got off the subject of self-destruction. With so much of the law knocking about he became terrified that he would be found out and punished for *felo-de-se*, but he couldn't resist an orgy of revelation to his mother, and I suppose that's what Tomlinson's girl friend overheard. A nice dance he's led me, the silly beggar, and a nice lot of my time he's wasted; but at least that accounts for his share of the crystals and leaves us only two spoonfuls unaccounted for, including the little that was spilt on the floor when Rachel Gay and Mrs. David first brought it into the shop, and the doubtful amount that was actually used in cleaning the hat.''

"You're sure no other poison was brought into the place?" asked Smithers.

"Oh, certain. No one went out through the showroom door till after lunch, when Cecil and Irene Best went off to their appointment; and the area steps were being watched by Mrs. Harris at all the relevant times."

"Have you inquired at the neighbouring chemists?"

"No, why should I? There was no opportunity to go out and get more, and no necessity. The poison was there and that's obviously what was used."

"I think I should have made inquiries all the same," said Smithers, smugly. "Shall we detail someone to do it now?"

Charlesworth squirmed but agreed.

"Now, this other small quantity of the poison—the stuff Miss Doon herself got hold of—are you sure that wasn't used?"

"Of course I'm sure, man. It was sitting there in the desk as large as life."

"The secretary girl, McEnery, had a very convincing motive, hadn't she?"

"Yes, she had, I quite agree; but there's stacks of evidence to show that she was not given a spot more poison than was found in the desk; she didn't leave the office for a moment between the time she brought it downstairs and the time she went into lunch. Bevan was with her and Doon and he swears to that. Besides, the charwoman was in the kitchen and would have seen her going through the dining-room and up the area steps, or up the stairs, whichever way she might have gone."

"She couldn't have gone up the stairs and into Bevan's office at the top of them and through the back door of that office out into the street?"

"No, she couldn't. First, she couldn't have passed Mrs. Harris; and secondly, the door of the salesgirls' little room, opposite the door of Bevan's room, was open the whole morning, and they could see anybody going up those stairs and into the office. Nobody did so the whole morning. Nobody could have gone up the stairs and out of the office door because nobody went into the office till Bevan came up at one o'clock."

"But the secretary was left alone with Miss Doon for a little while after Bevan left her office?"

"A few seconds, if that's any use to you; well, say two minutes, to be absolutely fair."

"A lot can be done in two minutes," said Smithers, sententiously. "You'll agree that she might have induced Doon to take something during that time."

"I suppose it's conceivable, but it's frightfully unlikely, immediately before lunch. Anyway, you can't get round the fact that the original amount of poison she brought down from the showroom remained untouched."

"It might have been used and replenished."

"Oh, no, I've gone into all that," said Charlesworth, who had been waiting for this. "The desk was locked up and Macaroni took both the keys home with her. There weren't any more keys and as the murder was an unpremeditated one—I suppose you'll agree it *was* unpremeditated?—there wasn't any time for mucking about getting new ones."

"So that your contention is that nobody could have used the poison that was originally given to the secretary, bought more poison overnight and, using her keys, filled up the little packet in the drawer before the police examined it in the morning?"

"Nobody," said Charlesworth, but even as he said it his voice faltered.

"Nobody, in fact," said Smithers, getting it in first, "except the secretary herself!"

The conference had taken a very long time. Charlesworth had been working for seven whole days upon the case and he was weary and fed up. "You can take the darn thing over for to-night," he said to Smithers, at six o'clock. "I'm going to have a real good dinner and then I'm going to a flick and then I'm going to bed. You can do what you like—arrest Macaroni, interview chemists, discover that Elliot was Cecil in disguise—I don't care what the hell you do. For to-night this is your baby and

147

I wish you joy of it." He stumped off ungratefully into the night.

Mr. Smithers sent for coffee and sandwiches and applied himself diligently to the notes of the case. The little secretary could very well wait until he was ready for her; she had been working quietly at the shop and was obviously relieved of all anxiety as to police suspicion about herself; on second thoughts, however, he detailed a plain-clothes man to keep a watch upon her home. Mr. Smithers was very free with the time and trouble of his subordinates.

His study of the notes furthered him not at all. It was obviously McEnery, he decided, and he would have her along to-morrow and get an admission from her. Really Charlesworth was a bit of a fool; the Chief had spoken a word and of course he, Smithers, must keep pretty quiet about his part in solving the affair; but he would see to it that everybody realized that it was he who had cleared up in a couple of hours what had puzzled the rest of them for a week. Motive, opportunity to administer, opportunity to obtain, Macaroni had them all; he tidied his papers and reached for his hat. At that moment the telephone bell rang.

"Hallo, yes?"

"P.C. Conrad on the line for you, sir."

"All right, put him through. Hallo, Conrad, have you got something for me?"

"Yes, sir. I thought I'd better let you know at once, sir. I've been round the chemists within a radius of half a mile of the shop, and I've found one that sold an ounce of oxalic acid on the day of the murder to a young lady. He doesn't remember much about it, but he's identified a photograph. It's number five, on the back, sir."

Smithers rang off. "Just like him," thought Constable Conrad. "At least old Charles always has a word of thanks for a decent piece of work, even if he is a bit of an ass . . . but not Smithers, not 'im. I 'ope this news gives 'im a 'eadache, that's all."

It did give him a 'eadache, for the photograph with number five on the back was not of Macaroni at all; it was of a small, dark girl, extraordinarily lovely, and the name on the back of it was Mrs. Irene Best.

# *Eleven*

## I

INSPECTOR SMITHERS made a half-hearted attempt to locate Charlesworth, but he was not sorry when it failed. Without waiting to consult the notes—which, indeed, he already knew almost by heart—he collected a sergeant and repaired to the flats where Irene was spending the night. The head porter referred him to Miss Gregory for the keys.

Gregory appeared sleepy and bewildered at her door. She resisted strongly Inspector Smithers' insistence that he should see Mrs. Best; Irene had gone to bed worn out, she said, and had taken a sleeping powder. Smithers, however, was adamant, and she finally handed over a key to the guest-flat. Smithers, having refused her permission to accompany him, marched downstairs.

A prolonged ringing at Irene's door evoked no response. "Asleep with the dope, I suppose," said Smithers. "She'll have to wake up, that's all, and do a bit of talking. I'm not going home to-night without an explanation."

They applied the key to the lock and pushed their way into the tiny hall. The first door they tried proved to be that of the bathroom; they knocked upon the second without result. "I hope she hasn't hopped," said Smithers over his shoulder and, turning the handle of the door, went in.

Irene hadn't hopped. She lay on the bed in a gradually deepening sleep, and already the tormented life was ebbing out of her tiny frame. Smithers rushed forward and caught her little wrist in his hand: "My God, she's going— ring up for a doctor and an ambulance, quick. . . ." He thrust his hand suddenly under the pillow and pulled out a small white card: "Good heavens, Jones, we *must* save her—here's the confession!"

It was an ordinary professional visiting-card, printed with Irene's name and underneath it the name and address of Christophe et Cie, such as the three salesgirls were accustomed to use when visiting clients outside the shop. On the back of it was printed in large, untidy letters: "I have made an end of my life because I killed Doon." On the table beside the bed lay a latchkey to the outer door. The glass held a dribble of whitish dregs and beside it were four small squares of paper, unfolded and empty.

The doctor arrived, a spruce young man, with hair brushed carefully over a premature bald spot. "Got her just in time," he said. "She'll pull through all right after the way you've managed her—you ought to have been in my profession, Inspector. What was it—suicide?"

Smithers rose to the hook so well baited: "Most people would think so," he answered, expansive in his gratified pride, "but one thing strikes me as odd, Doctor, which perhaps somebody else wouldn't take any notice of. . . . Why should a suicide *print* her last message? They hardly ever do, and the educated ones almost never—in such a moment of stress they use the medium that comes most easily to them . . . that's my experience, anyway." He spoke as if his experience were something very much worth taking into account.

The doctor was duly impressed. "Very cute of you, that. . . ." He glanced at Irene again. "Good lord, isn't this one of the girls in the dress-shop case? I've seen her photograph in the papers."

"That's what makes me wonder, Doctor. She's already mixed up in a murder case and one can't be too careful. . . ."

He telephoned the Yard and while he waited for assistance decided that a talk with Miss Gregory would be interesting. She reappeared, highly indignant, at her door. "Really, Inspector, or whoever you are, this is the limit. What on earth do you want now, at this hour of the night?"

Smithers gently forced her backwards and followed her into the flat. "I've just been down to Mrs. Best's room."

"Good gracious, that was an hour ago. If you can't wake her it's because, as I told you, she's taken a sleeping draught. Can't you leave it till the morning?"

Smithers decided to test her reaction, and put the news in startling form. "I found your friend dying," he said bluntly.

"Dying? . . . dying? . . ." She looked blankly at him. He could not resist adding smugly, "Fortunately I was able to apply medical aid until the doctor came, and I've pulled her through. . . ."

But Gregory had fallen forward in a dead faint upon the floor.

Once again Smithers applied the skill that would have made him such an ornament to the medical profession, but it was ten minutes before Gregory was revived and, sitting shakily on her chintz-covered sofa, could give him any account of the evening that had been spent at her flat.

"Really, after all we've been through, the shock of this is too dreadful," she said through white lips. "How can Mrs. Best have—did she take too much of that sleeping draught?" she asked, suddenly.

"Well, I think she must have, Miss Gregory. Perhaps it was not a very wise thing to have given her at a time like this. Who suggested her having it, do you remember?"

"No, I don't remember at all—one of the girls. Now that I come to think of it, I believe it was Rachel Gay."

"And who actually gave it to her?"

"Mrs. David did," said Gregory, still, of course, unaware that there was reason to suspect anything but a simple suicide. "I boiled up some milk and Mrs. David got the powders from the bathroom and mixed one in."

"I suppose she couldn't have put in more than one, by—er—by mistake?"

"Oh, I don't think so. Each dose was wrapped up by itself in a little square of paper."

"Can you swear that not more than one packet was used?"

"Well, no, I can't swear to it," said Gregory, doubtfully. "Mrs. David was standing by the bathroom cupboard and I handed her the glass of milk and turned back into the room. She came out of the bathroom, holding the glass in her hand and stirring the milk; but there was only one little bit of paper left on the edge of the basin, because I threw it away, later. Here it is in the wastepaper-basket."

Smithers solemnly collected this relic and returned to his attack. "Did Mrs. Best take the box with the remaining powders down to her room with her?"

"Yes, I'm afraid it was I who suggested that. She was very nervy and overwrought and I thought that one powder might not be enough. It never occurred to me for a moment that she would use them in this terrible way."

"And how many papers were there left in the box?"

"I don't know. Three or four, I suppose. There were originally six, and I think I'd only used one. That would be five, counting the one she'd taken with the milk."

"Can you be certain, Miss Gregory, that there were four powders in the box when you handed it to her?"

"Well, I can only suppose so; the box was closed and I simply took it off the shelf in the bathroom and carried it downstairs in my hand, and gave it to her in her room. I can't see why you should think she took an overdose up here; she may simply have taken some more when she went downstairs. Perhaps it was simply an accident."

"Oh, I think not, Miss Gregory. You see, she left a letter."

"A letter? A suicide letter? Good heavens—what was in it? What did it say?"

"That I am not in a position to reveal," said Smithers, ponderously. "It certainly gave the impression that Mrs. Best intended to take her life, but one has to work out every possibility. Now, about the keys to the flatlet. I gather that they were originally handed to you?"

Gregory explained the confusion about the keys. "I

gave one to Mrs. David to slip in at the letter-box on her way home. I kept the other one as we had agreed that I should go into Irene's room on my way to work and see whether she was awake."

"Couldn't you have taken the second key to her then?"

"Well, I suppose I could, Inspector, but I simply never thought of it. Mrs. David was passing the door and I asked her to slip it in. I don't think anything else occurred to her either."

"Did you yourself go to Mrs. Best's room after the other young ladies had gone home?"

"No, of course I didn't—what would I have done that for?" asked Gregory, looking puzzled and a little scared. "I went downstairs and posted a letter, but I imagined her as being fast asleep and I didn't go near her flat."

"You went and posted a letter, did you? Why didn't you ask one of the other young ladies to do it for you on their way home?"

"For the plain and simple reason," said Gregory, growing irritable as her nervousness increased, "that once again I didn't think of it. As soon as Mrs. David had gone I noticed the letter lying on my desk; it had to be posted before midnight, so I wrote another one, and put both of them in the letter-box in the hall."

"Did anyone see you do this?"

"Not that I know of, unless there was a porter about. What is all this leading to, Inspector? I don't see what it has got to do with Mrs. Best."

"Neither do I," said Smithers, smiling pleasantly, "but, as I said before, I have to go into all these things. One more question and then I won't bother you any further: did any of the other young ladies go into this flatlet that Mrs. Best had taken for the night?"

"Only Mrs. David. I went in with Irene when she arrived and took her some things for the night, and so on, and helped her to settle in; then we came upstairs and all the others came on up to my flat. Afterwards Mrs. David and I went down and tucked Irene up and left her for the night. I don't think that at that time she had anything like this in her head; but she was dreadfully upset and unhappy and I blame myself terribly for having given her the extra sleeping powders. In the light of what has happened, Inspector, it seems a criminally stupid thing to have done; but you must believe me when I say that the thought of it just never entered my head. And none of the others seem to have thought of it, either," she added, brightening considerably. "They all heard me offer her the box, and none of them suggested for a moment that it was unwise."

"No, I quite appreciate that, Miss Gregory, I'm sure you need feel no responsibility in the matter." He produced a small chamois leather case and, taking out of it a square of dark glass, held it out before her so suddenly that she took it before she was aware of what she was doing.

"Whatever is this?" she said.

"Oh, I beg your pardon—what on earth am I thinking of? I meant to offer you a cigarette. I'm afraid you are in need of one after all these questions," said Smithers, unobtrusively slipping the glass back into its case. "Now you go back to bed and try and get some sleep. . . ." He left her with the promised cigarette, and on his way back to Irene's room handed the case to his sergeant. "I want these finger-prints compared with any in the room downstairs. When the man gets here, ask him to 'phone through to me as soon as he gets any results. I'm going to Mrs. David's. . . I shall be at that number."

Bobby Dazzler had left a large drawing on the studio mantelpiece, depicting himself and his sister, she with very fat legs and he with very untidy hair, dining in great state at a palatial restaurant and with a couple of theatre tickets conspicuously displayed in the foreground, and this Victoria took to be an indication that they would not be back until late. It was a huge, square room with an overhead light, one corner occupied by the paraphernalia of painting, one by a dining-table and four chairs, and a third by a fireplace surrounded by easy chairs and a sofa. The easel and model's throne stood in the centre and around them Victoria was obliged to make a careful detour as she fussed about picking up her sister-in-law's scattered possessions and making up the sofa into a tolerably comfortable bed. She cried quietly to herself as she moved and her hands were shaking, but she completed her tasks and began to prepare for bed. As she slid into her nightdress, the doorbell rang.

"Curse Bobby," said Victoria, without venom. "He always forgets his key." She hung a gay blue dressing-gown about her shoulders and went to the door.

Three strange men pushed their way unceremoniously into the flat.

Victoria stared at them open-mouthed, automatically adjusting her dressing-gown. Smithers repeated his act with a second glass, but this time did not trouble himself to explain. One of his henchmen departed with the chamois leather case, and the other propped himself up against the door and pulled out his little book. Smithers took a look round the room, sniffed at the sight of the easel and the canvases piled round the walls, and sat down on the arm of one of the easy chairs. Victoria, frankly terrified, gasped out a protest at his intrusion.

"I'm afraid I can't waste time on fancy speeches, Mrs. David," said Smithers, in his excitement reverting, as usual, to type. "I have to tell you that Mrs. Irene Best 'as bin found dying in 'er room; I think you already know something about that, don't you?"

Victoria did not swoon as Gregory had done. She stared at him with horrified eyes and said faintly: "Why should you come to me about it?"

"Because I believe that you and Miss Gregory were the last persons to see Mrs. Best before she went to bed."

"Yes, yes, of course," said Victoria, looking a tiny bit relieved. "We went down to her room with her and saw her into bed. How—how could she have been found dying?"

"She was found by me. There is a suggestion that she may have taken, or been given, an overdose of sleeping draught."

155

"She did have a sleeping draught. I—I gave it to her myself, in Gregory's flat."

"You don't suppose you can have given her too much—*by any chance?*" asked Smithers, smiling unpleasantly.

"Too much—no, of course not! I gave her one powder, like Gregory said. You don't imagine. . ."

"I'm not 'ere to imagine, Mrs. David. I'm 'ere to find out."

"Where's Mr. Charlesworth?" said Toria, suddenly. "Why isn't *he* here? Why hasn't *he* come to see me?"

"Because I've taken over part of the conduct of the case from Mr. Charlesworth and I'm here in his place."

"Well, I don't think I ought to talk to you," said Victoria, pulling herself together. "I'd rather see Mr. Charlesworth; and I don't think I ought to say anything till my husband's here. I'm not going to tell you any more."

"I'm afraid you haven't got very much choice," said Smithers, nastily. "You can refuse, of course, but you're putting yourself in a very peculiar position if you do. I must warn you, Mrs. David, that I have reason to believe that you know more about the supposed suicide of Mrs. Best than you pretend to, and that, in fact, you are under grave suspicion of being concerned in it. I should advise you to tell me frankly what you know about it." He disregarded her gasp of terror and went on, relentlessly, "Miss Gregory gave you a key to Mrs. Best's flat. *What did you do with that key?*"

Victoria turned her head nervously from side to side, and passed her dry tongue over her lips. Smithers repeated his question, and as she still made no reply, urged: "Come on, now, if you have nothing to conceal, you can surely tell me what became of the key."

"I put it through the letter-box," said Victoria, desperately.

"Then how do you account for the fact that it was found on the table at Mrs. Best's bedside?"

Victoria went terribly white. "How can you explain

that?" repeated Smithers, watching the expression on her face.

"I can't explain it—I don't know," said Toria, frantically. "Gregory asked me to put it through the letter-box, and that's what I did."

"I suggest to you that you did not put the key through the letter-box. I suggest that, having given Mrs. Best an overdose of sleeping powder before she went to bed, you entered the flat with the key Miss Gregory had given you, and printed on one of Mrs. Best's own cards a confession of murder and suicide?"

"Did Irene leave a confession?"

"A 'confession' was found under her pillow before she was taken to hospital."

"To hospital!" cried Victoria, and now every vestige of colour had left her face, and her hands shook as though she had the ague. "Do you mean to say that Irene isn't dead?"

"That frightens you, doesn't it, Mrs. David? No, she isn't dead; you have to thank me for saving you from, perhaps, a double charge of murder."

"I don't understand what you mean?"

"I mean that it may have been to conceal your implication in another murder that you staged this apparent suicide."

"No, no," cried Victoria, mad with fear.

"How else can you account for the fact that the key you speak of had not been pushed through the letter-box at all and that a forged confession of suicide was found under Mrs. Best's pillow? How can you account for that?"

"A forged confession? I can't understand what it's all about."

"No, I wouldn't expect that you could. Now, Mrs. David, I want to ask you one or two questions about the glass which was found beside the bed. When you and Miss Gregory went into the room to put Mrs. Best to bed, did you handle the glass?"

"I didn't touch it. Miss Gregory put the glass, full

of water, beside Irene. But I'm sure Miss Gregory doesn't know any more about it than I do."

"Perhaps you put the box of powders—full or empty, whichever it was—beside the glass?"

"I didn't. I didn't touch them after I put the box back in the cupboard in the bathroom upstairs. Gregory took them out and brought them down with her, and she put the glass on the table and handed the box to Irene; and Irene put it on the table beside the bed. Not that I mean to suggest that Gregory . . ."

"Don't you worry about Miss Gregory, Mrs. David. You've got troubles enough of your own. Now, about what happened upstairs. . . ."

He took her through the events of the earlier part of the evening. Who had suggested that Mrs. Best should go to the guest-room in the first place? Toria thought it had been Judy. Who had thought of giving Mrs. Best a sleeping draught? Well, that was Rachel . . . her eyes kept straying to the door, watching for her husband's return, and when the telephone rang she started towards it eagerly and her face lit up with relief; but Smithers was as quick and he took the receiver out of her hand.

"Hallo, yes? Oh, Davies, is that you? You got the two lots of prints I sent along?"

"I'm checking up the whole room," said the finger-print expert, speaking from Irene's guest-flat. "So far I've only got three lots of prints, except for some old ones which I take to be a servant's, left while cleaning the place and so forth. The others all belong either to Mrs. Best herself or to the other two lots you sent me; at least, as far as I can tell, until I get them back for testing, but I don't think there's any doubt about it. I haven't finished yet, but I understood you were anxious to know about the glass which was standing on the table by the bed. The outside of it had been recently wiped absolutely clean, and there are two lots of prints on it; the thumb and four fingers of Mrs. Best, very clear, as though she had gripped the glass with her hand, possibly drinking from it; and the thumb and three fingers of the second lot you sent me—Mrs. David's. What I think may be of special interest to you, from what I've heard from your man here, is that the prints of Mrs. David must have been made *after* Mrs. Best had handled the glass. They're superimposed."

Inspector Smithers put down the receiver with a sigh of pure satisfaction and turned to Victoria, huddled in one corner of the sofa, staring at him with panic-stricken blue eyes. "Mrs. David," he said, savouring every word, "it is my duty to ask you to come to the police-station with me for questioning regarding the attempted murder of Mrs. Irene Best; and I must warn you again that anything you say will be taken down and may be used in evidence."

2

Charlesworth, returning gaily from his night off, was met by the persistent ringing of his telephone bell. Victoria's husband was on the other end of the line, frantic with fear and anger. The Dazzler had taken a liking to Mr. Charlesworth, and having obtained his private number, now placed himself and Victoria unreservedly in that young man's hands. "There's been some ghastly mistake," he said down the 'phone. "Do get hold of this bloody fellow, Smithers, and make him see reason. What on earth had Toria to gain by harming Irene Best? . . . The whole thing is so utterly monstrous and fantastic that I can't seem to see daylight anywhere. I'm going to get hold of my mother now, she has a bit of a pull with the big noises at your place; meanwhile, be a good chap, Charlesworth, and get hold of this Smither, and tell him. . . ."

Charlesworth got hold of Smithers and told him. His language surprised that acute young man into a fairly accurate summing-up of Mr. Charlesworth's feelings for the lady in question, for his reputation for susceptibility was not unknown to his colleagues. Smithers produced his proofs triumphantly, but found Charlesworth obstinately unimpressed.

"What if her prints *were* on the glass? I thought you said the overdose was administered upstairs?"

"Yes, by Mrs. David."

"Then what's the significance of the finger-prints on the glass? Why should you get so excited about them?"

"Only that Miss Gregory says that Mrs. David didn't touch the glass while they were all three in the room."

"She may easily be mistaken."

"No, no, Mrs. David herself says that she didn't touch it."

"What difference does it make, if the stuff was administered upstairs?"

"We can't be certain of that. Very possibly Mrs. David put an extra dose in the glass and gave it to Mrs. Best when she went into her flat later."

"I don't even see why you can be so sure she did go into the flat. Anybody could have entered it after she had put the key through the letter-box, and picked up the key from the mat inside and left it on the table. It needn't necessarily have been Mrs. David."

"Anyone?"

"Well, Miss Gregory, then. She had a second key, she gave it to you herself. She even admits that she was snooping about downstairs, long after Mrs. David had gone home. Why pick on Mrs. David? Why not Miss Gregory?"

"For half a dozen excellent reasons," said Smithers, joyfully. "Firstly, I'm not prejudiced in favour of Mrs. David!" He looked pointedly at Charlesworth, who had the grace to blush. "Secondly, because it was obviously a genuine shock to Miss Gregory to hear that Mrs. Best had been found dying, and it just as obviously wasn't a surprise at all to Mrs. David. Thirdly, because Miss Gregory has, as far as I can see, told the truth all the way along, even volunteering the information that she went downstairs with the letter, which she needn't have done, because she knows that there was nobody about to see her; fourthly, because nobody handled the key after Mrs. David for the simple reason that her finger-print is the last to have been made on it—oh, I grant you it may have been picked up by a gloved hand, but is it likely, my dear man? and lastly, because if Mrs. David didn't leave her finger-prints on the glass when she went into the room with Mrs. Best and Miss Gregory, she must have entered the room later and left them then. Will that satisfy you?"

"Why in the world should she wipe the glass clean and then put a full set of prints clearly upon it? A child would know better than that in these days of the public's interest in crime."

"Well, you have me there," acknowledged Smithers, thoughtfully. "However, I'm not obliged to explain everything, while she can explain nothing. I suppose, like any woman, she wiped the glass, got Mrs. Best to use it, and then got a bit panicky, forgot all about finger-prints, and picked it up again. Same with the key. If she hadn't left that on the table I should probably never have thought of her, till the finger-print complication cropped up . . . but I'd have been on to her then. It's a clear case, Charlesworth, ol' man, and you can't talk your way out of it."

"It isn't clear to me," said Charlesworth, stoutly. "Why should she want to kill the girl? The whole thing's absolutely pointless."

"Doesn't it occur to you that she might have had another crime to conceal, that was becoming dangerous to her? Perhaps Mrs. Best had found out more about the murder of Doon than you have!"

"Oh, don't be a damn fool, Smithers," cried Charlesworth, furiously. "Mrs. David no more killed Doon than you or I did. Mrs. David didn't even know that Doon was going to be in to lunch; she thought she was going out with Bevan."

"But she did have ample opportunity for getting the poison?"

"Earlier this evening you were convinced that the original poison brought into the shop wasn't used in the murder of Doon; you've even discovered that Mrs. Best bought some more poison on that day. What about that, may I ask?"

"The chemist says a small girl, very pretty. That describes Mrs. Best, but it also describes Mrs. David. He may have got mixed up in the photographs. He doesn't remember the transaction at all clearly, only that the girl was small and pretty."

" Good lord, man, you're just twisting the thing to suit yourself. When do you suggest that Mrs. David can have got it? She was in the company of several other girls during the entire morning; you don't imagine it was a concerted plan, I suppose, got up between the lot of them?"

"I haven't worked that out yet; I daresay we shall find that it fits in somewhere—if we aren't afraid of fitting it in," added Smithers, with a superior smirk for his heart-sick colleague.

"Anyway, you can't get away from the fact that Victoria David thought that Doon was going to be out to lunch; she was never in the dining-room after Bevan had changed his mind and said he was taking Gregory."

"Now, Charlesworth, don't start that all over again. Look here—you won't deny that the plate of food was actually served out, or partly served out, by Mrs. David?"

"Yes, but not for Miss *Doon*, Smithers," cried Charlesworth, weary and exasperated. "It was served out originally for Miss Gregory. Victoria thought that Doon was going out. Surely you can see that—Victoria thought that the plate was being served out for Miss Gregory!"

"And how do you know," asked Smithers, sweetly, "*that your precious Victoria didn't intend to murder Miss Gregory?*"

3

A detective sat solemnly beside Irene's bed and made meticulous notes of her incoherent babblings. Gradually she came out of her coma, but no sense was forthcoming until well into the morning. Then, after a long period of silence, she suddenly sat up in bed and made the usual inquiry as to her whereabouts.

"You're in hospital, miss," said the constable, who had dealt with this question a number of times. "You've been rather ill but you're better now. You lay down and keep still, miss, and I'll get the nurse for you." He made a solemn note in his book and rang for assistance.

Irene lay very quiet again. She had taken a sleeping draught and gone off to sleep and now here she was in a different place; it was all very puzzling. She dozed off again, and when she woke there was a' different young man beside her. She closed her eyes and gave herself gradually up to more lucid thought.

Inspector Smithers got very little help from her when she finally came to. She had had something in Gregory's flat to make her sleep and Gregory and Victoria had put her to bed and that was all she could remember. They had been ever so kind—*ever* so kind, repeated Irene, and drifted off to sleep again.

## *Twelve*

### I

THE Dazzler, having concluded his appeal to Charlesworth, rang up his mamma, who was a lady of title, and besought her to pull some strings. The lady of title reminded him that she had always known what would come of his mixing with that terrible artist lot, and marrying a girl who actually worked for her own living ("And for mine," put in Bobby Dazzler, blinking his sleepy brown eyes), but ended by replying that she would see what she could do. She then had recourse to a bottle which was kept hidden in her bathroom, a close secret from all but her husband, her servants and most of her acquaintances, and, fortified by this unfailing friend, proceeded cheerfully to disturb the midnight slumbers of the great. Whether it was the whisky or the title or a combination of both, a promise was finally extracted that her daughter-in-law should be treated with every consideration consistent with the rigours of the law; and should, moreover, be released as soon as her questioning was over, and not detained under any pretext whatsoever.

This was no more and no less than Smithers had originally intended, but it enabled him to make a tremendous favour of Victoria's release. He obtained an undertaking that she would hold herself in readiness to return for further questioning if required and, in the early hours of the morning, permitted her to return to her home.

The Dazzler put his wife to bed and the next morning rang up Bevan and informed him that Victoria would not be returning to the shop; he glanced in at the bedroom door and, seeing her sleeping quietly, let himself, with something of an air of mystery, out of the flat.

Half an hour later Charlesworth rang the bell, and Toria, once more wrapped in the blue dressing-gown, opened the door. "Oh, Mr. Charlesworth, I *am* so glad to see you; all this is too ghastly, it's the most awful mistake. . . . Of course I didn't kill Irene—how could anyone think I would do such a thing? Mr. Charlesworth, you don't believe all these terrible things, do you? Do say that you don't believe them! I couldn't bear it if you were against me too."

She caught his arm and dragged him into the studio. "Do come and sit down; I can't tell you how glad I am you've come. . . . "

Charlesworth struggled hard against a longing to take her small, forlorn figure into his arms. "Of course I don't believe a word against you, Victoria," he said. "I ought not to say so, I'd get the sack if anybody knew—but nothing on earth would make me believe you were a murderess; in fact," he added, belligerently, "I'd chuck up my job before I'd be party to such an idea!"

"Oh, you are kind, Mr. Charlesworth; now do tell me, I'm so worried about this confession they've found: what on earth was in it?"

"That I can't tell you, Toria. Smithers has got a bee in

his bonnet about not revealing the contents and as it's his own particular bit of fun and games I can't very well refuse. It's perfect nonsense, but I suppose it can't do any harm; the important thing is this: was it there when you went into the room?"

"But I didn't go into the room," said Victoria, avoiding his eyes.

"My dear, you must have. Smithers has proved that you went in. I'm on your side, Victoria, and I'm doing all I can to clear you, but I can't do a thing if you don't tell me the truth."

She looked at him wistfully. "I do want to tell you the truth, but—well, I put the key through the letter-box. I didn't go into the flat."

"Toria," said Charlesworth, patiently, "I *know* you went into the flat. I'm not asking you—I know it. What I want you to tell me is: why did you go in and what did you do while you were there?"

"I didn't go in."

"My dear, look. The key which you say you put through the letter-box was found on the table. How did it get there, if you didn't go into the place?"

"Somebody might have gone in afterwards and picked it up and put it on the table," said Victoria, as he himself had argued so short a time before.

"But your finger-prints? You and Miss Gregory left Irene with a glass full of water which you yourself say you hadn't touched. When Smithers found her, the glass was empty and there were no prints on it but hers and yours. And yours were what's called superimposed— they were on top of hers. In other words, between the time you and Miss Gregory left her and the time Smithers found her, Irene had drunk the water and you had handled the glass. Nobody can deny that."

"I don't see why only my marks were on it. Gregory put it on the table and it was she who filled it with water; she didn't wipe it then, because I was there with her the whole time. Not that I mean to suggest anything against Gregory . . . personally I think that Rene tried to commit suicide and there was no question of murdering her at all."

"That doesn't explain the finger-marks."

"Then why weren't Gregory's on the glass?"

"The glass had been wiped clean, Victoria, after you and Gregory left the room."

"Well, there," cried Toria, triumphantly. "Doesn't that just show—why should I have wiped it clean and then put my own marks on it? It doesn't make sense."

"My dear, I've argued all this out before," said Charlesworth, patiently. "There isn't any answer to that, but it doesn't make a bit of difference. Victoria, tell me, I implore you, why did you go into that room? Don't pretend to me: can't you trust me? You ought to know that I'm your friend."

"How can I know that?" said Victoria, sadly, lifting her lovely eyes to his. "You've always been very nice, Mr. Charlesworth, and awfully kind and sweet—but, after all, you *are* a detective and you may be saying all this to get something out of me that I don't want to tell you. . . ."

"You don't believe that?" he said, staring at her.

"How am I to know?" said Toria again. "I never thought of it till this moment, but, after all, how am I to know?"

"Because I happen to be in love with you," said Charlesworth, crossly. He leant against the mantelpiece, looking down at her as she sat perched on the arm of a chair. "I have no right to say this, Victoria, and I wouldn't have, if you hadn't driven me to it: but I *must* make you believe that you can trust me and the plain and simple answer is that I've been in love with you ever since I first met you. I don't say that if I thought you were guilty, I would let it make any difference; as you say, I'm a police officer and I've got to do what I've got to do. But you aren't guilty and I know it; and I'm not going to see you suffer, not if it costs me my job."

There was a little silence, and he looked at her anxiously; but she came and stood beside him and smiled up into his eyes. "Well, Mr. Charlesworth, it's very sweet of you—

and thank you. . . ." She hesitated, and then said, reluctantly: "After that, I can't possibly go on telling you lies. I'm not very good at it, anyway, am I? I did go into Irene's room, of course, and I did pick up the glass, and I suppose I put the key on the table, if that's where it was found; I was in such a panic that I didn't know what I was doing, and I'm not much used to crime! But I didn't—didn't even speak to Irene, I didn't touch her, and I didn't give her anything, and God knows, I didn't forge a confession and put it under her pillow. Anyway, I can't see why you think it was a forgery. Perhaps it isn't."

"That would mean that Irene was the murderer of Doon," said Charlesworth, "but, if so, why did somebody try to murder *her*?"

"I can't see why you're so sure that somebody did, unless you still think that I did."

"I never thought that you did, Toria, and I don't think so now. But you've got a lot more to explain—why did you go into Irene's flat in the first place, and what did you do while you were there?"

"I simply can't answer that, Mr. Charlesworth. Perhaps I just thought I would like to see how she was getting on—wouldn't that do?"

"Well, hardly, as you don't even pretend that it's the real answer."

"It's all the answer I can give. I suddenly thought that I would like to see if she had gone off to sleep all right; I went in and looked at her, and—and went out again."

"And was she all right?"

"She was asleep," said Victoria, abruptly.

"Are you sure, Toria?"

"Yes, I am. She was asleep. I stood beside the bed and I—I idly picked up the glass and—and put it down again. Then I went away."

"Didn't you see by the empty papers on the table that she'd taken a very big overdose?"

"There weren't any," said Victoria, quickly.

"There weren't any bits of paper? My dear, are you sure of that?"

"Of course I'm sure. There was nothing on the table except the glass and the little box. I didn't touch the box. Have they looked at that for finger-prints? They'll see that I didn't touch the box."

"You had it in your hand when you were upstairs in the other flat."

"Yes, but Gregory had it afterwards, and either she or Irene carried it downstairs. Their marks would be over mine, as Mr. Smithers is so keen on his superimposing and stuff."

"They may be, but it doesn't help us much. You could just as easily have put the stuff into the glass of milk she had upstairs. Victoria, you didn't, did you? I mean, you don't think you could possibly have made a mistake about the dose? You didn't go into Irene's room to make sure that you hadn't made a mistake?"

"Oh, Mr. Charlesworth, no! I swear there was nothing like that about it—I'd tell you if there were. I only wish it were as simple. Don't ask me any more, Mr. Charlesworth—I can't tell you any more than I have; and whoever else asks me, and whoever asks you, I shall stick to my story and you must too, that I put the key through the door."

He begged and badgered and bullied, but all in vain. Not another word would she say, and to all his protestations she simply replied that they couldn't pin it on her in the end; they couldn't find the slightest motive for her to kill Irene, whom she loved; and they would have to let her go in the end.

"You little idiot," he cried, distracted at the thought of the danger into which she was plunging herself. "Don't you see that it isn't going to stop here? Smithers is trying to fasten the murder of Doon on to you. For God's sake, open your eyes and look facts in the face."

"Oh, but, Mr. Charlesworth, they can't do that. It's just nonsense. Mr. Smithers said something about it, but it—it's just fantastic. I—I didn't even know the plate of lunch was for Doon; I thought she was going out. I couldn't have poisoned her—I couldn't have poisoned Doon!"

"Perhaps," said Charlesworth, as Smithers had said to him before, "perhaps it wasn't intended to murder *Doon*."

Not even Smithers had brought such terror to Victoria's blue eyes.

2

Charlesworth went back to the Yard. "Well, Smithers, you were right. Mrs. David sticks to her story that she didn't go into the flat, but put the key through the letter-box and went her way. All the same, you're barking up the wrong tree, my dear chap. There's more in this than meets the eye, and if you don't walk very warily you're going to make a ghastly mistake. I warn you, I'm not going to work with you along these lines; I don't believe Mrs. David is guilty of murder or of attempted murder, and if you think it's on account of her bonny blue eyes, then you're wrong. You carry on, if you like, but I'm out to disprove you. There are a dozen other byways we haven't yet cleared up: that note to Doon from Rachel Gay; what was the matter with Aileen Wheeler at the funeral, and why she lied to me in the first place about never having spoken to Doon outside her work; Bevan—he had motive and, to some extent, opportunity, and we've never properly checked up on him; Mrs. Harris could have done it and you've proved yourself that so could Macaroni. Here's this chemist swears that he isn't mistaken about the photograph and that it was Irene who bought the poison on the day of Doon's death. Have you considered that Irene Best may have committed the murder after all? How can you be so sure that it wasn't a genuine suicide?"

"Because I'm so sure that it isn't a genuine confession. Mrs. Best was horrified to hear of it, and swore she didn't write it. That was perfectly honest."

"How can you be sure when a woman's being honest?" said Charlesworth, whose own faith had been sorely tried in the last half-hour. "She may perfectly well be acting. And you haven't found any finger-prints on the confession."

"No, and who ever heard of a suicide taking care to

keep her farewell note free of finger-prints? Anyway, why should she have printed it in the first place? Why not just write it? The thing is a forgery, ol' man, and you'd better make up your mind to it.''

"Look here, Smithers, here's a theory. Why couldn't Gregory have done what you say Victoria David did? Why couldn't she have gone in after Mrs. David had left her; given Mrs. Best a further dose of the draught, forged the note and left her to it? What about that?''

"What about it? What about Mrs. David's denial that she ever went into the room? What about her finger-prints on the glass? Why doesn't Mrs. Best say that Miss Gregory came in and gave her a second dose of sleeping draught? Why should Miss Gregory have done it, anyway? Don't be damn silly, Charlesworth; your enthusiasm as counsel for the defence is running away with you.'

"Mrs. David may very well have gone in *after* Miss Gregory. The message was tucked under the pillow—you didn't see it yourself till you moved the girl; Victoria may have seen Mrs. Best sleeping peacefully and gone away again.''

"Then why doesn't she say so?''

"I don't know,'' confessed Charlesworth, with a sigh. "I'm sorry, Smithers. I'm being a fool, as you very justly remark; only you're making a mistake and I know it and I can't see any way out. Just tell me one thing before I go: Mrs. Best doesn't say anything about seeing Mrs. David in her room?''

"No,'' admitted Smithers. "I haven't asked her point-blank, of course, but she says that she went straight off to sleep after the two girls left her, and remembers nothing until she woke up in hospital, although she thinks she may have drunk some more water before dropping off.''

"Well, there you are, Smithers! Couldn't Gregory have introduced some more powder into the glass while Mrs. Best was asleep, or half asleep, then left the glass, and wiped off her finger-prints beside the bed? Mrs. Best wakes and drinks it, and later Mrs. David comes in, picks up the glass and puts it down again, and goes innocently out of the room . . ."

"Then why doesn't she say so?"

"I don't know. But it would work, Smithers. It would work, wouldn't it?"

"No, it wouldn't," said Smithers, impatiently. "Mrs. David's story is that she put the key of the flat in at the letter-box on her way down from Miss Gregory's flat; in other words, there wasn't time for Miss Gregory to have been there before her. You can't get out of it, Charlesworth. Mrs. David had it in for Gregory and when she got the opportunity of the oxalic acid, she decided to poison her food; Doon got the food and Doon died; then, for some reason it became necessary to get Mrs. Best out of the way as well; while she was doing that she might as well add a 'confession' and kill a couple of birds with one stone. There are a few loose ends, like the matter of the extra poison bought at the chemist's—I can't quite see why she should have wanted that—and then the thing's in the bag. Work away as you like, ol' man; I don't mind what you do; but that's my case and I'm sticking to it."

## 3

Meanwhile the Dazzler had returned from his morning's outing, and airily announced that he had found himself a job.

"A *job*!" cried Victoria, as though the idea of her husband in a position of bondage was the most incredible thing on earth, as indeed it was.

"I got hold of Mother and made her pull some more strings; she rang up her girl friend, Lady Somebody, who's something to do with the whats-a-name of education, and I went along to see the old trout this morning. You behold before you the assistant art-teacher at St. Maud's School for Girls, Paddington. The money isn't much, but the duties are light, and may lead to higher things—if there *is* anything higher than an assistant art-teachership at St. Maud's School for Girls, Paddington. I can go to the Central for a model in the evenings, if the light isn't good enough when I get back here, and I may be able to pick up another part-time job—this business is only four days a week."

"But Bobby, *dar*ling—what are you talking about? Can you *see* yourself teaching a whole lot of St. Maud's girls, all covered with spots and making painstaking copies of *Rebecca at the Well* and *Dignity and Impudence* and drawings by J. C. Smart. Don't be comic, my sweet; it's simply nonsense. You wouldn't last half an hour, much less four days a week. You'd start telling the fifth form a filthy story, or do a drawing of the head mistress with an enormous bozoom, and you'd be reported to the L.C.C. and probably deported. One criminal in the family's enough, darling. Do for goodness' sake give up this fantastic idea."

The Dazzler, unmoved, merely reiterated his determination to start work at St. Maud's School for Girls on the following Monday. "And what's more," he said, "you aren't going back to Christophe's—I've fixed all that."

"I certainly am!"

"You certainly are not. Do you think I'm going to have you gaped at by a whole lot of Bevan's ruddy clients, wondering whether you're a murderess?"

"You're not serious about this, Bobby? The whole thing's absolute tripe. What do I care if the women stare at me? They've been staring at us for the last week, and they'd be thrilled to death with me if I *was* a murderess. I put up with it before, why not now? I'm no more guilty than I was then; anybody with any sense can see that I didn't try to kill poor little Rene: she did it herself and I don't believe for one moment that the letter was a forgery."

"But that makes Irene the murderer of Doon."

"Well, I don't mean that; what I think is that Irene was fed up with all this hell of the anonymous letters and things, and she couldn't stick it any longer. Life wasn't

172

too marvellous for her at the best of times. There was the sleeping draught, and she decided to end the whole show; and as she was doing it anyway, she thought she might as well say that she killed Doon and then it would all be done with and we at least would be safe. She didn't really like Doon, and she didn't approve of her goings on, and she probably thought that whoever killed her must have had a very good reason for doing so and might as well get off—something like that, anyway. . . ."

"Victoria," said her husband, seriously, "have you any conception of the terrible danger you're in? I know you didn't kill anybody, my sweet, and anybody who knows you must realize the same thing. I think that chap Charlesworth sees it, too," added the Dazzler, innocently, "but the police aren't going to trust you just because you're you, and outside people aren't either. I won't have you going anywhere public where you can be stared at and talked about, until this blasted thing is over and everything's settled down again—if things ever do settle down again," he ended, with a sigh.

"It's terribly sweet of you, darling, but . . ."

"Don't argue any more, my dear. I don't mind the school business a bit—it will be rather humorous, actually, and I shall be terribly careful about not telling the fifth form filthy stories and drawing the head mistress with an enormous bozoom. As a matter of fact, by the purest coincidence, she *has* got an enormous one, so it wouldn't be libel at all, but a very magnificent portrait, and would probably be bought by the L.C.C. for a large sum of money, and hung up in the seniors' room."

Victoria sighed and laughed and sighed again. "All right, my darling, just till it's over. You'll have to teach the St. Maud's girls to draw terribly pathetic pictures of me in my cell and put under them, "Stone walls do not a prison make. While suffering for another's sake," and you can all come in a crocodile and push them to me through the bars. . . ."

She put her head on her husband's houlder and suddenly burst into tears.

# *Thirteen*

IN the meantime there was pandemonium at the shop. Doon was dead and Irene was ill and Victoria was mysteriously absent; customers poured in more eager than ever after the Press accounts of Mrs. Best's overdose of sleeping draught, and Rachel, most nobly assisted by Gregory, was left to cope with the rush. Cecil was invisible, closeted in the workroom with the cutters and fitters, feverishly bringing out new designs and altering and adapting old ones to cope with the new demand; Bevan struggled with the books and at intervals rang up the employment agencies for extra help. Aileen was anxious and nervy these days, and Judy avoided Rachel's eyes and went about her work like a ghost; Macaroni wept vaguely, little realizing how near she was to having something to weep about, and her work was a nightmare of inaccuracy. Mrs. 'Arris, co-opted into the general rush, ran messages and fetched and carried and even answered telephone calls, to the immeasurable surprise of the callers. " 'Ang on, duck," she would say, cheerfully, shouting into the receiver with all her might. "We're in a bit of a muck 'ere, but I'll see if I can't get someone to 'ave a word with you. What was the name, agen, dear? Lady 'Oo, did you say?"

Mrs. 'Arris was sorely puzzled at this time. If it were true that there was somethink rummy about this trouble of Miss Irene and if dear Miss Victoria was to be blamed, wasn't it 'igh time that she, Mrs. 'Arris, should speak up and tell what she 'eard in the keb that day? Not that she wanted to get Miss Rachel into any trouble; Miss Rachel was as nice a gel as ever stepped, and that Miss Doon was no loss to anybody, 'er and 'er bit o' fish, and 'iding 'er brooch in 'er cape and laying the blame on a pore old body what never did no worse than take 'ome a few cold potatoes; if Miss Rachel had killed Doon, well and good; she wouldn't 'ave done it without a very good reason, and it wasn't for Mrs. 'Arris to interfere, especially as Miss Judy seemed to be of the same mind. Not but wot Mrs. 'Arris would ever feel quite the same to Miss Rachel agen, you couldn't expect it; but now, 'ere was Miss Victoria getting the blame. . . . Mrs. 'Arris decided to pay a visit to Scotland Yard. That Mr. Charlesworth, 'e was a nice, good-'earted lad. . . . ". . .'Allo? Mrs. 'Oo? Well, 'ang on a minute, duck, and I'll see if I can't get someone to 'ave a word with you. We're in a bit of a muck 'ere. . . ."

Midday brought news of Irene. She was sleeping peacefully and would be at work again in a day or two. "Couldn't one of us take a bit of time off and go and see her?" said Rachel, poised for flight with a couple of evening dresses over her arm and an order book in her hand. "None of us will get lunch-hours, of course, but I think someone might snatch a few minutes—it wouldn't take long. What do you think, Judy?"

"I think Aileen had better go," said Judy, shortly, zipping herself into a dinner frock with feverish hands.

Charlesworth was at the hospital when Aileen got there. He could extract nothing from Irene, but that she had taken the sleeping draught in Gregory's flat and gone straight off to sleep. It was perfectly possible, she volunteered, however, that she had woken up and drunk some water; in fact, she had a vague idea that she had done so—she might even have put some more powder in it; Gregory had suggested her doing so, and if she had gone to sleep with that in her mind, she might have done it almost in her sleep. The more she thought about it the more she thought that she had. . . .

"You're telling lies to protect someone," said Charlesworth. "You don't really think that you did that, do you?"

"I do think it, Mr. Charlesworth. It may be my imagination, but I have a distinct idea that I sat up in bed and drank the water and went off to sleep again."

"You may easily have drunk the water—but you didn't put any more powder into it, did you?"

"I have an idea that I did," said Irene, feebly.

Aileen brought "love from all the girls" and a message from Mr. Bevan that Irene must stay in bed till she was quite all right again. "We're managing all right at the shop, and although we miss you, dear, you mustn't hurry back till you're quite better. Of course, with Victoria being away. . ."

"Victoria—why isn't she there?"

"She isn't very well," said Charlesworth, hurriedly. "Come along, now, Miss Wheeler, we mustn't stay any longer. No point upsetting her," he went on as he and Aileen left the ward. "She's had a bad time and she would be miserable at this suggestion against Mrs. David."

"They can't really imagine that Toria had anything to do with it?" asked Aileen in her languid Mayfair voice. "It's simply silly, Mr. Charlesworth. It was Rachel that suggested giving Irene anything at all in the first place; Gregory offered the sleeping powder and also said she could take more. Victoria had nothing to do with it, except that she did mix up the dose in the milk. Gregory told her at the time only to put one powder in—she couldn't have made a mistake."

Charlesworth looked down at her, walking so carelessly along in her close-fitting silk frock (bought for a guinea from Christophe's at the end of the previous season), her gay little hat and her faultless stockings and shoes. "This girl is a marvel," he thought. "At home her mother probably takes in washing for a living—and except for the twang in her voice, I'm hanged if you could tell her from a debutante. She looks as if she hadn't got a thought in her head, as if butter wouldn't melt in her mouth: and yet Bevan could buy her for money, and a ghastly plump youth called Arthur has her heart on a string." He took her arm in a rather uncomfortable grip and marched her along Mortimer Street.

"I'm glad to have this opportunity to talk to you, Miss Wheeler. Do you remember the first time I saw you? You said then that you'd never seen Miss Doon outside the shop. Was that strictly true?"

"Of course it was," said Aileen, trying to wriggle free her arm.

"I don't think it was," said Charlesworth, gripping hard, "I think you'll remember that Doon actually came to your house, at least once, and saw you there. She said it was very urgent. Why didn't you tell me that?"

"She may have—I believe I remember that she did once. Not for anything in particular, though. Just to see me."

"She could see you at the shop, couldn't she?"

"Yes, but she came round to—to have a drink, and so on. There's nothing very odd about that, is there? We often go to each other's homes."

"I understand that you weren't very fond of Miss Doon?"

"No, I wasn't very fond of her. Everyone's free to know that. But I didn't particularly dislike her, and I certainly had no reason to kill her, if that's what you're getting at."

"Is it true that your fiancé was at one time rather attracted to her?" asked Charlesworth, ignoring this sally.

Aileen went scarlet. "No, it is not," she said, sharply, and back came the Hoxton edge to the Mayfair voice. "My young man has never seen Miss Doon in his life, unless it might be at Christophe's, when he called for me. He certainly never spoke to her." She added naïvely, "I wouldn't of let him—she was much too dangerous for that."

"How do you mean—dangerous?"

"I mean nothing. Simply that Doon was a girl that couldn't keep her claws off other girls' boys. She took away Judy's fellow and I wasn't going to take any chances with mine. If you think I was jealous of Doon, Mr. Charlesworth, you're wrong; I saw to it that I had nothing to be jealous about."

"But your young man did go to Doon's funeral."

"Good lord, that's nothing to get het up about.

Mr. Bevan said I was to go in a taxi with some of the other girls, but there was no call for us to go home that way. I knew it would be depressing and horrible and I didn't want to go back with Macaroni snivelling like a drain, so I asked Arthur to come along in the car and fetch me home. He never came near the place; he stood at the gate and it was only—only when I passed out that he came in and looked after me. You're all wrong about this, Mr. Charlesworth, honestly you are."

They turned down Upper Regent Street. "About this passing out," said Charlesworth, thoughtfully. "Why should you have fainted at that particular moment, Miss Wheeler? If you weren't much attached to Miss Doon, it seems odd that you should have been so much upset."

Aileen was steadily losing poise. "That wasn't anything either," she said, uncertainly. "The girls'll tell you—I'm just an easy fainter, that's all. Some are and some aren't. I've fainted several times in the shop, bang in front of the customers, and I'm always passing out at fittings; they keep a bottle of sal volatile in the workroom for me, special, and they'd always rather have Judy to model on; she can stand for hours. I suppose it was so depressing in the graveyard and there was nowhere to sit down in that little chapel place; I'd 've been surprised if I *had*n't 've fainted."

Across the Circus and down Regent Street. "One thing more, Miss Wheeler. Don't mind my asking this—I have to know, you know. Just what were your relations with Mr. Bevan before you became engaged to your present fiancé?"

"My relations with Mr. Bevan?" cried Aileen, apparently overcome with astonishment. "Whatever do you mean? You don't think I'd let that beast mess about with *me*, do you? How dare you say such a thing—I shall tell Arthur, I shall. . . ." Her voice faltered but after a moment she said more quietly: "You've got it all wrong, Mr. Charlesworth, honest you have. I never spoke to Mr. Bevan outside Christophe's in all my life;

except the very first time I met him, at a party that was, and he said he had a job going and that I would do for it. I went round next morning and saw him in his office and he gave me the job; I've never spoken to him outside the place ever since. You may believe that, Mr. Charlesworth; I didn't tell you the truth about Miss Doon, she did come to my place once, and had a bit of a talk with me; but it's true about Mr. Bevan. Don't go suggesting that sort of thing, Mr. Charlesworth, *please*. Arthur'd never forgive me if he thought I'd got me name mixed up in anything like that, and I couldn't explain to him, I don't see how I ever could. He's ever so perticalar and I just don't know what 'e'd say. Mr. Charlesworth, you do believe me? You must believe me!"

All Aileen's languor and gentility had deserted her now. She was back in Hoxton, a little guttersnipe with a voice like tearing linen and hardly an aitch to her name, and Charlesworth liked her all the better for it. It was impossible to doubt the passionate sincerity of what she said. He patted her gently on the arm. "All right, don't worry, Aileen. I won't let a whisper of it reach Arthur's ears, if I can possibly help it. It was only an idea I had. I expect I was wrong."

But was he wrong? Bevan himself had admitted to an affair with the girl; he remembered the interview in the dead Doon's flat. . . "but you had dismissed at least one young lady in Miss Doon's favour?"

"Ah, but that was different," Bevan had said.

"The redhead?"

"The redhead," Bevan had agreed, mildly astonished.

"Miss Wheeler?"

"Miss Wheeler, yes." He had added later, "Filthy Lucre are, I regret to say, Miss Wheeler's first and second names." Charlesworth remembered how surprised he had been at this sidelight upon Aileen's character. Perhaps, after all, she had led him up the garden path; perhaps she was just a damn good little actress. . . . He watched her run down the area steps and, sighing, went his way.

Smithers and Charlesworth together escorted Victoria to the little chemist shop where the mysterious ounce of oxalic acid had been purchased on the day of the murder. It was a neat, clean room, lined with glass cupboards and decorated with innumerable boxes and bottles, packets and jars, and printed promises of relief from every known disease. Charlesworth, in the presence of his beloved, turned his back upon one embarrassing article only to find another staring him in the face; his eyes seemed powerless to fix themselves anywhere but on a large structure of toilet rolls and he was much relieved by the chemist's invitation to step into the back room and carry on their conversation there. Under the gaze of a weedy youth with his mouth permanently ajar, they sat down on three wooden chairs and Smithers, taking the initiative, asked the chemist to remember whether he had ever seen Victoria before.

To Charlesworth the first denial was conclusive. Who that had once seen it could ever forget that lovely face and those great blue eyes? Smithers, however, remained unconvinced. Mr. Brown confessed that his recollection of the whole transaction was extremely dim.

"I have a note that a young lady came in and bought an ounce of oxalic acid; and I do remember now that a girl came in on that day . . . she was a very pretty young lady, but it wasn't *this* pretty young lady . . ." he made a courtly little bow to Victoria. "I can't tell you the time of day and I can't tell you anything else about it; a police officer came round here and showed me some photographs and I thought I recognized one; that's all I can say."

Charlesworth fished out a sheaf of Press cuttings. "These are the other girls—just see if you can pick her out again." Two of Rachel, with her mouth open; one of Aileen, immaculate and exquisite; three of Judy, looking furious; one of Victoria, with her eyes shut, and one coming out of the shop with Gregory, both with their hands over their faces; several of Macaroni, giggling or in tears; and one of

Mrs. 'Arris, shaking her fist at the photographer. Finally one of Irene, looking nervously at the crowd around the court-room door after the inquest, her mouth rounded in protest and distress. "There she is," said the chemist, without hesitation. "It isn't very good, and perhaps that's why I didn't recognize her before when I saw it in the papers—but that's the girl."

Charlesworth was triumphant, Smithers still unconvinced; they parted from Victoria, and Charlesworth rushed round to the hospital. After a stormy scene with the Sister he was allowed to go up to Irene's bed; here, however, Irene emphatically denied that she had bought any poison, or even thought of buying any poison, on the day in question. "How could I!" she pointed out. "I was in the showroom the entire morning; first in our room with Victoria and Rachel and then helping Cecil with a customer. Then I went downstairs and had my lunch right under Mrs. 'Arris's nose; then I helped her to put the things out for one o'clock lunch; then I went up to a customer, and *then* I went out with Cissie. It's simply silly."

Charlesworth was tired of being told by young women that he was simply silly. He left her abruptly and went back to the chemist, and as he went a wonderful idea began to take form in his bewildered mind. He thought over the events of that Monday morning: Aileen had been in the workroom, Judy had been . . . ? Well, never mind Judy for the moment, she had known nothing about the proposed purchase of oxalic acid . . . say that she had just been sitting quietly in the mannequins' room. And what had happened then? Irene had advised the two girls to buy some oxalic acid and had *sent them out to buy it*. How long had they taken over their purchase? Quite a little while, he imagined, knowing their easy, pleasant ways. Would it have been possible for Irene to have slipped out of the empty showroom, run down the back streets to this other little chemist's and brought back some oxalic acid for another purpose than that of cleaning a hat? But wait a minute—could she have got past Judy, sitting in the mannequins' room? Wouldn't the risk have been too great?

His mind took another turn. Judy herself. Perhaps she *had* heard the conversation about the crystals, perhaps she had watched the two girls go off across the road, and Irene retire to the salesgirls' room. Perhaps it was she who had skipped through the showroom door and run down the back streets with murder in her heart. But here again he was up against the same thing; what a risk! Supposing Irene had seen her . . . supposing Irene had seen her coming back . . . was that perhaps why Irene had had to die?

"Oi, now, this is ridiculous," said Charles to himself, firmly. "Judy couldn't have got at Irene, it just wasn't possible." He thought carefully over the events of the previous night and confirmed: "It just wasn't possible. No, Irene herself is involved in this somehow. . . . My God! I've got it . . . the back door of Bevan's office! Judy couldn't have passed Irene, sitting in her little room; but Irene could have gone out that way and Judy need never have known she was not in the showroom. Irene saw those two off the premises and hopped out through Bevan's office and through that back door, and down the street to Brown's. All I want is proof of the time, and we're off. Fool that I was not to see it . . . fools that we all were. . . ." His long legs broke into a run.

The chemist smiled politely and concealed any impatience he might have felt at the repeated visits of the police, but he could remember nothing more than he had already told. "I wouldn't have remembered it at all," he said, "except that I have a habit of making a little/note in a business diary of every time I sell an unprotected poison . . . that is to say, a poison that can be sold across the counter without formality."

"Your diary wouldn't help, I suppose?" said Charlesworth, clutching at a straw. "Couldn't you work out, from the other entries, about what time the sale was made?"

They fell to work upon the little book. Here was a

note: "Low in AgNO₃." He knew he had written that first thing in the morning. This was the amount that was to be banked that afternoon, but it might have been put down any time. Here was an address of a customer who wanted something special, there was another; they didn't help at all. Nothing else but, immediately before the entry about the oxalic acid, a couple of capital letters, F. R. "What's this?" asked Charlesworth. "Initials? I suppose they wouldn't help you."

The chemist grew quite excited. "I do believe they might. That's a gentleman who comes in for—well, for a drug, Inspector. It's quite all right and all above board, but he seems to have been in rather frequently lately, and I kept a little private mark of it, just in case I was asked. Now what time would that be that he came in? Percy, come here a minute," he called to the adenoidy youth who had watched them that morning. "You don't remember the gent from number 12 coming in last Monday, a week ago, do you?"

"Do, I doat, sir," said Percy, appearing at the door. "He bust of cub id after I'd god hobe, sir; I saw id the diary next bordig that he'd beed id, and I thought that you was od the right track there, sir, I rebbeber thickig so; but it wasn't id the diary wed I left to go hobe, Bister Browd, of that I'b sure."

"And what time do you go home?" asked Charlesworth, thinking that he had never before realized how many m's and n's there are in the English language.

"Six o'clock, sir."

Realization began to dawn upon Charlesworth. "But this is impossible . . . don't you see what this means . . . the poison must have been bought after Christophe's closed. You must be mistaken."

"Oh, do, I'b dot, sir," said Percy, with an obstinate shake of his head.

"I can't understand it. How long do you remain open, Mr. Browd . . . Brown, I mean?"

"Eight o'clock, Inspector. I stay here myself till then."

"We must get hold of this gentleman from number 12.

Can you ring him up?  Ask him what time on the Monday he came in for his drug . . . it'll come better from you than from me."

The gentleman from number 12 confirmed the hour. He thought he had called in about six.  He had arrived home at . . . yes, that's right, he must have come to the chemist's at about five-past six.  He hoped, rather anxiously, that nothing was wrong.

Charlesworth dragged himself out of the shop.  Well, there went all his bright ideas.  All gone phut on the word of a youth with adenoids.  Gradually, however, light began to break; it was true that his theory about Irene was all gone west, but what about Victoria?  Smithers would have to believe it now—for at six o'clock Doon had been in hospital and already near to death; and Victoria had been in a cold and dreary waiting-room where she had sat with Rachel through the long night hours till Doon was dead.  Whoever had bought the poison on Monday night it had not been Victoria; but why she or anybody else could have wanted to buy it when the victim was already in her death-throes, he did not pretend to know.  Unless the murderer, frightened by success, had made sure of a suicidal dose in case of discovery.  But in that case Irene must be the murderer—and Irene herself was the victim of an attempted attack.  It was all too complicated for words.

He went back to the Yard and had another look at the famous forgery, though without much hope.  "I have made an end of my life because I killed Doon."  Its contents were being kept a close secret, he hardly knew why.  The experts had given a decided opinion that it was not the handiwork of Irene herself, but as to whose it was they would not be sure.  It might be Victoria's, but then, confronted with Gregory's handwriting, it might be Gregory's, it might be Aileen's or Judy's or Rachel's.  "In fact, anybody's," said Charlesworth with irrational sarcasm.

"Exactly," said the expert, smiling politely.  "We only discount Mrs. Best because in her case it would appear to have been a genuine suicide note, and there are indications that it wasn't that. Anyone might have written it who was not in a violent emotional state at the time; if forgers would always say as little and print it as unevenly, our job would be a lot more difficult than it is. Actually, if I were asked an off-hand opinion, I should be inclined to say that it wasn't done by any of these young ladies at all—it's very straggly and inky; not as neat and small as one would expect; but, of course, that may all be part of a particularly intelligent disguise."

"It looks as if it had been done by somebody in gloves much too big for them," said Charlesworth, holding the card before him, arm outstretched.

"Or with a handkerchief or some such things held round the pen to prevent marks."

"There was a pair of Mrs. Best's gloves lying on the dressing-table with her handbag," said Charlesworth, thoughtfully, "and the card was taken out of her handbag as we already know. I wonder if the murderer could have put on Irene's gloves to protect their fingers. . . ."

"Mrs. David would have had her own, as she was on her way home," put in Smithers, who was standing by.

"Mrs. David wasn't wearing gloves," said Charlesworth, sharply. "In the height of summer she doesn't even carry them; in fact, she says she hasn't got any, though that may be one of her light-hearted exaggerations."

"Well, if there is anything in your 'light-hearted' suggestions against Miss Gregory," countered Smithers, "for example if she is supposed to have dropped in and overdosed the girl on her way to post her letter—she wouldn't have been wearing gloves either, not in the height of summer, as you point out. And what is very much more important, Charles, ol' man, is that Miss Gregory is a big, tall girl, and Mrs. Best and Mrs. David are little, small-boned women; Miss Gregory couldn't possibly have got into Mrs. Best's gloves—but Mrs. David could. . . . I must check that up." He fished out his odious little notebook.

"I suppose Mrs. David removed them, so as to make her marks on the glass?" scoffed Charlesworth.

"Would you two blokes mind finishing your argument outside my room," said the finger-print expert, patiently. "I've given you all I can; the thing may have been written by any of these girls, probably with the hands impeded by very thick or ill-fitting gloves; or it may have been the work of someone comparatively illiterate; or it may even conceivably have been the work of Mrs. Best herself, but if that's so she has deliberately counterfeited forgery—too elaborate to be done by anyone in a suicidal state of mind, I think, but that's only my opinion. Now, if you will kindly push off I can give my attention to a little matter of a suicide pact in Epping Forest: yours isn't the only case on hand, you know, though anyone would think so from the way you both go on."

Smithers retired to his room and to the tireless prosecution of the case against Victoria. He had decided to leave all side issues to Charlesworth, knowing that no stone would be left unturned to provide an alternative murderer; and he confined himself frankly and exclusively to proving his own theory. In his own mind he had not the slightest doubt as to its correctness, but he fully realized that he had little in the way of concrete proof; he applied his damp pink nose to the grindstone and sniffed happily as he ground.

### 3

Charlesworth, with the afternoon before him, decided to follow up the lead that had been given him by Aileen. He called upon Bevan and requested the name and address of the host at whose party he was supposed to have offered her the post at Christophe's, dating it for Bevan's benefit as the "day before Aileen had called for her first interview at the shop."

"What on earth can you want to know that for?" said Bevan, impatiently. "I don't see what it's got to do with you."

"It would help me very much if you could let me know the name of the people who gave the party."

"A Mrs. Rayne gave it; it was a most dismal affair and I only remember it because she and I had a few words about my taking the Wheeler girl there. Damn nonsense."

"Could I have the address."

"No, you could not," said Bevan, angrily. "What on earth have my private friends got to do with your investigations?" The telephone rang and he took up the receiver. "Hallo! Oh, yes, Miss Raymond. A request for payment? *Have* we? Already? Well, that's too bad— we mustn't begin troubling one of our favourite customers for money . . . these things go through a regular routine, you know, there's nothing personal about them, and I often don't know when the bills are being sent out. Suppose we split the difference and you send us a little something on account. . . ." He put his hand over the receiver and, still listening at the ear-piece, said to Charlesworth in a savage whisper: "You get out, please. I'm not going to give you another word about it. . . . Yes, yes, Miss Raymond, that's all very well. . . ."

Charlesworth went straight to the nearest telephone booth. There was one Mrs. Rain in the book and half a dozen Raynes. He proceeded to ring them all up.

A woman's voice answered his third call. "I hope you will forgive my troubling you," said Charlesworth, sticking to a formula, "but I should be grateful if you would tell me whether you are acquainted with Mr. Frank Bevan, of Christophe's, in Regent Street. . . ."

The voice answered before he had finished. "Yes, I am *acquainted* with Mr. Bevan, or rather, I used to be. Why do you ask?"

"I am a police officer engaged in investigations concerning the murder at Mr. Bevan's shop," said Charlesworth, mentally congratulating himself upon these well-rounded phrases. "I wonder if you would be so kind as to give me a few minutes' interview?"

"What on earth has it got to do with me?"

"Nothing to do with you at all, madam," said Charlesworth, soothingly. "I just wanted to ask you something about the young lady who came with Mr. Bevan to your house one evening. I can't ask you on the telephone . . ."

"I couldn't tell you on the telephone!" said the voice, laughing. "All right, come along round . . . ."

She was a pleasant, dark young woman, with bright eyes and a sense of humour. She settled him in a large armchair, gave him a cup of tea, and obviously thrilled and amused at her sudden importance in the affairs of Scotland Yard, asked him what he wanted to know.

"I wish all women were like you, Mrs. Rayne," said Charlesworth, beaming at her over the rim of his teacup. "Most of them are much too busy wanting to know, themselves, to bother about what *I've* come to find out. Now all I want you to tell me is this: do you remember a party you gave at which Mr. Frank Bevan was present and at which I believe he had 'a few words' with you about a young lady who accompanied him?"

"I should say I do," said Mrs. Rayne, emphatically. "It was the last time he ever came to my house and the last time he ever will. He turned up with this awful female, Ann Waller or Jane Whistler or something . . . she was most frankly and blatantly a daughter of joy, and though I know these people have to live, Inspector, I don't see why I should be asked to entertain them. I gave an invitation to Frank alone, and he turned up with his woman and another couple; I did think it was a bit thick."

"Would you say the name was Wheeler?" asked Charlesworth.

"Yes, I believe it was; something like that, anyway. Several of our friends had seen Frank with her before; they said he had been running her for some time. She was a pretty girl except that she was plastered with make-up; but, after all, there are pretty girls enough in London without bringing them in off the streets."

Charlesworth handed over a bunch of photographs and she rather doubtfully picked out Aileen's. "This might be the girl, but if so she's cleaned up a lot of the war-paint. I saw one in the paper the other day and thought I recognized it. . . . I pointed it out to my husband and said that Frank Bevan still seemed to be running her, which was something of a record, for it's a long time ago now."

Charlesworth left her pleasant flat. "I'm afraid our Aileen has been leading poor Charles up the garden," he ruminated sadly, tucking himself into his little car. "All the same, she must be a damn good actress!" And if Rachel also were a damn good actress, as now he knew, why not Irene? Perhaps Irene hadn't been telling the truth either, when she had seemed so surprised at hearing of that confession under her pillow. And if Irene—why not Victoria? Why should Victoria have looked so terribly frightened at the suggestion that the poison might not have been meant for Doon? He closed his heart against the thought.

So Aileen had known Bevan and had lived with Bevan before ever she came into Christophe et Cie; and Doon had taken Bevan away from Aileen and now Doon was dead. But in the meanwhile Aileen had become engaged to her Arthur . . . so why should she have cared? "Ah," thought Charlesworth, nearly mowing down a group of pedestrians in his excitement. "Blackmail, that's what it was! Doon knew all about the affair with Bevan and she had threatened to tell Arthur; that was what she had come to Aileen's house about, that was the visit that Aileen had at first denied." What Doon could be blackmailing her for, he could not imagine; she had not a penny beyond the three or four pounds a week she earned at Christophe's and she could have nothing very valuable in the way of possessions. Letters? Perhaps she had kept some of Bevan's; but Bevan had said that he was not the man to write indiscreet letters to women, and Charlesworth could well believe it. Could Aileen in her turn be blackmailing Bevan, and Doon had found out and so Doon had to die? Aileen had had the two necessary opportunities and Aileen had fainted across Doon's open grave. Aileen had had the spirit and wit to work up her little act of languor and grace, her refined accent and her ladylike manners; might she not have had the brains to blackmail, and the courage to strike when danger threatened? But what about Irene? Aileen had gone most of the way home from Gregory's flat with Judy; could she have left Judy and come back to the flats? But if so, how could she have got access to Irene's room? Gregory had had both keys, had given one to Victoria long after the others had left the flat; could Victoria be protecting Aileen? Was that whom Irene was telling lies to save? Mr. Charlesworth decided after long and complicated thought that it was not.

4

He sat at the Yard scribbling dolefully on a clean piece of blotting-paper, trying to see some way out. Six o'clock struck and at twenty minutes past a visitor was announced. He roused himself, pushed the now ruined blotter into a drawer and turned round in his chair. At the door stood Mrs. 'Arris.

Mrs. 'Arris had had a trying time; there had been a crowd for the bus and her hat was crooked and she was out of breath. She was, moreover, frightened and depressed. Rachel was second only to Miss Victoria in her affections, and here she was to give Miss Rachel away. But Victoria came first and the evening papers had been most alarming about Miss Victoria. The girls had brought one in—they were always running out for a paper in these terrible days—and she had seen an account of Toria's midnight visit to the police station and her subsequent release. "On bail!" thought Mrs. 'Arris, darkly. Many of her friends had known liberty on these terms and it had finally decided her to act. Besides, one of the customers had supposed aloud that it was that Mrs. David all the time. "Such a sweet-looking girl, Mrs. Gay, who would have thought it?" It was true that Rachel had hotly denied it and said that Miss Toria was the most innocent of them all. A note had come for her in Victoria's writing just before, and afterwards she had been whispering in a corner with Miss Judy every time there was a moment free, warning her perhaps to say nothing, and perhaps threatening her. "You don't want to die, Judy, do you?" It had made Mrs. 'Arris's blood run cold that day in the keb.

Supposing they hung Miss Rachel, and all through her, Mrs. 'Arris. But here was her dear Miss Victoria out on bail, and somebody had to do somethink about it. She wondered Miss Judy didn't speak up; but Judy was a Yorkshireman and her word was her sacred bond.

Charlesworth asked her to sit down and she overflowed on to one of his small office chairs and folded her grubby old hands. "I don't like to trouble you, sir, but you was that kind about the brooch and the bit er fish; I thought as 'ow if I 'ed somethink to tell I ought to come to you; well, I 'as got somethink to tell and 'ere I am." She produced the black-edged handkerchief which she had taken to the funeral and which was still doing duty and, after a few preliminary sniffs, unburdened her soul.

"You actually heard Mrs. Gay admit to the murder," said Charlesworth, flabbergasted, when she had done. "Can you be sure of that, Mrs. Harris? It's a terribly serious thing, you know."

"Don't I know it," said Mrs. 'Arris, sobbing afresh. " 'Aven't I laid awake all last night, worriting meself to a shred, trying to make up me mind what to do. But there it is, sir. 'Ere's my pore Miss Toria out on bail and that's decided me."

"But, Mrs. Harris, the whole thing's incredible. Would Mrs. Gay ever have said such a thing in front of you? Surely you must be mistaken?"

Mrs. 'Arris explained her innocent little habit. " 'Mrs. 'Arris,' the young ladies says, very soft-like, to see if I'm listening, and if I don't answer, they thinks I don't 'ear and goes on with what they 'as to say. I don't mean no 'arm, sir; it's a bit lonely in the shop sometimes, 'aving the people all talking between theirselves, and keeping you out as you might say; of course, if I'd 'ad any idea what was to come out in the keb—but there," amended Mrs. 'Arris, with a gleam of humour, "I suppose there's no denying I'd 've listened twice as 'ard!"

"Now, tell me again, Mrs. Harris, just what Mrs. Gay said to Miss Judy . . . she said, 'You know who killed Doon, don't you?' and Miss Judy said 'Yes.' "

"That's right. And then Miss Rachel she says, ''Ow do you know?' and Miss Judy says, 'I see you picking up the poison off the floor.' And then Miss Rachel she threatens 'er not to tell, and then she says, '*I* 'aven't admitted anythink, 'ave I?' and Miss Judy promises. It's as true, sir, as true as I'm sitting 'ere."

Mrs. 'Arris was most manifestly sitting there and, as manifestly, most earnestly telling the truth. Charlesworth could hardly believe his ears, but he remembered the pencilled note he had found among Doon's papers and the fact that Rachel had been an actress and might be adept at hiding her real feelings. He dismissed the old woman with words of comfort, and put the whole story before Bedd.

Bedd was at first incredulous, then inclined to believe that they had the answer in their hands. "She had the opportunity to drop poison on the plate, sir, and she knew the plate was for Doon; no nonsense about meaning to murder Gregory. She was instrumental in bringing the stuff into the shop and she might easily have kept a bit back while she was cleaning the 'at; and now here's this story about her picking some up off the floor."

"That would be when they first brought it in, when Mrs. David spilt some on the showroom carpet?"

Bedd considered, flipping over the earlier pages of his notes. "Yes, I think it would, sir. Everybody seems certain that Mrs. 'Arris cleared up *all* the stuff that Macaroni spilt at the table where they were cleaning the 'at, and gave it *all* to Mr. Cecil." He stopped suddenly as a sentence in his notebook caught his eye. "But this attempt at Mrs. Best's life, sir; I don't see 'ow Mrs. Gay could 've been concerned in that. Here it says: She left with Miss Judy and Miss Aileen after the party in Miss Gregory's flat, and walked down the street with them."

"Yes, but she parted from them at 'her turning'; I wonder if she could have gone back? Is *that* who Victoria's trying to protect? She's very fond of Rachel Gay—it seems much more likely."

"Collusion, sir?" suggested Bedd, with much temerity.

"About the keys, you mean? I suppose Toria might have given her key to Rachel; no, she must have gone into the room with her, because of the finger-prints, and that involves Toria all over again. What about Rachel and Gregory? But why? Could Rachel have threatened Gregory, as she threatened Judy? D'you think that's possible? This Rachel's a cool customer if the conversation in the cab is correctly reported."

"I must say, sir, I don't think collusion in the murder *is* very likely. Two girls don't get together to murder another girl, do they? If they do it at all, they do it secretly, 'iding it almost from themselves, if you get my meaning, 'alf pretending even to themselves that they're not doing it . . . of course that's psychology," said Bedd, proudly, "and it don't 'old in a court of law; but there's somethink in it, sir. As for Mrs. Gay threatening 'er— well, Miss Gregory's a strong young woman with 'er 'ead screwed on all right, Mr. Charlesworth. She wouldn't have no funny ideas about honour and promises and things, Miss Gregory wouldn't. She'd pretend to agree and then she'd come straight to the police."

"*She* couldn't have given Mrs. Gay a key? I wonder if she did, quite innocently, and that's why she passed out when she heard of the attempted murder. I think I'll go and see Miss Gregory, Sergeant."

Gregory had come home a little early from the shop. She was sitting darning a pair of stockings in her chintzy room, with a vase of roses, arranged without skill or imagination, by her side. Gregory was of the school who, never having missed a meal in their lives, are wont to declare that they would rather go without food than without flowers. She greeted Charlesworth with her joyless smile and begged him to have a glass of sherry.

"No, thanks, Miss Gregory, I don't think I will. I don't really like to drink on duty."

"Well, let's pretend this is pleasure!" said Gregory, archly.

It was not much pleasure for Charlesworth. Once again he ploughed through the story of the previous evening, and the porter was summoned to assist in the matter of the keys to the guest-flat. There were no duplicates and no other means of access to the flat. The windows? Impossible, said the porter, and obviously thought Charlesworth a fool for asking. The main door to the flats would be open until midnight and anyone might have come in or gone out without being observed; but he believed that, after the young ladies left that evening, nobody had. "I made a few inquiries on my own, sir, 'aving a bit of a theory, you see . . ."

"Ah! and what was that?" said Charlesworth, politely.

"The same as you're getting at—one of them young ladies came back; but it won't wash," said the porter, and sadly took his leave.

Charlesworth refused a second offer of sherry and embarked on a new tack. "Tell me, Miss Gregory, you're all very fond of Irene Best, aren't you? I was wondering how anyone can have brought themselves to try to murder her; they must have had a very strong reason. She seems to be such a kind, affectionate little person—can you think of a grudge anyone might have held against her, sufficiently bad to have led them to do such a thing? Leaving out all question of the first murder, of course."

"Oh, no, Mr. Charlesworth, everybody's devoted to her. I must say she isn't a girl I could make a friend of—she has no, well, no personality, has she? But, as you say, she's a kind-hearted little thing, and the girls in the showroom are all devoted to her. She was extremely good to Rachel over her divorce. I don't know the ins and outs of it," confessed Gregory, who would dearly have liked to find out, "but Irene has a brother who is apparently a bad hat, and he has made her life a misery, sponging on her and turning up at awkward times; she was very anxious that Rachel should not come to some sort of half-and-half arrangement with her husband and leave herself open to the same kind of thing; and she persuaded her to try and get a divorce, and took care of the child while it was actually going on, and I think even lent her some money. . . . She's not exactly Rachel's soul-mate and they get terribly on each other's nerves, but Rachel has often said what a debt she owes to Irene and that she can never be grateful enough for all she did. Rachel is perhaps a little given to exaggeration, and she is always unnecessarily frank about her affairs."

"What about the others? What about Judy and Aileen?"

"Oh, Aileen—I don't think she has it in her to care for anyone; she's a very common little girl, Mr. Charlesworth, as I expect you've discovered in spite of her airs and graces. Not that I mean to say that for that reason she isn't fond of Irene; I think she is quite, and of course I always say that the lower classes probably feel just as much as we do, though perhaps not so *intensely* . . . "

"And Judy?"

"Well, Judy again was very much attached to Irene. She's a bit irritated by some of her fussy ways, but some time ago, as you may have heard, there was a little trouble between Doon and Judy, when Judy's fiancé fell in love with Doon. Irene actually took it upon herself to see this wretched boy and tell him that he was breaking Judy's heart or some such nonsense; it was very unnecessary and did no good at all, but Judy thought it was kind. As for Victoria, she likes everybody and I think she is devoted to Irene. She hasn't got very much *depth*—I don't think many of these universally loved and loving people have; it's mostly that they haven't got the intelligence to see the faults in other people or to have any in themselves. . . . I mean, there's nothing to dis*like* in Victoria . . ."

"I quite agree," said Charlesworth, pointedly, and changed the subject. "Now, what do you think yourself about this business of Mrs. Best? You're a very intelligent girl and you see more clearly than most, I should say. I wish you could give me your own opinion as to how she came to take this overdose."

Gregory was flattered and delighted. To be considered intelligent and level-headed was second only to being considered attractive and marriageable. "I have a brain like a man's," she would say, spreading out hands also regrettably like a man's. "I'm not taking any credit for it, I was just born like that; but I really do reason things out more than most women, I think, and Mr. Bevan says . . ." What Mr. Bevan said would keep Gregory happy for hours.

She gave her whole attention to answering Charlesworth's question. Then she said, weightily: "Have you ever heard of an involuntary suicide, Mr. Charlesworth? Does such a thing ever happen? Because, do you know, I really think that that is what must have happened to little Irene. She went to bed worn out and miserable after a terrible day. She was dopey and confused by the draught which she had had upstairs, and she only knew enough to tip the rest of the powders into the glass by her bed and swallow them. Perhaps she came to a little bit with the cold water and, realizing what she'd done, she thought she might as well make capital out of it for the sake of her friends; she scrambled out of bed and scrawled on one of her cards that she had decided to make an end of her life, and she tucked the card under her pillow and went back to bed. Perhaps the confession was even true. It's a terrible thing to say, but I've sometimes wondered whether—well, Mr. Charlesworth, I realize that Irene Best could not have intended to murder Doon, but it was *I* that was going to Deauville. . . ."

Charlesworth sat staring at her unseeingly, and as he stared his eyes grew bright with excitement. He stared and stared and stared and thought and thought and thought and when, ten minutes later, he left her and stumbled out into the evening, the whole thing was crystal clear in his mind.

# Fourteen

## I

"I WANT to go home," said Irene, sitting up in bed.

"Now, Mrs. Best, you must lie down again and keep quiet and comfortable. We'll send you home just as soon as you're fit to go."

"I want to go home," repeated Irene, obstinately.

The nurse sent for the staff nurse and the staff nurse sent for the sister. Finally the sister sent for the house physician, and a young man in untidy grey flannels and a tweed coat came and stood by her bed.

"What's all this, Mrs. Best? Sister tells me you want to leave and go home."

"I'm going now," said Irene, firmly. "I've just remembered something and I want to go at once. What's the time?"

"It's nearly seven o'clock. Why not just stay for the night, and to-morrow morning I'll make arrangements for you to leave?"

"I want to go now."

"Well, Mrs. Best, we can't stop you; but we don't think you're fit to go and you'll have to sign a statement that you go at your own risk and against our advice. Are you willing to do that?"

"I'll sign anything," said Irene, impatiently.

"And we shall have to notify the police."

"Tell them anything, I don't care. Only do let me go, I'm late already."

She crept down the wide steps, a pathetic figure in the thin summer dress she had worn to Gregory's flat the night before; with troubled eyes and a pale, pinched face under her big straw hat. Beneath one arm she clutched a bundle containing Gregory's pyjamas and a few things Aileen had brought round to her from the shop; she scrambled on to a bus and jogged wearily home to her flat.

197

Once indoors she flung the bundle on to the bed and, running to her little desk, got out her diary and feverishly searched through the pages of addresses. When she had found what she wanted, she took a warm coat from her wardrobe and hurried off out of the flat again. The diary remained lying open on the mantelpiece.

Charlesworth saw it there when, arriving twenty minutes later, he finally obtained entrance by means of the hall-porter's key. He glanced round the room, noted the bundle on the bed, and went quickly back to his car. At an address in South Kensington he knocked on the door and a lugubrious maidservant answered his call. "Yor late," she said.

"Has the séance begun?" asked Charlesworth, breathlessly.

"Yers, I think she's gorn orf," said the woman, casting an anxious glance at a closed door to her left. She said again, severely, "Yor late."

"Can't I go in?"

"Werl you could go in and stand, I suppose. You musern't break the circle. Do you want a mask?"

"A mask?" said Charlesworth, incredulously.

"Yers, a mask. 'Aven't you bin 'ere before? Lots of them wears them; they can talk more natural, I suppose. Not but what they keeps the room very dark—you couldn't see much, anyway."

"Oh, we must have a mask, I think," said Charlesworth, grinning, "if only for the fun of it." She looked a little dazed at such levity, but produced a small black square and a grubby pink ticket and said that that would be seven-and-six, and ninepence for the mask. She opened the door and Charlesworth slipped inside and propped himself against the wall.

A ring of shadowy forms sat round a table, on which burned a dim red light. A woman was breathing stertorously and now and again giving a sort of moan. At intervals a voice said in a thick whisper: "Is anyone there?"

Charlesworth checked an impulse to make an irreverent

reply; nobody spoke. Somebody near him was wearing too much scent.

It seemed a long time before at last the medium stirred and began to make small, plaintive noises in her throat. This time, when the thick whisper spoke, a man's deep voice replied: "I come!"

"It's the Indian boy," cried a woman's voice, excitedly, and everybody else said, "Hush!"

The thick whisper started asking questions.

A woman had lost her husband and the deep voice told her that she must pray for him. "But he isn't in purgatory, is he?" asked the woman, and the table rocked beneath the linked hands and the voice cried, "No, no, no!" "Don't mention hell and purgatory," whispered another voice, and the table rocked again and the spirit cried, loud and harsh: "No hell, no purgatory, no pain!"

A man asked, hopelessly, for "Mary," but there was no reply. "She never comes," he said, and the spirit took up the cry: "She never comes; she never comes; she never comes." "Why does he have to repeat himself?" thought Charlesworth, irritably. "We heard him the first time. What nonsense all this is."

Nonsense and yet worse than nonsense; the exploitation of sorrow for the sake of seven-and-sixpence and ninepence for a mask; a husky voice, a superficial knowledge of the cravings of the human heart, and the price of a ground-floor room three evenings a week . . . no ghostly hands, no unearthly lights, not even a tambourine: just a voice, answering questions in the dark. He began a calculation of the takings in seven-and-sixpences. . . .

The voice that he had been waiting to hear broke softly into his thoughts. "I want you to help me—to advise me," said the tiny whisper, and the deep voice cried: "I help!"

"If one has done wrong and—and something terrible has come of it—I want you to tell me: even if it's too late to repair the wrong—must one confess?"

"Confess your sins," said the spirit.

"But if it was all a mistake; if it was just that things

went wrong; if no more harm will come to anyone else . . . should one—must I—confess?"

"Mistakes are not sins," said the spirit, speaking with a glimmer of sense for the first and only time.

"But may one benefit by those wrongs? Supposing—supposing I go to pick a rose and somebody else gets pricked, can I keep the rose? Ought I to keep the rose?"

"Keep the rose, keep the rose, keep the rose," cried the Indian boy, and his voice began to fade.

"The rose is red," said the whisper, fainter still. "The price of the rose was a life. . . ."

"Keep the rose, keep the rose, keep the rose," cried the voice, and as it cried it grew higher and thinner and fainter until it died away in the breathless hush of the room.

A woman's form slipped past Charlesworth, running down the steps and out into the rain. · He cut across the garden and was in time to see her face as she hurried past. It was Victoria.

2

Victoria was standing in the doorway with Rachel and Judy when Irene got home. "We want to talk to you," they said, and led the way into the flat.

Irene looked weary almost to death. She took off her hat and her warm coat and pushed back her soft, dark hair from her aching head. "I'm tired," she said, looking at them drearily. "I couldn't stay in hospital; I had to come out this evening. I've just been to a spiritualist séance."

"So have I," said Victoria.

There was a ghastly silence. Then Irene said, quietlly: "So you know?"

"We've known for a long time," said Victoria, while the other two stood, a little behind her, silent and miserable. "I came here this evening to talk to you about it. I rang up the hospital to inquire about you and they told me you'd left, so I came on here. I could see that you'd been in and gone out again, but your diary was open on the mantelpiece and I saw a note of the séance and the address. I knew you had a lot of faith in that sort of thing, so I guessed that was where you'd gone. I was sure you couldn't be fit to be running about London by yourself, so I thought I'd better follow you and bring you home; but after what I heard, I couldn't stay. You killed Doon, didn't you?"

"Yes," said Irene.

It was a little, square room with an uninteresting wall-paper and ugly, chipped brown paint; there was a divan bed in one corner, unskilfully camouflaged, a washbasin with a screen round it, and one armchair in front of the small gas fire. Rachel took Irene by the arm and pushed her into the chair. She said, looking round: "Have you got any drink anywhere?"

There was only one place where Irene would keep drink. She said: "There's some brandy in the medicine cupboard."

Rachel found the little bottle and poured half its contents into a toothglass. "Here you are, drink it." She waited till the glass was empty and replaced it on the washstand; she and Victoria and Judy stood leaning against the mantelpiece, looking down at the little figure in the chair. Judy said, kindly: "We know the worst, now, Irene; it'll be easier to tell us the rest."

Irene looked at the three lovely faces and saw in them horror and pity, but no uncharity. She said eagerly: "I didn't mean to kill her; whatever you think of me, you must believe that. I intended the poison for Gregory, of course, but I didn't mean to kill her."

"What did you want to do, then?" asked Rachel, half incredulous.

"I meant to make her ill, Ray. I wanted to go to Deauville so much, and I thought if she were ill, only a little bit ill, just for a few days, Bevan would have to send me. They wanted someone there urgently. . . ."

"But Doon would have gone, Irene."

"Not if Gregory had been ill. Bevan couldn't have left himself to Christophe's without either of them. It was touch and go between us three, only Gregory put Bevan off me by telling him things behind my back. Why should she have done me out of the job? *She* didn't care whether she went or not, she was perfectly happy as long as she could be near Bevan; in fact, she was a fool to let him think of sending her, because as soon as she was safely parked over there she'd have lost him for ever. But she just couldn't bear that anyone else should get it, so she did me out of my chance by saying cruel things about me; she deserved punishing, if it were only for that . . . she's been hard and treacherous and unkind always, to all of us; she deserved to suffer and I wish she had!"

"*Irene!*"

"Well, it's true, Victoria. But I didn't mean it for Doon, and God knows I didn't intend it to kill. I saw the little crystals lying there on the carpet where you spilt them as you brought them into the showroom, and it seemed like providence; but I had to put some back on to the heap on the table and I'd only picked up a few—I didn't keep more than three or four grains of the crystal and I never dreamt for a moment anyone could die of that much."

Rachel and Victoria and Judy looked at one another and shrugged their shoulders in a sort of bewildered dismay. Rachel moved over to the bed and sat down on it: "Well, anyway, you put some on the curry?"

"I meant it for Gregory," repeated Irene, with childish insistence. "I put it on the curry while I was serving it out and I specially marked the plate for Gregory; how could I know that anyone else would get it?"

"Couldn't you have stopped Doon having it?"

"But I didn't *know*, Victoria," cried Irene. "I was upstairs with my customer all during your lunch hour and then I went straight on with Cecil to the Ritz, and I wasn't downstairs at all. By the time we got back, Doon had been taken to hospital; but even then it never occurred to me that she would die. I was afraid to say anything and it's been a nightmare to me ever since, because, if

I'd spoken then, there might have been time to save her."

"There wouldn't have," said Judy in her blunt way. "By the time you got back from the Ritz, the doctor knew there was a possibility of her having taken oxalic acid; it was already too late to do anything. You can spare yourself that much anxiety, anyway."

"I didn't know what to do," said Irene, leaning forward in her big armchair, her aching head in her hands. "I thought I would go mad, but I just had to carry on. I lived in a sort of daze last week, and I was dreading having to go to the funeral and pretend—well, of course, it wouldn't have been pretending because no one there could have been more wretched than I, but—you know what I mean. I simply couldn't have gone. Then, when Bevan suggested that I should stay behind, imagine how thankful I was! But after that, the letters came . . . and you were all so sweet . . . do you mean to say that you knew all the time?"

"Don't think we weren't sincere about that, Irene," said Victoria. "We knew that the things they said weren't true, all the filth about your revelling in her sufferings and so on; and you looked so ill and desperate that we couldn't bear to see you—we knew you must be going through hell, knowing the dreadful truth behind it all. Aileen was the only one that didn't know. . . ."

"When did you realize, Victoria?"

Rachel and Victoria looked at each other. "It was Wednesday," said Rachel at last. "We were sitting, talking things over, after Gregory made her speech; Toria, do you remember? You said that Irene couldn't have got hold of any of the poison, because she hadn't been near the table where we were doing the hat. . . ."

"And then I suddenly realized that she might have kept back some of what she picked up off the floor; but I was just going to say that even so she couldn't have murdered Doon because she'd thought, as I thought, that the lunch was for Gregory, and it flashed upon me that the poison might not have been meant for Doon at all, but for Gregory. The detective thought the same thing afterwards about me."

"I saw it at the same moment," said Rachel, from the bed.

"And Judy . . .?"

"I saw you as you were picking up the crystals, Irene, from the showroom carpet; and I saw your face. . . . Of course, I didn't understand until much later, and by that time Doon was dead. While I was making up my mind what to do, Rachel told me that she knew, too, and that if we weren't going to tell Mr. Charlesworth, we must keep the whole thing an absolute secret and not let you guess that we knew. . . ."

"Why not?" said Irene, staring at her.

Rachel looked embarrassed, but she said, gravely: "We didn't know then, Irene, that you hadn't intended to murder Doon—or rather Gregory. Mr. Charlesworth told the Dazzler on the day of the inquest that the murderer wouldn't kill anyone else *unless they knew too much*. It suddenly came to me, while I was dressing for the funeral, that I had noticed Judy standing at the door of the mannequins' room, while we were picking up the poison; I thought she might have put two and two together, so on the way to the funeral I asked her if she knew; and she said that she'd seen us picking up the crystals. I told her that we must both say nothing to anybody about our suspicions; but when Victoria began to get into a mess over your attempt at suicide, of course we couldn't allow that. We talked it over at odd moments in the shop to-day, and this evening we got hold of Toria and agreed to meet you here and tell you that we couldn't let Victoria suffer to protect you."

Victoria looked miserable. "I don't see why we shouldn't let it go on a little longer. . . ."

"No, no, darling, of course not," said Irene. She looked at them wistfully. "It was terribly loyal and marvellous of you all."

"It was terribly wrong of us all," said Rachel, without a smile. "I don't know what we'd have done in the end,

Irene; I think we all expected that the police would inevitably find out, and we didn't want to feel responsible for—for giving you up. Each of us had something to be grateful to you for; we were all so fond of you. . . ."

"Well, we just couldn't give information against you," said Judy, "that was all. We knew you were suffering; it wasn't as if you were just going gaily on and showing no remorse or anything. . . ."

"I've never been through such hell in all my life," said Irene, looking up into their eyes, twisting her little hands. "The letters were the last straw; knowing that they were true, having you all so good to me; when I went to bed after the party at Gregory's, I felt I just couldn't go on. Gregory had given me a box full of sleeping powders and it seemed the best and happiest and easiest way out; I sat up in bed and tipped the powder all into the glass and drank it down; I hardly thought at all. Then, just as I was fading off to sleep, I realized dimly that I hadn't left any sort of message to say what I was doing. We'd been living in such a world of poison and suspicions and dreadfulness that it came to me that perhaps nobody would realize I'd done it myself and that one of you might be suspected. I was getting drowsier and drowsier and I couldn't drag myself out of bed to write a note, but with a last sort of dying effort I took the edge of my sheet and wiped round the outside of the glass, and then I gripped it hard with my hand to show that my fingers only had touched it. That was the last thing I remember before I woke up in hospital. I couldn't understand what had happened, but when I realized that I'd been saved, I had the sense to close my eyes and think things over before I said anything."

"Naturally you couldn't have admitted that you'd tried to commit suicide, or the police would have begun to realize why you'd done it?"

"No, of course. And then, when they found the confession . . . who could have put that there?"

"I thought you'd written it yourself?" said Victoria, staring.

"No, of course I didn't. I've just explained that to you. This afternoon that man Smithers came and questioned me again and he told me that you were supposed to have been in my room; I thought perhaps you'd guessed what had happened and had written the message then. . . ."

"I never even saw the message," said Victoria. She went and sat beside Rachel on the bed. "I did go into your room, because on my way down from Gregory's I suddenly realized that it had been foolish to put an overdose of sleeping draught right into your hands, as it were, when you were already in a state of such depression. I imagined you doing just what you say you did do—the others hadn't thought of it, but then they didn't know what I knew about you; at least Gregory didn't, and it was she who suggested giving you the extra powders. As I'd got the key, I thought I would just slip into your room and see if you were all right; if you'd been awake I could have given you a second powder and put the rest away. . . ."

"I suppose I had taken the stuff by that time. I didn't see you come in."

"Yes, as soon as I got there I saw that I was too late; the packets were empty, unfolded on the table. I picked up the glass, more or less automatically, and looked at the dregs, and I suppose at the same time I must have put the key down on the table—that's where it was found. I was just going to rush to the telephone for a doctor when suddenly I thought: 'What's the use?' I thought that it would be too cruel to wake you up to face all the horror of a trial and—well, at best, prison and disgrace. I thought you had chosen your own way out and perhaps it was the best one, after all."

"Victoria, you might have got into terrible trouble for leaving me like that?"

"She did," said Rachel.

"I didn't know about it, Toria. They didn't tell me in the hospital. . . ."

"No, I know, my dear. It's all right, don't worry."

"I couldn't believe that anybody could be so—so generous and brave," said Irene, tears in her eyes.

"It wasn't really," said Victoria, a little impatiently. "I didn't think for a moment that anyone would find out I'd been in the room; when they did I thought for my own sake I'd better stick it out and not admit it if I could possibly help it; but, of course, when I realized that you were still alive—well, then I was terrified. I couldn't own up if I'd wanted to, because it would have meant explaining *why* I'd left you to die."

"But she's got to explain now, Irene," said Rachel, coming and standing with Judy by the mantelpiece. "Victoria's under suspicion for Doon's murder, because they think she tried to kill you."

"You wouldn't want anybody to suffer for what you did, would you?" said Judy, anxiously. "Least of all Toria, when she's been so marvellous."

Irene was on her feet, staring at them with big blue eyes, her face white and terrified: "Of course not; of course . . . I didn't know, I didn't realize. . . . I'll go to the police. . . . I'll tell them it was me. . . ."

Judy turned away and buried her face in her hands. Victoria said, humbly: "It isn't my fault, Irene. I wanted to go on with it, but Rachel and Judy think things have gone too far. They won't keep silence any more. We thought we should warn you first and—and bring you this. . . ." She thrust a small white packet into Irene's hand.

Irene looked down at it stupidly. "What is it?"

"Morphia," said Victoria.

Irene smiled for the first time that evening; the despair seemed to have lifted from her and she spoke quite coolly, handing the package back. "No, you keep it, darling. It's all right, I'll do what you mean me to do, but I won't risk using anything of yours. The night that Doon died I went to a little chemist behind the shop and bought some oxalic acid and hid it away in case anything went wrong. . . ."

Judy looked up, startled. "Irene, you can't do that.

It's the most ghastly death; you didn't see her, but poor Doon . . ."

"Yes, exactly—poor Doon!" said Irene, still in her cool, quiet voice. "It's only fair, isn't it? You people go away and leave me now, and I'll write it all out quietly, so that there can be no more mistakes, and to-morrow morning you can wake up knowing that all my troubles are over." She added, smiling again: "The spirit said, 'Take the rose.' Do you think this is what he meant?"

"No," said a voice, and Charlesworth stood at the door.


# Fifteen

I

IRENE snatched at the packet in Victoria's hand and, tearing it open, put her hand to her mouth. Charlesworth caught her wrist and forced it back.

"Mr. Charlesworth," implored Victoria, "let her! Let her take it! It won't hurt you and she can't go through all this horror of trials and things. . . ." She put her hand on his arm and looked up at him with pleading eyes. "Let her end it in her own way! I beg of you. . . ." And as he shook his head, she added desperately: "You told me you loved me—well, for my sake . . . don't make her go through a trial, and—and be condemned and—and—hanged. . . ."

Irene was frightened again now, but she said, looking straight at Charlesworth and standing very still: "I killed Doon."

"Oh, no, you didn't," said Charlesworth, cheerfully.

Irene stared at him. "But I did; for heaven's sake don't let's have any more mistakes and misunderstandings; I did kill her; I poisoned her."

"No, you didn't," repeated Charlesworth, smiling. "You're a very foolish and naughty girl, and how we're going to cover up your misdeeds goodness knows." He looked at Bedd, who had sidled in and now stood quietly just inside the door. "Unless we can persuade the sergeant to enter into a conspiracy with us!"

"I'm 'ere to obey orders, sir," said Sergeant Bedd, with a grin.

"As for you three," said Charlesworth, beaming round upon the others as they stood in a bewildered row behind Irene, "I'm ashamed of you, conniving at suicides all over the place. And your detection is no better than your ethics; what about that forged confession? You haven't worked that in yet, and you can't leave a case with loose ends lying around."

"But Irene says . . ." faltered Victoria.

"Irene knows nothing about it. Irene put a few crystals on Doon's food, we know, but somebody else put a more than lethal dose. . . ."

"Then I didn't—I really didn't? . . ." Irene swayed and caught at the mantelpiece for support. "It wasn't really I who caused Doon's death?"

"You didn't even contribute towards it," said Charlesworth, looking with pitying eyes at her white face.

"I think I'd better put her to bed," said Victoria, taking Irene's arm. "She's been through a terrible time and she really isn't fit to stand any more." As Charlesworth moved towards the door, she added: "I won't be long. Don't go away without me. I want to talk to you."

"And I want to talk to you," said Charlesworth. "Come on," he said to Rachel and Judy, "we'll wait for her outside."

Toria tucked Irene up in bed and bade her a gentle good-night. "Don't worry any more, my dear. It was a terrible thing to have done, and utterly unlike you, but it's over now and God knows you've suffered enough. You'll be going off to Deauville and life will start all over again. Judy and Rachel and I are the only people who know, and we won't tell; you'll be safe and happy in your new life and, even if things are never quite the same between us all, at least we can meet sometimes and still be friends."

Irene sat up in bed. "Victoria, I couldn't go to Deauville. I couldn't benefit by Doon's death! I didn't mean to kill her, it's true, and it seems now that I really didn't, in the end; but I don't see how I can . . ."

"The spirit said, 'Take the rose!'" said Victoria and, smiling, closed the door.

## 2

Charlesworth was standing alone outside the flats. "I've sent the other two home with Bedd," he said. "I wanted a word with you, so I'll see you home and then I've got to meet Smithers and . . . well, make this arrest, you know." He took her arm and they walked down the steps to his car. "There's a guard watching the place, of course, and Smithers is doing a bit of final checking up, though I haven't any doubt as to the results. I wanted to get one or two things straight first, and when I found Irene had left the hospital I was afraid of what might happen. I followed her to the séance—have you ever heard such rot as the Indian boy talked?—and then I followed you back here. Since then I'm afraid I must plead guilty to a spot of eavesdropping. I ought to have interfered sooner, but I thought she deserved a few bad moments before it was all cleared up for her. . . ."

"It isn't cleared up for *me*, Mr. Charlesworth," said Victoria, as she climbed into the little car. "Who? . . ."

"I don't owe you any consideration at all, Victoria, after the dance you've led me, holding back vital clues, telling the most awful fibs. . . ."

"Yes, but Mr. Charlesworth, you *must* tell me. Who? . . ."

They came to Irene's "corner" and followed the bus route south. "All right," said Charlesworth, automatically correcting a small skid on the wet road, "you've asked for it and here it is: it was somebody who, on Wednesday morning of last week, was closeted in Bevan's office, resisting his attempts to kiss her. It was you, Victoria."

Victoria spoke before the full significance of what he said had dawned upon her. "That wasn't me. That was Rachel."

"But you said, 'Not a sausage' like Aileen does, and laughed like you always laugh when you copy her."

"Ray copies her too. I remember on that very day Irene said she couldn't tell us apart and that we soon shouldn't be able to talk the King's English ourselves. . . ."

"Then it was Rachel."

"If you mean to suggest that it was Rachel who killed Doon, it certainly wasn't," said Toria, sharply. "Why should she, anyway?"

"Because Doon had been blackmailing her. I found a letter among Doon's papers, a letter from Rachel threatening thunder and lightning and all sorts of things." He pulled it out of his pocket.

"You found this among Doon's papers? Good lord, this wasn't written to Doon—it was to Bevan. It was never intended for anyone but Bevan."

"Why was it ever written?"

"Because Rachel's an idiot. She's so impulsive and ready to fly off the handle, Mr. Charlesworth, but it doesn't mean a thing, honestly it doesn't. It all happened a long time ago; Bevan was rather keen on Rachel and she quite liked him until she found him out. She had dinner with him one evening and went back to his flat and—well, Mr. Charlesworth, Rachel's a married woman and all that and Bevan's quite an attractive sort of man, I suppose, when he's on his best behaviour. I don't say that anything very dreadful took place, but the point is that Rachel is in the thick of her divorce now, and it's terribly important to her to get the custody of her child and what not, and she was terrified of anything leaking out. On the night that Doon died she got back to her flat and found that her husband had been there and had asked the kid questions about her and Bevan. She wrote a frantic note to Bevan, and posted it before midnight, asking him to see her about it next morning and—well, there it is, you can read it for yourself. It must have been in his pocket when he gave you the rest of the letters of Doon's."

"How do you know he gave them to me?" asked Charlesworth.

"He told us so himself," said Victoria, laughing. "He said you led him up the garden path and let him make a fool of himself pretending to look for the letters when he already had them, and you knew it. Poor old Doon used to write poetry and stuff; he thinks she must have destroyed it, because he couldn't find it there, but he, rather decently, I think, didn't want it found, for her sake."

"I wondered at the time why he should have taken so much trouble for the letters," said Charlesworth. "They were a bit lively, but they didn't tell us anything we didn't already know."

"Anyway, Mr. Charlesworth, the note had nothing to do with Doon. You didn't really think Rachel had killed her?"

"Oh, no, not really," said Charlesworth, still laughing. "I was just getting a little of my own back for all those awful lies you told me."

"You devil—you terrified me! But now, do tell me, honestly . . ."

"Well, then, think for a moment. Lots of people had motives, but who had the most serious motive of all? Mrs. 'Arris had a grievance about fish, Mr. Cecil had lost his boy friend, Bevan was getting tired of his mistress, Judy had had a small tragedy, perhaps rather a big tragedy, but that was a long time before; Macaroni had had a little worry that you will never know anything about; but who was it who had lost Bevan to Doon's superior charms? Who had lived with Bevan and loved Bevan and battened on Bevan before Doon took him away?"

"Gregory!" said Toria.

"Gregory had no mercenary claims on Bevan; but there was one person who, in losing him, lost everything. She got someone to make up for it afterwards; but perhaps she didn't forget . . . perhaps she didn't forgive!" He lifted his hands for a moment from the steering-wheel and waved them dramatically in the air.

Victoria regarded him in amazement: "I don't know what you're talking about, Mr. Charlesworth."

"I'm talking about Aileen," said Charlesworth, and now he was perfectly grave.

### 3

Victoria turned right round in her seat to stare at him. "*Ai*leen! Aileen never lived with Bevan; she doesn't care tuppence about him. She's terribly proper and, anyway, she's potty on Arthur."

"I'm talking about pre-Arthur days. Aileen hasn't always been proper, has she?"

"Of course she has. Always. She was born proper."

"But Bevan himself told me that she was his mistress."

"Good heavens, that wasn't Aileen! That was her sister. She's the most terrible female; some people say she's actually on the streets, though I don't believe that. Poor Aileen's terrified of Arthur finding out; he's the most awful little tick, really, and he'd chuck her over for two pins if he thought she was connected with anyone like that. Didn't you see the sister at the funeral, a creature with henna'ed hair . . . no wonder poor Aileen passed out. There was Arthur among the crowd at the gate and Anne as large as life in the audience or whatever you call it at funerals, all dressed up like a sore finger and covered from head to toe in silver fox. She looks very much like Aileen, except that she's so made-up, and Arthur might easily have recognized her."

"Why on earth should she have gone to the funeral? Did she know Miss Doon?"

"She knew Bevan! He'd given her up for Doon and now that Doon was dead I suppose she thought she might get Bevan back and went along to see how he looked and let him know she was still on the tapis. She daren't come near the shop; he'd put a stop to that. She made a bit of a pest of herself after Bevan left her and tried to get a few pounds out of Doon by threatening to make her affair with Bevan public. She was a fool because Doon didn't give a hoot in hell who knew about it; but Doon did get a bit fed up and once, after the girl had rung her up, she went round to see Aileen and told her that she must keep her sister quiet. I remember her telling Rachel and me about it in her room one day. Doon never cared who knew all about her affairs."

"In the light of all this, perhaps you know something about a party at which Aileen is supposed to have met Bevan for the first time, just before she came into the firm?"

"Oh, yes, it was while Bevan was still running the sister. I supposed he wanted to do her a good turn, and we needed a new mannequin. He told her sister to bring Aileen along to this party and he got another man and made up a four. Aileen has told us since that it was perfectly ghastly, because the girl who was giving the party was furious at Bevan turning up with all these extra people and didn't make any secret of her annoyance. I expect Ann Wheeler had something to do with it, too— she would hardly be a very acceptable guest at a decent party. Anyway, the next day Aileen came round to the shop and we all had a look at her and thought she was marvellous, so Bevan took her on."

"And it couldn't have been Aileen after all?" asked Charlesworth, laughing again.

"Mr. Charlesworth, you knew that perfectly well! Don't pull my leg any more. Do tell me—tell me the truth! Who was it? How did you find out?"

"I found out by a piece of brilliant deduction, Victoria. For once I came all over like a detective in a story-book . . . insight flashed about like lightning and the little grey cells whizzed round and round and round; and when they stopped whizzing I knew who my murderer was. From that I worked backwards, which isn't according to the rules at all, and in the end I found myself left with two questions. First, how could anyone come out of a room if they'd never gone into it? And second, wouldn't it be as difficult to write a note in gloves that were too small as it would in gloves that were too large? Find the answer to my questions and you'll know the answer to your own."

They approached the turning that would take them to Victoria's door. "Go straight on, Mr. Charlesworth," said a small, sad voice at his side. "I'll come with you."

"You can't do that, my dear. I'm going to . . ."

"Yes, I know. Couldn't I come too? Whatever they've done, it's rather dreadful to let anyone go through this without—without someone to hang on to. . . ."

He said no more, but headed the car further west. They stopped at a door guarded by two constables in uniform; Bedd had got there before them, and Smithers also joined them, too crestfallen to make more than a feeble protest at Victoria's presence. The four of them went along a familiar corridor; a plain-clothes man stood aside to allow them to ring the bell.

Even as she opened the door, Gregory knew why they had come.

4

Victoria, sick and dazed, heard Smithers mumble words he had once repeated to her. She pushed past him and, taking Gregory by the arm, led her to a chair. "You must sit down, Gregory; there's no need to stand out here. Wait a minute, Mr. Smithers, give her a moment; get a glass of water . . . there in the bathroom. . . ."

Smithers, like a little dog, obeyed. Gregory drank some of the water and lifted a face that, in those few moments, had grown old and gaunt under her clumsy make-up. Her cold grey eyes met the gentle blue ones; she said harshly: "Victoria . . . please go away."

"But, Gregory—I came to tell you . . . I came to offer you . . . I just wanted you to know that you have a friend. . . ."

Gregory did not answer. She sat hunched in the big chair, her hands dangling listlessly at her sides, and made no further movement. "Do speak to me, Gregory," stammered Victoria, miserably. "I only want to help you if I can. Is there anything I can do for you?"

Still there was no reply. "Come along, my dear," said Charlesworth, putting his arm round Victoria's shaking shoulders. "You can't do any good. If Miss Gregory wants to see you some other time, she'll know she can send for you. Smithers will look after her now. I'd better take you home."

Victoria stopped in the doorway. "Gregory—do just say one word to me!"

But the figure in the big armchair was silent and still.

5

Once more they got into the car. "Drop me at a Tube station, Mr. Charlesworth, if you will," said the sergeant tactfully, and they watched his broad, friendly back disappearing into the gloom. "He's a good old stick," said Charlesworth, letting in the clutch. "He's stood by me solid all through this blinking affair. What a mess I've made of it, Victoria, haven't I?"

"I think you've been marvellous," said Toria, a trifle mendaciously.

"Do you? Well, I return the compliment. For sheer misguided loyalty, commend me to the staff of Christophe et Cie."

Victoria smiled for the first time since they had left Gregory's flat. "Well, we were all fond of Irene, you know, and there wasn't one of us she hadn't been good to in her own little way. It's an impossible thought to go to the police with accusations against someone you know so well. I think we all believed you would discover the truth in the end—we just couldn't bear to be responsible for your finding it out. But now, Mr. Charlesworth, I *must* know about this Gregory affair . . . you thought of your two questions—and then what?"

"Well, I thought of my two questions—how could anyone come out of a room they hadn't gone into? And wouldn't it be as difficult to write in too small gloves as it would be to write in too large ones? . . . you yourself saw the answer as quickly as I did."

"It was a wild guess, really, now that I come to dissect it; I didn't think about the room—I suddenly had a vision of

Gregory's big, bony hands thrusting themselves into Irene's little gloves, and there didn't seem to be any doubt any more."

"That was how it hit me. I was sitting talking to her at the time and she said something that put me on the right track. I took one look at her hands, and I seemed to know. I thought it over for a while, and then I went round to a big chemist's just opposite her flats and talked to the people there; after that I rang up Smithers and for once we found ourselves in perfect agreement. I told him to put a watch on the place and to make a few inquiries here and there, and it was then he mentioned to me that Irene had left the hospital."

"But, Mr. Charlesworth, why should Gregory have done it? She had the job they all wanted. . . ."

"Ah, that was where I went wrong in the very beginning," said Charlesworth. "I suspected people of murdering Doon because they wanted the job in Deauville; it never occurred to me to suspect anyone of killing her because they *did*n't want it! But there it was—Gregory was being sent away and Doon would have Bevan all to herself in London. Smithers got hold of Bevan after I rang him up and questioned him on this point. Bevan says that that Monday was the first time he had told her she was to go, and that he didn't take much trouble to conceal his reasons; he says—he really is a filthy bounder, that chap—that he thinks that up to then Gregory had really had some idea that he would marry her. I suppose she realized that morning that if she had to leave London she would lose him once and for all, and when directly afterwards she saw the poison lying on the floor in the shop the idea of killing Doon must have flashed on her as a solution of all her troubles. Firstly, she would get her rival out of her way, and secondly, she would make it impossible for Bevan to send her abroad; it was essential for him, wasn't it, to have one or other of them at Christophe's? That masculine brain of hers worked very coolly and quickly and she took good care to keep well away from the poison that was already in the shop.

She went downstairs and told Mrs. 'Arris to go up and sweep it away; and in the few moments while the basement was empty she went up the area steps and out into the street; once there she went to a different chemist altogether and bought an ounce or so of oxalic acid. She came quietly back and in at the back door of Bevan's office and when lunch was ready she walked calmly out of the office and downstairs, and as soon as an opportunity presented itself she put a lethal dose of the poison on to poor Doon's lunch. It was simple and daring and it worked; but what I can't make out is why she should have gone to a chemist so near her own block of flats."

Victoria thought for a moment. "I think I can tell you why," she said, slowly. "She heard Rachel telling Mr. Bevan that a chemist won't give you oxalic acid unless you're fairly well known to him. I believe that's wrong, actually, but we thought at the time that Mr. Mitchell only let us have the stuff because, though he may not have known our names, he knew who we were and where we came from. If Gregory went to a large chemist's near her flats it was probably because they knew her there as a regular customer, though they wouldn't have associated her with Christophe's. It was a terrific risk, though."

"It was the only one she took and it was justified. A lot of people buy oxalic acid, and it isn't at all an event in the day of a large chemist's shop to sell an ounce or two. It's used for cleaning brass, you know, as well as hats."

"One ought to work in a joke about brass hats, I suppose," said Victoria, wanly. "But I can't think of one."

Charlesworth smiled down at her: "Well, anyway, you must be recovering, to have even had the idea."

Her eyes clouded. "I don't think I am, actually; but still, after all, she was a murderess, and Doon died a terrible death; I must try to remember that. Anyway, go on about the chemist."

"Oh, yes. Well, the point is that it's nothing out of the way to sell an ounce or two of oxalic, and though the particular man who served her read about the case afterwards in the papers he had no earthly reason to connect her with it. He didn't even know her name, or that she came from the flats opposite; only that she was a fairly regular customer. She took care to put her hand in front of her face whenever there were Press photographers about, and the only pictures that appeared in the papers were almost unrecognizable. He thought no more about the whole affair until I rang up this evening and even then it took a good deal of digging to unearth it from his memory. Meanwhile, as I say, Gregory had gone quietly back to the shop and through the back door into Bevan's office; and when the lunch was ready she marched downstairs as large as life, and it was so natural for her to do so that it didn't occur to any of you to wonder how she got there in the first place, although the door had been visible to you all the morning and none of you had seen her go in. I ought to have realized it, of course; she didn't come upstairs while Mrs. 'Arris was brushing up the poison, she didn't pass Mrs. 'Arris and Mr. Cecil on their way downstairs, and Mrs. 'Arris didn't set eyes on her the whole morning . . . when could she have left the cloakroom?"

"Surely that was a bit of a risk?"

"Well, not much. When she came downstairs at lunchtime she still hadn't burned her boats, had she? If anyone paid any particular attention to her or so much as asked her where she had sprung from, she had only to sit tight and keep the poison in her pocket till another time; but nobody took the faintest notice and so she went ahead with the dirty work. It wasn't very difficult for her to have got the crystals on to the plate of food; you were all sitting at the table by then, and the plate was in the farthest hot-cupboard, so that her back would have been turned towards you, more or less; and then there was nothing more to do but to lead her victim to the table and persuade her to eat. It was bold, but it wasn't foolhardy."

"It was vile!" cried Victoria, recoiling. "The treachery! The cruelty! I do feel sorry for her now, poor devil, but when one thinks of it—how can she have gone about among us and been so sweetie-pie and seen us suffer, and seen Irene suffer? . . ."

"Well, she may have been genuinely sorry about the anonymous letters; she's a woman, after all, and though she was hard enough about killing poor Doon, it doesn't follow that she would want to see Irene so wretched and upset, and of course she didn't know the part Irene had played; all the same, when she went into the flatlet and found her lying in a coma with four empty packets beside her that had contained sleeping draught—well, she was quick enough to see where her advantage lay. She didn't touch the glass or leave her marks on anything in the room—I suppose you are all rather detective-minded by now!—but she cramped her fingers into Irene's little gloves and scrawled a confession of murder and suicide and crept upstairs again."

Victoria shifted her position, curling one slim leg under her on the seat of the car, but her mind never left the problem before her. "Yes, but how could she have known Irene was dying?"

"Oh, I don't for a moment suppose she did, do you? Smithers will get all this out of her, but I imagine what happened was that, as she went down to post her letter she suddenly thought, just as you did, that it had been rather stupid to let Irene, when she was in such a depressed condition, have a fatal dose of sleeping draught to take to bed with her. I don't imagine she had any but the most altruistic thoughts as, using the key she still had in her handbag, she crept into the flat to see that all was well. But, like you, Victoria, she was too late; and, like you, but for a very different reason, she decided to leave Irene to her fate. She didn't think anyone had seen her outside her own flat, but just in case there had been a porter about, she candidly admitted posting the letter after you had left. Of course it must have been a shock to her when Smithers turned up in the middle of the night, demanding to see Irene, but she didn't lose her head. She tried to persuade him to put it off till the morning, but finally she gave him the key and settled down in her flat to wait."

"But she was so sur*prised*. She actually fainted when she heard that Irene had been found dying. Was that just pretending?"

"Oh, no, you couldn't get round Smithers with a fake faint. I got him to repeat, this evening, what he actually said to her; he told her first that Irene had taken an overdose, and then that she had been found while there was still time to save her. That was why Gregory fainted: at the knowledge that Irene wouldn't die—that she would be alive to deny that she had written the 'confession.' Gregory didn't know, of course, that you had been in the room before her to leave your beautiful finger-prints on the glass; if the key was on the table then, I don't suppose she noticed it . . . she had a lot to think about and it just wouldn't have made any impression on her. Why did you tell me, Toria, that there were no papers on the table beside the glass? It put me off horribly."

"I thought that if I said there were it would show that I knew Irene had taken too much," said Victoria, apologetically, "and then I should have had to explain why I left her to die—I couldn't do that for her sake, and also, of course, for my own. If I'd had time to think I'd just have said that I didn't notice any papers: in fact, if I'd thought it out properly and not been so miserable and worried about leaving her and so on, I could have made up a much better story altogether. When Mr. Smithers came to see me I thought at least that Rene was dead; it was terrible when I realized that she was alive and I should never be able to explain why I'd gone away and left her. I was frightened then!"

"I'll tell you another time you were frightened, poor little thing," said Charlesworth tenderly, "when I told you Smithers had got on to the idea that it might have been intended to murder Gregory, not Doon."

Victoria shuddered. "I saw then that it was between Irene and myself, and as long as he suspected me of trying to kill Irene, it had to be me! The only way out would have been to tell you all that I knew or thought about Rene—and, of course, in the end that's what I would have done. I explained that to the Dazzler, after you came to see me; we both knew that I should be safe in the end . . . all the same, I had some nasty moments."

Charlesworth took a corner rather badly. "So did I!" he said.

"But, Mr. Charlesworth, what first gave you the idea that it was Gregory? What about the flashes of insight and the little grey cells? Tell me how the mind of the great detective worked. You told me it was something Gregory said that put you on the right track. What did she say?"

They were approaching Victoria's door. Charlesworth passed it and drove slowly round the block as he explained. "She said she thought Irene had decided to make an end of her life."

Toria shrugged her shoulders: "Well, how could that help you? You know we all thought that."

"Thought what?" said Charlesworth.

"Thought that Irene'd decided to put an end to her life."

Charlesworth was pleased. "Ah, there you are! When I ask you, you say that Irene had decided to *put an end to her life;* but when I asked Gregory she said she thought that Irene might have intended to *make an end of her life.* Have you ever heard the actual wording of the forged confession?"

"No, I don't think any of us have. You wouldn't tell us; and Mr. Smithers—well, Mr. Smithers wouldn't tell anybody anything," said Victoria, viciously.

"Well, don't waste your spume on Inspector Smithers. Smithers is a very sick and sorry young man at this time, Toria, eating large quantities of humble pie . . ."

"I hope it chokes him," said Victoria.

Charlesworth laughed. "Well, I think we may safely say it does. Anyway, the point is that when Gregory used that phrase I recognized it as the one used in the confession—the confession that nobody outside Scotland Yard had seen. I was sitting there innocently talking to her with nothing but beautiful thoughts of her in my mind; but when she used those words my tummy turned right over in my inside. It was a little thing—not even a wildly unusual phrase—but it seemed odd that she should have used exactly those words, and I thought the whole thing out, all over again, with Gregory in the name part, and I began to see how it would fit. Ye gods!" said Charlesworth, going quite weak at the memory of his brainwave, "I've never been so relieved in all my life. I thought of those little gloves of Irene's and I looked at Gregory's big, bony hands, and then I think I was certain. I stalled her off with fair answers, and as soon as I could get away I rang up Smithers and we got on to all the chemists in the neighbourhood. And there we were."

"And here we are," said Victoria, as again they approached her front door.

Charlesworth stopped the car. "I suppose this is good-bye."

"I suppose it is, though I hope you'll come and see us sometimes, Mr. Charlesworth. You've been most terribly kind and the Dazzler and I are both very grateful for all you've done for me. All the same, I'm thankful it's over. It's been so cruel and hateful and sordid—I've never come up against such black and terrifying things before. It's different for you; you're used to this kind of thing, I suppose, and it's just another murder . . . our worries and fears and troubles, Gregory's feelings now, this minute—I suppose they're all part of just another murder case?"

"Well, that's true in a way," admitted Charlesworth. "Most cases are 'just another case,' really. The corpse is just a corpse and the murderer is just a murderer and you're out to get him if you possibly can. But . . ." he hesitated and then went on with a little rush . . . "let me say this, Victoria, and then I'll never mention it again, I swear. This case hasn't been just another case to me. Every night I've gone to bed and thought, 'To-morrow I shall see Victoria.' Every morning I've woken up and thought, 'To-day I shall see Victoria.' I've made excuses to come up to the shop just to talk to you, and when I've got there my knees have given way under me and I haven't had a word to say. I do love you, Victoria, with all my heart and soul." He leant his forehead against the steering-wheel and looked down at the toes of his shoes. "All my life I've been falling in and out of love and it hasn't meant a thing; but this time it's serious and now, when I get it really and deeply and truly—it has to be you! Happily married and in love with your husband and utterly out of my reach—it has to be you!"

There was a small silence. Toria put her hand on his arm and gave it a little shake. "Mr. Charlesworth, dear," she said, "I think it's high time I said good-night and went in."

6

At Scotland Yard Mr. Charlesworth's chief pressed several buzzers and returned again to his morning's reports. As each buzzer was answered he handed over a file with hardly a word; but to Charlesworth he murmured: "A murder in a racing yacht!" and regarded him with an indulgent eye.

"A racing yacht; that sounds rich and glamorous, sir."

"Beware of the lovely women!" said the great man, smiling still.

"Women!" cried Charlesworth, gloomily. "Preserve me from any more women. Honestly, sir, I don't care if I never set eyes on another girl for the rest of my life."

The superintendent looked anxious. "Now, now, Charlesworth, you're not still breaking your heart over that little Mrs. David in the Doon case? I know you took it badly at the time; but she was a married woman, and, after all, my dear boy . . ."

"Mrs. David!" said Charlesworth in accents of the liveliest astonishment. "Good lord, sir, this isn't Mrs. David that I'm talking about. Victoria was the sweetest thing, absolutely the dearest thing, and I'm the greatest possible friends with them both to this day; but, no, this isn't Victoria David . . . if all girls were like her. . . . Oh, well," said Charlesworth, with a heavy sigh. "I beg your pardon, sir. The racing yacht?"

# FINE MYSTERY AND SUSPENSE
# TITLES FROM CARROLL & GRAF

| | | |
|---|---|---|
| ☐ | Gilbert, Michael/THE DOORS OPEN | $3.95 |
| ☐ | Gilbert, Michael/GAME WITHOUT RULES | $3.95 |
| ☐ | Gilbert, Michael/THE 92nd TIGER | $3.95 |
| ☐ | Gilbert, Michael/OVERDRIVE | $3.95 |
| ☐ | Graham, Winston/MARNIE | $3.95 |
| ☐ | Greeley, Andrew/DEATH IN APRIL | $3.95 |
| ☐ | Hughes, Dorothy B./THE FALLEN SPARROW | $3.50 |
| ☐ | Hughes, Dorothy B./IN A LONELY PLACE | $3.50 |
| ☐ | Hughes, Dorothy B./RIDE THE PINK HORSE | $3.95 |
| ☐ | Hornung, E. W./THE AMATEUR CRACKSMAN | $3.95 |
| ☐ | Kitchin, C. H. B./DEATH OF HIS UNCLE | $3.95 |
| ☐ | Kitchin, C. H. B./DEATH OF MY AUNT | $3.50 |
| ☐ | MacDonald, John D./TWO | $2.50 |
| ☐ | Mason, A.E.W./AT THE VILLA ROSE | $3.50 |
| ☐ | Mason, A.E.W./THE HOUSE OF THE ARROW | $3.50 |
| ☐ | Priestley, J.B./SALT IS LEAVING | $3.95 |
| ☐ | Queen, Ellery/THE FINISHING STROKE | $3.95 |
| ☐ | Rogers, Joel T./THE RED RIGHT HAND | $3.50 |
| ☐ | 'Sapper'/BULLDOG DRUMMOND | $3.50 |
| ☐ | Symons, Julian/BOGUE'S FORTUNE | $3.95 |
| ☐ | Symons, Julian/THE BROKEN PENNY | $3.95 |
| ☐ | Wainwright, John/ALL ON A SUMMER'S DAY | $3.50 |
| ☐ | Wallace, Edgar/THE FOUR JUST MEN | $2.95 |
| ☐ | Waugh, Hillary/SLEEP LONG, MY LOVE | $3.95 |
| ☐ | Willeford, Charles/THE WOMAN CHASER | $3.95 |

Available from fine bookstores everywhere or use this coupon for ordering.

Carroll & Graf Publishers, Inc., 260 Fifth Avenue, N.Y., N.Y. 10001

Please send me the books I have checked above. I am enclosing
$_____ (please add $1.00 per title to cover postage and
handling.) Send check or money order—no cash or C.O.D.'s
please. N.Y. residents please add 8¼% sales tax.

Mr/Mrs/Ms _____

Address _____

City _____ State/Zip _____

Please allow four to six weeks for delivery.